IT'S NOT THEM, IT'S ONLY HER

Young in Love

Book 4

ELLE WRIGHT

Elle Wrights Books, LLC
Ypsilanti, Michigan
www.ElleWright.com

Copy Editor/Proofreading:
Paulette Nunlee
5-Star Proofing

Cover Design:
Sherelle Green

It's Not Them, It's Only Her

My mission in life is simple. Family. Food. Freedom. Most people don't question my love for my family. And I make my living as a celebrity chef. The freedom part? The thought of being confined—behind bars, at a desk, or in a monogamous relationship—is not something I want for myself. Unfortunately, it becomes a problem when women want to make me their Forever Bae. Even after I make it clear that I'm not looking for more than short interlude.

Except… when I think of her, when I'm with her, I don't feel stuck. I actually want uninterrupted time with her. Surprised? Me too.

Want to know how I ended up in this predicament? I wish I knew because I definitely wasn't looking for it. Maybe it's the way she takes care of me? By listening to the things I say and everything I don't say.

Want to know why changing our relationship dynamic is a bad idea? I'm not the only one who wants her. Which makes it very complicated.

Want to know another reason why this is a bad idea? My track record speaks for itself. And she deserves someone good. I'm… not.

The choice is hers, though. I hate to lose so I'm playing to win. And I will show her that it's not him that she needs. It's me.

Dear Reader

Duke is finally here!!

This character has to be one of my favorite characters in my Universe. He grabbed a hold of my heart when I wrote The Way You Tempt Me, and hasn't let go. Now, it's his turn!

Brace yourself, because he is not for the games. He's ready to risk it all for *her*... And *only* her!

Thank you for joining me on this ride!!! I hope you enjoy them!

Love,

Elle

www.ellewright.com

Content Notes

Hi again,

I love to be surprised when I read a book. But I fully recognize that every reader is not like me. If you haven't read an Elle Wright book before, I feel like I should let you know a few things before you dive in.

IT'S NOT THEM, IT'S ONLY HER contains sexual content, profanity, and sensitive subjects that some may find triggering.

Trigger Warnings include but are not limited to:

Violence and Death
Child abuse
Child abandonment
Humiliation
Family estrangement
Grief

For all the women who found love with that guy.

Dick Interrupted

A DUKE YOUNG ORIGINAL

Duke

Part I

A Long-Ass Time Ago

*I*t had been hours. Hours of uncertainty. Hours of Tristan throwing shit around the house. Hours of unanswered phone calls to my parents. Hours of threatening messages from her father. Hours of her crying. I couldn't find a bright spot, but I knew I couldn't take it much longer. If only this was the first time this had happened. I was younger then, but the helpless feeling I'd had then still applied now. It might have been worse today.

Years ago, Demita Strong had come to the house,

soaking wet, with only the clothes on her back. And my brother Tristan and I were home alone then too. She needed our help that night, and she needed it now. Taking care of her was important to all of us. The fact that she was my sister's best friend was irrelevant. She was family. *My* family. From the moment she'd darkened our doorstep, cold and afraid, my parents had set things in motion to ensure she'd never have to return to that hellhole her father called home. She'd been with us ever since.

Everything she'd witnessed still affected her, though—even years later, after she'd been accepted into our family. Everything her father had done still propelled her to do better in life, to *be* better. And everything she'd accomplished was a *fuck you* to the two people she should've been able to trust with her life.

"Duke?" Chastity called from next to me, squeezing my dick with her small palm. "Are you okay? What's going on?"

I waved her off and tried to get my head back into the matter at hand. Sex. "Nothing." I pressed my mouth to her neck and untied her bikini top, letting it fall open, revealing her breasts.

A loud crash drew my attention toward the wall. *What the hell is she doing in there?*

"What was that?" Chastity was my plus one to the senior activities my mother made me attend. For pictures. She was also our pastor's niece. And judging by the look in her eyes and the accusatory tone in her voice, she thought she was my girlfriend. The loud wails started again. "Is it your sister? I thought your family was out of town. Are you hiding someone here?"

"Stop talking," I grumbled.

She sucked her teeth, which I hated. "Don't tell me what to do."

Ignoring the next sequence of probing questions, I slipped my jeans back on and tossed Chastity's shorts at her. "You gotta go."

"But…"

"This is over," I told her.

Chastity blinked. "What do you mean? Our night is over?"

For once, I was torn. It wasn't my style to sugarcoat anything, but… *Do I want to risk the wrath of the entire congregation for breaking Chastity's heart?* My mother would kill me. Even though it was her damn fault for encouraging me to ask the girl out in the first place. She knew I wasn't a nice guy. After all, she did give birth to me.

Before I could formulate the right words to let her down gently, realization dawned in her brown eyes. "You're breaking up with me?"

"We're not together."

"We've been together all year," she said.

Sighing, I met her watery gaze. "We went on a few dates."

"We had sex!"

I shrugged. "Okay…? Still doesn't make you my girlfriend."

"I gave you my virginity." *Doubtful.* But I kept my face void of emotion. "Duke?" She approached me. "You're my first love."

Frowning, I said, "How?" Her chin trembled and I rushed to apologize. "I'm sorry. It's nothing against you."

She hugged herself. "I don't understand. I thought you liked me."

I dropped my head and let out another slow breath. This was some bullshit, but I would suck it up. For Mom's sake. For her church relationships. "I had a lot of fun with you. You're a good person. Better than I deserve. There's

3

someone out there that wants the same things you do. A successful career and a committed marriage. A big family with a dog and… the Lord." Silence hung in the air for a moment, and I added, "Go to New York and live your life. Start fresh without me."

Chastity pouted. "Can't we just talk about it?"

"There's nothing more to say." I checked my watch and tried to ignore the muffled cries from the room down the hall. "I don't want to hurt your feelings, but I really have to take care of something."

Chastity seemed to accept my decision and gathered her things. "I hope whoever that is crying will be okay," she said.

"She'll be fine," I told Chastity as I led her downstairs toward the front door.

Once Chastity left, I considered my next move. Upstairs or kitchen? Visions of Demi's sad, doe eyes taunted me. I'd seen despair in her eyes before. The memory had been seared on my brain, almost like the first time I'd cooked dinner for the family—pan-fried ribeye, served with oven-roasted vegetables, baked sweet potatoes, and white cheddar mac and cheese. It was a rare sight, but when she cried, it tore me up inside. Decision made, I walked away. Downstairs in the kitchen, Tristan was staring into the refrigerator.

Without looking at me, he mumbled, "She still crying?"

I joined him, leaning against the countertop. "She won't stop."

He sighed. "Maybe you should check on her."

"Why don't *you* check on her?"

My big brother glared at me. "You know why."

"That's bullshit." I folded my arms over my chest. "She's basically our sister."

Raising a challenging brow, he said, "Is she really? To you?"

The question caught me off guard, but I didn't take the bait. "Yes," I lied. I knew what sisterly love was. Paityn, Dallas, Blake, Bliss, and even my best friend, Skye, were my sisters. But Demi? While she was family, and she'd lived with us for years, I'd never really felt like her brother. Don't get me wrong, though. I'd fuck some shit up over her, but the thought of seeing her naked didn't make me want to throw up. And Tristan understood it because he felt the same way.

"You still have company?" my brother asked.

It wasn't uncommon for me to sneak girls home, especially since I was technically still a minor—until Halloween. My parents didn't have many rules. Mostly, they trusted us to make good and bad decisions. In fact, a bad decision landed me on house arrest while the rest of my family was out of town on vacation. To make matters worse, Ma had given Tristan strict instructions to keep them informed about my activities.

To my surprise, though, my oldest brother hadn't obliged her request. Surprised the hell out of me because, in the past, he'd taken his oldest sibling role seriously. Tristan had never passed up an opportunity to take the fun out of every activity. Yet, since he'd returned for a short visit before he shipped out again, he'd pretty much left me alone. While I appreciated the reprieve and he still failed at enjoying life, I was glad he'd seemingly mellowed out a little.

Tristan eyed me over his glass. "I'm going to take your silence as my answer. Maybe it's time for your girl to leave."

I realized I might have given him too much credit because the dour expression on his face told me this would not be a pleasant conversation. "She's not my girl." I grabbed a bottle of water from the fridge. "And she's gone. Do you plan on telling Mom and Dad that she was here?"

He shrugged. "That's up to you."

"And what do I have to do so that you won't tell them?"

"Clean up your shit." He gestured to the sink full of dishes. "And check on Demi."

For some reason, that irritated the fuck out of me. "I wondered when you'd revert to your natural self. You're full of shit."

"Just do what I said."

"Or what?" I taunted.

"I can show you more than I can tell you."

"I don't need you to tell me what the hell to do." A couple of years ago, Tristan had at least three inches on me in height. Today, I stepped to him, looking him straight in the eye. "And you never have to tell me what to do with Demi. Maybe that talk should be with the man in the mirror."

Tristan shoved me. "Back the fuck up, Duke," he growled. "Don't play with me. You don't know what you think you do."

I smirked. "I know when I've hit a nerve. You know the old saying. Hit dogs…?" Without another word, I left him standing there, fury in his eyes.

As I made my way back upstairs, I thought about that conversation with my brother. Things hadn't been right between us in some years. Time and distance hadn't helped with his issues. Even becoming a father hadn't dulled the anger and resentment that radiated from him. Unfortunately, I didn't think anything would change until he accepted his role in the deterioration of all his relationships.

Stopping at the bathroom door, I pressed my ear

against the wood. The water was still running, and she was... *Still crying*. With a heavy sigh, I pushed the door open and immediately turned my back to the shower.

I half expected to have something thrown at me for barging in, but when nothing whizzed by my head, I announced, "I'm going to give you five seconds before I turn around." The time was for me more than it was for her. Strangely, I'd been in this exact position before. And once again, it was the first night she'd come to our house for help. Slowly, I counted to five. I wasn't sure what I'd see when I saw her, so I counted to ten. Then, twenty. She still hadn't answered. As far as I could tell, she hadn't even moved.

My heartbeat raced as I called to her. "Demi?" I grabbed a towel from the hook on the door and tossed it behind my head. "I'm trying to respect your privacy but you're making this hard as hell. Use that shit to cover up."

"Please," she whispered breathlessly.

Finally. But her voice was so soft, so unsure, so wounded, I instinctively whirled around. My shoulders sagged in relief at the sight of her, so small in the huge tub. Swallowing, I sent up a silent prayer of thanks that she hadn't hurt herself. Then I sent up another one asking for help. Because, while she was fully clothed, she was drenched. I approached the tub and turned the faucet. Bending down, I cradled her in my arms and carried her out of the bathroom.

When I entered her room, I kicked the door closed and set her on her feet. I tipped her chin up and studied her face. Her fair skin was red and her eyes dark. "You're okay."

Tears burst from her eyes. "I'm not."

Pulling her into my arms, I assured her that she was. Over and again until she stopped crying. "Demi," I pulled

7

away, squeezing her shoulders, "I promise you. Everything will be alright. Trust me?"

She nodded.

"Do me a favor and put some dry clothes on."

Demi gripped my arm when I reached for the door-knob. "Don't leave me."

"I'm just getting you food and something to drink. And some Carmex for those lips."

She let out a small laugh. "You're a fool."

I lifted my arms. "Hey, I'm honest."

After I changed my own shirt, I went back to the kitchen. Luckily, Tristan wasn't there. I made Demi's favorite sandwich, cut it in half, grabbed a bag of chips, and poured two glasses of lemonade. By the time I made it back upstairs, she'd changed her clothes.

"Thanks for following instructions," I told her with a wink. "Makes everything easier."

"I'm not hungry."

"You need to eat," I insisted, holding up a joint. "Especially since we're going to smoke this."

An hour later, the sandwich was gone, and I'd pulled out the chocolate. And Demi was giggling uncontrollably. "I can't believe I'm high." She fell back on the mattress next to me. I passed her the joint and she put it to her lips and inhaled. "I needed this."

"Don't tell anyone," I murmured. "I'm already on house arrest."

"I'm glad you stay fucking up," she admitted. "I don't know what I would've done if you weren't here."

"Are you ready to tell me what happened?"

"I saw both of my parents today."

I frowned and met her hooded gaze. "Together?"

Demi's parents divorced when she was in elementary school and had never gotten along. Her father was verbally, emotionally, and spiritually abusive, which prompted her mother to leave everything behind to get away from him. Unfortunately, that left Demi to take the abuse. Until she couldn't anymore.

Demi sat up and stared ahead. "No. Dad blamed me for everything wrong in his life. Things went to hell." She glanced at me over her shoulder. "He informed me his obligation to me ended on my eighteenth birthday and that I had to make other arrangements to pay for college. Mom came to town for a court proceeding. When I told her what he said, she shrugged me off and basically told me I was on my own." Tears streamed down her face, and she wiped her cheeks with her hand. "Then she asked me to cosign for my sister's car because I don't have messed up credit." She let out a humorless chuckle. "My life is so fucked up."

I smoothed a hand over her back. "It might not seem like it now, but you have options."

"Community college? Because I damn sure can't afford Hampton now." Demi had been accepted to Hampton University and would be leaving with Dallas and Dexter in a matter of weeks to attend the HBCU. "Do I really want to be saddled with thousands of dollars of debt just to go there?"

"You won't have to." I didn't know the particulars of the arrangement between my parents and hers, but I knew my mother and father wouldn't leave her future up to chance. "Let's not panic. When Ma and Pop get home, you'll talk to them and see what they can do."

"They've already helped me too much, Duke. They took me in. I can't ask them to pay for my college."

"Have you met my parents?"

She giggled. "Stop making me laugh."

"Anything is better than that crying. Damn, Demi, I can't take it."

9

She laid down again and turned on her side. "Thanks for listening. But I'm not asking them to help me."

"I say this with all respect in the world for you. But that's bullshit. You live here. They feed you. And not just food. They make sure you're good because you're one of us. Shit, you put your money in that damn cursing jar just like the rest of us."

Demi giggled, resting her head on my shoulder. "It's not even just the college."

"I know."

She glanced at me. "You always do."

I smirked and held out the joint. "Now, hit this shit so you can go to sleep and stop the tears."

The door cracked open, and Tristan poked his head inside. He looked at Demi, then me. Then at Demi again. His eyes narrowed on mine, but he didn't speak. He just closed the door.

Demi cracked up. "I guess he doesn't want to get fucked up."

I barked out a laugh. "Trust me. He already is."

&

Part II

Several years ago

The first hit didn't faze me. Because that muthafucka was weak. Always had been a punk. I was able to knock his ass out before his brothers joined the fight. I held my own for about ten minutes before I felt the blade slice into my side. Dropping to my knees, I placed pressure over the wound as another assailant knocked the wind out of me with a swift kick to my stomach. When I reached out to grab his ankle, I noticed my hands were covered with blood. My blood. *Shit.*

"Stay the hell away from my wife," the weak muthafucka spat from behind his brother.

I snickered, even as a sharp pain radiated down my leg. "Maybe if you knew how to take care of her, she wouldn't be trying to get in my bed." The right hook to my jaw caught me off guard, but it wasn't delivered by that asshole. Once again, one of his brothers had delivered a devastating blow. "The fact that you can't even fight me yourself tells me all I need to know."

I lunged for him, getting a few punches in before another brother—the one who looked like he spent his days lifting weights—slammed me onto the ground. In my attempt to shield my head from the hard cement, I landed on my hand, causing sharp pain to shoot from my finger to my elbow. *Shit, it's probably fractured.* I groaned, rolling over onto my back. And his big ass laughed. "You just don't learn, do you?" he taunted.

"Fuck you," I growled. "You better hope you kill me, because when I find yo' ass, when I'm not potentially bleeding out, I'm not coming to play."

His answer was a kick to my other side.

After taking several more severe hits, I couldn't find the strength to get up. As I struggled to catch my breath, I wondered if this was it for me. If the brutal beating and blood loss didn't kill me, dehydration and this damn Louisiana heat would. Them dusty-ass niggas probably thought the same because they scurried away like the pussies they were. I forced my eyes open but could only see out of one. The excruciating pain in my side had dulled to a small ache, but it still hurt to breathe. *Probably a broken rib.* Or several.

A moment later, I'd given up on driving myself to the hospital or even walking to my car. Luckily, I couldn't even feel the sweltering hard concrete beneath me anymore. My brief time in medical school made me acutely aware of my precarious situation. Dizziness. Shortness of breath. I was cold. And tired as hell. If I lost consciousness, I could die.

I managed to lift my arm, relieved that my Apple Watch wasn't damaged. Using all my energy, I asked Siri to dial the first name I could think.

She answered on the third ring. "What the hell is wrong with you? Calling this early in the morning."

Under normal circumstances, I would've told her she wasn't doing anything but sleeping anyway. Talking shit was my love language, but I especially loved the banter between *us*. But because I could barely get a word out, I simply muttered, "Come."

My arm fell under the weight of my injuries, and I promised myself I would fuck them muthafuckas up the next time I saw them. It took a damn stab wound and five big-ass niggas to knock me down. *But is this going to take me out?*

As the minutes ticked by, I found myself thinking of my family, of my parents, Always so giving, so understand-ing. They'd given us a blueprint to live by, taught us how to navigate the world while Black. They'd shown us unconditional love in action every day. Never made me choose between what *they* wanted and what *I* wanted.

They'd only encouraged me to go after what made me happy.

My mother once told me to stop taking so many risks, to stop tempting fate. If she only knew the shit I'd done... Aside from this particular situation, I'd fucked up more times than I'd ever admit to her. What would she do if I died in the street alone over some bullshit? I chose to mess around with a married woman and now bore the brunt of her husband's anger. In my defense, she'd told me she was separated. I didn't believe her ass, though. I just didn't care. Maybe because I was young and cocky. More likely because she was fine as hell, and I was a man-whore. At least, according to my sisters and Skye.

In my weakened state, I sent up a silent prayer, going through the Lord's Prayer and asking for forgiveness and protection as my mom and Sister Pearl had taught me back in the day. All those years in Sunday School mattered. A moment after I sealed my prayer with an "Amen," I wondered if God even heard me. It wasn't like I'd spent so much time talking to Him. But I wanted to plead my case, though, to argue that my brothers and sisters needed me. Well, six of them needed me. Not Tristan. He didn't need shit, but I could imagine even he would be devastated if I was no longer here to blame for his shortcomings.

Who's going to tell everyone when they're fucking up? Paityn would blame herself, for not being there, for not giving me enough love and understanding. But she'd always been a person I could count on and the only person that might be able to beat me in the kitchen. *Maybe.* My baby sister, Blake, would probably go to jail or die trying to avenge my death. My chest tightened when I thought of Blake's twin sister, Bliss. All I could see is her sad face in my mind. Dex and Dallas... They called us "The Triples". Dex and I were identical twins and Dallas was our fraternal sister. She

13

always thought that made her an outsider, but she was the best of us. Hell, they all were a hell of a lot better than me. And Asa? My baby brother would probably just leave. He was good at disappearing. Guess he got that from Tristan. Demi would probably be quiet. She wouldn't speak, she wouldn't cry, she wouldn't engage. It was her defense mechanism, but also her most comfortable state. And she would retreat to that space. X, Zara, Skye… They weren't just friends. They were as much my family as my siblings and parents.

Tears filled my eyes. I wanted all of them to be happy, to know how it felt to be in love, to be loved. I hoped someone would pick up a spatula and cook something besides Paityn. Maybe my niece, Raven? I needed my father to know how much I admired him, how he inspired me to be great. And I prayed my mother didn't blame herself for my mistakes.

As my eyes drifted closed, I whispered my love for them to the night air and imagined their faces in the stars. And then everything went black.

"Duke?"

A voice. *Her* voice pulled me back to the present.

"Please," she whispered, emotion in her voice. "Don't do this to me. Don't make me explain this to Dallas. And your parents? Oh God." I felt her forehead against the side of my face. "I'm sorry. I'm so sorry. I shouldn't have left you there. You were drunk, and I knew it wasn't a good idea."

I winced as a needle pierced my skin. Coolness replaced the sting and I realized someone had started an IV. Other sounds registered next. Male voices, spouting vitals. A hand wrapping a blood pressure cuff around my arm and another set of hands applying pressure on my side.

"Stay with me," she pleaded.

It's not your fault. I wanted to tell her this was on me, that she did nothing wrong, but the darkness pulled me back.

Sometime later, I awoke to unfamiliar voices around me, the sound of a blood pressure cuff deflating, and the consistent beep of the heart monitor. Opening my eyes, I scanned the area and realized I was in a hospital room. Two doctors were off to the side, discussing my care with a nurse while another nurse flushed my IV. And Demi was sitting in the chair next to my bed, her eyes on their movements.

"Not your fault," I managed to say finally.

She jerked back, meeting my good eye with a watery gaze. "Thank God." She stood and hugged me. Gingerly.

"I'm sorry," I whispered.

Demi peered up at the ceiling, before leveling her gaze on me again. "You scared the shit out of me. And you're right, it's not my fault. It's yours." Tears fell down her face. I wanted to wipe them away, but I still couldn't move. "I prayed."

"Me, too." I closed my eyes.

Demi flashed a wobbly smile. "You need to pray harder, because you look like you've been walking through the valley of the shadow of death. Face all fucked up, eye looking like Rocky's after Apollo Creed won the match."

I would've tried to smile, but I knew it would hurt so I murmured, "You're silly."

"Adrian!" she called, mimicking Rocky in the movie.

"Stop," I chuckled. "You're killing me."

The doctors walked over to us and gave me the rundown of my injuries. They'd operated to stop the internal bleeding and started me on intravenous antibiotics to prevent infection. The good news was the knife didn't hit an artery and my ribs were bruised, not broken. *Just like my life.*

When they left the room, Demi brushed a finger over my brow. "Are you in a lot of pain?"

I shook my head. "Not right now. Did you call my family?"

She quirked an eyebrow. "Did you want me to?"

"No."

"That's what I thought." Her chin trembled. "You could've died."

"I didn't."

"But you *could've*," she reiterated. "I'm glad you didn't, though. Get some rest."

Later, I woke up in a different room. Demi stood by the window staring outside, her arms folded across her chest. She'd changed clothes and pulled her curls back into a smooth bun. *What day is it?*

A nurse entered the room and smiled. "Hi, Mr. Young. I'm Ariana. I'll be the nurse on call today." I nodded at her and glanced at Demi again. "The attending physician will be in to speak with you momentarily. Can I get you anything right now?"

"No," I grumbled.

Another nurse walked in. She looked vaguely familiar, and I assumed she'd taken care of me before. "Hello, Mr. Young. I wanted to stop in before I head out. I'm on vacation the rest of the week, but I wanted to give you my phone number. Call me if you need anything at all." She handed me a business card.

Demi snatched it out of my hand. With her eyes on mine, she told the nurse, "He won't need this." Then, she met the nurse's horrified gaze. "Enjoy your vacation."

"Ma'am, I—" the nurse sputtered.

"Really?" Demi scoffed. "Ariana seems perfectly capable of taking care of Duke."

"She is," the nurse agreed. "She's one of our best."

"Good to know. Is there a reason you felt the need to hand a patient your personal number—" she threw up finger quotes, "—in case he needs you?"

"No, but—"

"You're that desperate that you're giving a strange man your phone number? A strange man that entered the hospital under mysterious circumstances, obviously beaten to a pulp, with another woman. He could be a drug dealer or a murderer. He could be *my* man and you're, what... flirting with him? Does he look like he's going to call you anytime soon? Because from where I'm standing, he looks pretty fucked up to me."

"But," the young nurse said. "I—"

"Is it protocol to pass your number to patients?" Demi continued relentlessly, her skill in the courtroom shining through with her interrogation of the poor nurse. "Do all patients receive the same level of care at this hospital that you would be on call, even during your vacation, to serve him? Or is it just the fine ones? Maybe I need to verify the rules with your supervisor?"

The nurse stuttered an apology—or fifty—before scurrying out of the room. Demi turned her attention to Ariana and smiled brightly. "Thanks for bringing me breakfast this morning. I appreciate you."

Ariana grinned. "You're welcome. And thank you," she whispered.

I looked back and forth between the two women and realized I'd missed something important. Context. A few minutes later, Ariana was gone, and Demi was back in front of the window.

"You told her," I mumbled, wincing as I shifted to face her. "Ma'am."

"Seriously? She tried it. She's probably older than me." Demi rolled her eyes hard. "Calling me ma'am, like I'm someone's mother."

"And we're not in court, counselor."

"It doesn't matter. The last thing you should be doing is hooking up with anyone else in this city."

"I take it Ariana was in on this takedown."

Demi shrugged, finally turning to me. "She mentioned being harassed by the mean-girl group of nurses led by that heffa who couldn't even start your IV yesterday."

I chuckled. "Alright, then. You did the right thing."

She sat on the edge of the bed, her forehead creased with worry. "Duke, you could've been killed."

"But I wasn't," I reminded her. I focused on her, relieved that I could now see her with both eyes, although the one was still swollen. "We've been over this already. Stop worrying."

"Easy for you to say. You didn't find *me* passed out in some alley, in a pool of blood."

"You already told me off yesterday. What happened?"

"*You* happened," she snapped. "I've thought of nothing else since I saw them wheel your ass into the back of an ambulance. I couldn't sleep, I couldn't eat. I had no idea what I would tell the family if you didn't make it. The initial shock of seeing you like that and the relief I felt when you opened your damn eye has worn off. I'm pissed now. You better be glad I was only a block away. All of this for some woman?" She stood and paced the small room. "I knew something wasn't right about this trip. But, once again, I let you lead me astray." Demi went on and on about warnings, fucking around, and finding out. "I don't blame you, though. This is all on me."

18

"Right." I'd been around Demi long enough to know that her ire was directed at me because I was there. And she was scared. The real target of her anger wasn't around to feel her wrath. "Did you do what you came here to do?"

She sighed and sat on the edge of the bed. "He stood me up. Again."

"Are you finally ready to let him go?"

The question hung in the air for a moment. It was no secret that Demi had a thing for my brother Tristan. Everyone knew it, including him. As far as I was concerned, he'd led her on, made her think there could be something between them, made her hope that one day they'd be at the same place in life and ready for forever. And she'd let him, through college, law school, and even now that she'd made a name for herself in her career as a divorce attorney. He'd leave. Come back. She'd accept him back in her life and heart, then he'd pull away. Then, the cycle would start over again. Wash. Rinse. Repeat.

Demi averted her gaze, fiddling with the strap of her purse. "Enough about me. This is about you."

"I keep telling you it's never going to work." Most likely because Tristan was an asshole on his best days. And Demi deserved better, but *she* hadn't learned that lesson yet.

She looked at me finally, then changed the subject. "Why would you sleep with that woman knowing she was married? You told me those days were behind you."

I told myself that it was my injuries and not the disappointment written on her face that made my chest tighten. The truth of my past wasn't pretty. I'd had several affairs with unavailable women, mostly because it worked for my lifestyle. No labels. No commitment. No expectations. But I'd vowed to be better in recent years. Not because I had a sudden epiphany about love and marriage, but because I realized I had too much to lose. *Family. Career.* I had many regrets, but dropping out of medical school to pursue culinary art wasn't one of them. I excelled in front of the stove. Food was my safe place. Cooking was my passion. The kitchen was my office.

"I didn't know she was married," I admitted.

Her green eyes flashed to mine. She bit down on her bottom lip. "Really?"

"Do I lie?"

Demi's shoulders sagged. "Never to me," she said. "When did you find out?"

"Tonight. I broke it off, and she called her husband."

"Bitch," she muttered.

"It's over."

Demi met my eyes. "No revenge." When I didn't answer, she squeezed my hand. "Duke? Please, don't go looking for him. Think about the plans you have for your life."

In the past, I wouldn't have thought twice about finding that punk and beating the shit out of him. But Demi was right. I'd come too far to fuck my life up. Maybe *I* wouldn't get to him, but I knew people. "I won't," I assured her.

"And no calling someone else to do it either," she said sternly.

I closed my eyes and burrowed into the pillow. "Fine."

I felt her hand on my chest and rested mine on top of hers. "Good. Now, get some rest." Demi walked to the door and peered back at me. "I'll be back in about an hour."

"If I can't go after him, you damn sure better not go see her."

"Shit," Demi hissed, stomping over to the chair next to the bed. "I was just going to have a little talk with her."

A smile tugged at my lips. "A talk with your fists?"

She crossed her arms over her chest and glared at me. "It's alright."

"And you can't tell Blake."

"Damn," she mumbled. "Anyway, we're out of here as soon as the doctor releases you. Go to sleep."

"Whatever you say." It didn't take long to drift off because I knew I was in good hands. That meant more to me than Demi could ever know.

Chapter One

HERE WE GO AGAIN!

Duke

Present Day, November

*E*verywhere I turned, someone was planning a wedding. From Blake to Skye to Dexter... I was inundated with meetings and teas and engagement parties and all that stupid shit I didn't want to be doing. Today, I found myself following Skye around as she shopped for her wedding night lingerie while simultaneously texting my siblings about Blake's wedding date. *Da fuq?*

"Duke?" Skye emerged from the dressing room, clad in a black corset with lace panels and matching panties. She lifted her arms and twirled around. "What do you think?"

I glanced at her briefly and grunted before turning my attention back to my phone.

Skye Palmer-Starks had been a part of my life since I was a kid. When I thought of "locked and loaded" and "ready to cut a nigga," Skye was up there with my siblings as far as her willingness to take a bullet or kick off her high heels and fight. She'd seen me through my crazy younger years and had even saved me from myself several times as I grew into adulthood—even now. Skye was bossy as hell, always all up in my business, and got on my damn nerves, but I loved the hell out of her. There wasn't much I wouldn't do for her, and her ass knew it too. I was seven years old when Skye forced me to babysit her baby doll while she got her hair combed.

"Duke!" she shouted, pulling me from my memories. "Thoughts?"

"I think you needed to bring your girls with you to the damn lingerie store. Seriously, Skye, you're taking this Man of Honor thing too damn far."

"Best person," she corrected. "You have a dual role in this wedding. I agreed to let you stand with the fellas during the ceremony, but you have to come to all the ladies' events with me. Didn't you read the emails."

Hell no. "All five thousand of them? You know the answer to that question."

Skye gave me yet another rundown of my important wedding duties, while I returned my attention to my phone, just in time to see the text from my sister Blake.

Blake: *Fuck all y'all!*

My little sister's message was met with a string of GIFs making fun of her outburst. Until Paityn responded.

Paityn: *Who the hell are you talking to? I'm very disappointed in you, Sissy.*

My big sister was the nurturer of our group. Paityn had taken care of all of us, especially when my mother went back to work. It was nothing for her to patch up a wound, help with homework, hide us from the world when we needed to get away, and cook a good-ass meal. We all respected her, so I wasn't surprised when Blake sent another message.

Blake: *Fine. Fuck all y'all. Except Paityn.*

Bliss: *Really? Because I asked you to pick the fuckin' date?*

Bliss: *Whatever. Plan your own damn wedding. Shit.*

I cracked up when another string of shocked emojis followed, probably because it was rare for Bliss to lose it. And she'd said three curse words in a matter of seconds. I even had to respond to that: *See what y'all made Bliss do!*

On cue, Dallas chimed in: *'Bout time your late ass joined the party. Talk to your sister because she's pissing everyone off.*

Skye snatched my phone out of my hand. "You didn't hear a word I said. You're supposed to be here for me. Stay in the moment."

I pinned her with a glare. "I understand that, but," I gestured to the outfit, "we're not fucking. Why would you pick me to come here?"

With a heavy sigh, she walked back into her dressing room. "You're the subject matter expert. You think with your dick, and you know what men like."

I chuckled. "Oh, you got jokes."

Meanwhile, my phone buzzed with a text from my best friend, Xavier.

X: *Underwear shopping with Skye?*

I snickered, then replied: *Lingerie. Kill. Me. Now.*

X: *Bruh... What's next? Hair appointment? Waxing eyebrows?*

He was right. It was lingerie today, but tomorrow it might be pedicures and champagne. Soon, I'd be carrying her purse while she was scanning shit for her bridal registry. *This has to stop. Now.* Instead of responding with words to my friend, I simply sent a middle finger emoji and opened the other text thread. I took a minute to skim the messages, but the last one caught my eye.

Dallas: *Demi is headed your way, Duke.*

My thumb hovered over my phone. Demi rarely visited Atlanta without telling me, so it caught me off guard to find out she was coming to town and hadn't reached out.

Me: *Why?*

Then, my phone rang. I accepted the call. "You could've answered the question in the text thread," I told Dallas.

"Maybe I wanted to hear your voice," she said. "Your niece misses you."

After a dramatic pregnancy, my sister had given birth to my beautiful niece, Dominique. The last time I saw her, she slept, pooped, burped, and slept some more. "She can't even say 'Ma' yet," I pointed out.

"She called Preston 'Da' the other day. I was pissed. All those labor pains and shit. I still have nightmares about my waddle."

I chuckled. "You were definitely over-the-top." She wasn't the only one either. When Bliss was pregnant with Naija, she'd turned into a whiner. I gave her a pass because she'd already been through so much with her baby daddy.

"Shut up," Dallas said. "Anyway, Demi is meeting a client there. And, you can't say anything, but she's having dinner or drinks with Tristan."

My relationship with my brother was pretty much non-existent. Tristan could've lived in Atlanta, and I'd never know. That's how bad it was. "He's in town too, huh?"

"I guess so."

Unfortunately, his relationship with the rest of my family wasn't much better. He'd made a habit of popping up at random times and then disappearing for long stretches. "I hope he doesn't stand her up again," I murmured.

Demi and Tristan had been circling each other for over a decade. The *will-they, won't-they* of it all got on my nerves because I knew it was never going to happen. For one, Tristan wasn't emotionally capable of commitment. And Demi wasn't willing to see Tristan for the flawed human being he was.

"This one is nice," Skye said from the dressing room. "I'm coming out."

"Okay, DD," I said. "I gotta go." After I hung up the phone, I sent Demi a text telling her to call me when she got in.

Skye returned to the waiting area. "I need a break from all the wedding planning." She shoved me lightly. "Are you okay?"

I blinked. "Huh?"

"I asked if you were good." She did a quick turn in the full mirror. This time she wore a sheer white kimono. Thankfully, she'd had enough sense to wear something under it to cover the parts that were none of my business. Skye peered at me over her shoulder. "You look like you just got bad news."

Waving her off, I said, "I'm good. Why do you need a break from planning? You love this shit."

She shrugged. "It's not fun if my girls aren't here. Rissa is back in LA, your sisters are in Michigan, and Zara is being Super Agent and Super Mom."

It wasn't that long ago when Xavier realized Zara wasn't *just* the girl next door. After they realized they were better together than apart, Xavier and Zara procreated— *at my birthday party actually*—and then married. Our families —the Youngs, the Starks, and the Reids—had spent a lifetime as friends. My father and Jax Starks, X's father, were like brothers. And we met Zara and her family when they moved into the house next door to the Starks. For a brief time, we'd even lived in the same Brentwood, Los Angeles neighborhood. *Damn, those were good times.* Lazy summers in Xavier's backyard doing shit we shouldn't have been doing, group vacations to popular and obscure locations, Christmas parties, and everything in between.

Skye perched herself on the arm of my chair and picked at her nail. "I want a perfect day," she said, her voice low. "I want Garrett to be so enamored, so captivated by me that he won't have time to regret anything."

Skye had built her public relations business by protecting her celebrity clientele from themselves. She was confident, talented, and knowledgeable. Yet, this side of her—the vulnerable Skye, the overthinker, the anxious woman afraid to fail, the sometimes-self-sabotaging Skye—had been carefully hidden beneath her take-no-shit exterior.

I gripped her hand. "I told you to stop doing this to yourself. You know I'd tell you if Garrett was full of shit. He's not. That man has loved you for as long as I've known him."

Tears filled Skye's eyes. "I love him too."

"I know you do."

She shot me a wobbly smile. "I'm so ready to be his wife."

"I'm ready for you to be his wife too," I grumbled.

"Stop." She smacked my shoulder. "Weddings are stressful."

"The wedding is one day with an open bar, uncomfortable shoes, and bland chicken. Focus on *after* the wedding."

She hugged me. "You should be nice more often."

"I'm nice," I argued. "Get dressed and let's go eat. And, for the record, men like skin. Naked is always better than any piece of lingerie. No need to spend hundreds of dollars on shit that will just end up on the floor or ripped to shreds."

She giggled. "See! I needed this! Thank you." She rushed into the dressing room.

Several minutes later, we were walking down Peachtree Boulevard. The clouds had moved east, and the sun was shining. Being from Michigan, I'd take the mild temperatures any day over the unpredictable weather.

After more shopping and a quick tour of the wedding venue, Skye led me into a restaurant she wanted to try. We talked about work and family over ramen and sake, and I was pleasantly surprised at the quality of the food.

"You like it?" Skye asked, dipping her chopstick into my lobster ramen. She moaned. "So good. Let's switch." She slid her garden ramen my way.

"This is good," I told her once I tasted it.

"I'm glad you're enjoying it. You're so damn picky with food."

"That's because I can make everything better myself."

She shook her head. "So cocky. How's the YouTube Channel going?"

Recently, I'd started to venture into digital marketing. Social media had never really been my thing, but my agent suggested I use it to expand my brand. So far, it was working. My following had grown tremendously once I started making Instagram Reels and videos on TikTok. "It's going… I probably need to hire an assistant. I don't have time to be posting all day."

"Isn't Raven still helping you?"

My niece had been a godsend because I didn't know what the hell to do, but she lived in Michigan. "Yeah, but she'll be going into her final year of college soon. She needs to concentrate on that."

Shrugging, Skye said, "If she's willing, why not let her at least handle your social media? It's good experience for her since she wants to go into marketing. You can always hire a manager, like I've been telling you. Or even a local producer for your YouTube videos. Influencers are making money out here."

"Already on it." I gave her a high-five. "X gave me some names." My friend was a former child star and had stepped into his father's role as CEO of Pure Talent Agency. They'd recently expanded their digital division, which benefitted me because I was a client of the agency.

"Love it." She sipped her drink. "Just don't sleep with your manager or your producer."

I smirked. "I can't make any promises."

She rolled her eyes. "Do better." Skye focused on something behind me. "There's Sasha."

I didn't bother turning around. "Really?"

Grinning, she explained, "I just saw her yesterday. I want to invite her to the wedding, but isn't that too close? She *is* my therapist."

"Do you think she'll come?" When Skye didn't answer right away, I glanced up at her. "What?"

"Did you sleep with her?"

I leaned back in my chair. "Come on, now. Stop asking me that."

"You told me—"

"I told you not to ask questions if you don't want to hear my answers." I finished. I remembered what I'd told her because I meant what I said. From the moment Skye started seeing the therapist, she'd been on me about Dr. Sasha Williams. Although, Sasha and I did have a complicated history, I wasn't the one that had a romantic past with her. I didn't go around telling other people's business either. "Let it go."

Skye frowned. "Oh." She gasped. "She's with Tristan."

I craned my neck to see what Skye was talking about. Sure enough, Sasha was seated at the bar, all smiles, with my brother. To some, the interaction might seem innocent. After all, the clinical psychologist was good friends with my sister Paityn. She knew our family well. I knew it wasn't merely two friends catching up over drinks, though. I'd seen them with my own eyes, huddled up together, sneaking off to quiet places. He'd admitted there was something between them himself. He also told me their relationship was over. But watching them now, the way she placed her hand on his knee and the subtle brush of his palm against her arm, only confirmed that he'd told me a bold-faced lie.

Demi. I closed my eyes and sighed. Picking up my phone, I noticed she'd texted me back from earlier that she'd arrived.

Me: *Where are you?*

The bubbles on the screen jumped around as I waited for her response. Heat flushed through my body as I thought about the hurt look in her eyes the last time he'd stood her up.

Demi: *At my hotel getting ready to eat dinner.*

I didn't need to ask which hotel. She always stayed at the Loews Atlanta.

Me: *Hit me up when you're done.*

I set my phone down and noticed Skye staring at me curiously. "What, Skye?"

"Are you jealous that Tristan is here with Sasha? Because you look pissed."

"I'm fine."

"Should we go say hello?"

"Hell no."

She bit down on her bottom lip. "I don't like this."

"Like what?"

"I wish you'd talk to your brother. Y'all are family."

"Skye," I warned. The last thing I wanted to do was talk to Tristan. Our last few interactions had ended with fists. "Don't."

"Okay, okay." She held up her hands in surrender. "I'll drop it. I'm worried about you, though."

"I'm fine," I repeated. "Finish eating."

Later, I dropped Skye off at her house and headed toward my place, only to veer off in the opposite direction. The lobby of the hotel was quiet, which I expected on a Tuesday. I greeted a front desk attendant as I headed toward the restaurant. An acquaintance of mine stopped me at the entrance. I talked to him for a few seconds, then excused myself to find Demi. Scanning the dining room, I spotted her in a corner booth near the back of the place.

On my way to her table, I stopped at the bar and ordered two drinks—an old-fashioned for her and Bulleit neat for me. Demi was looking at her phone when I approached the table. I set the glass down in front of her and slid into the booth across from her.

She frowned. "Duke? What are you doing here?"

"He's not coming," I told her.

"How do you—?"

"I just know."

"I knew it," she breathed. "I should've never..." Her shoulders fell on a heavy sigh. "Never mind."

I pushed the glass closer to her. "Drink. And then I'll order you another."

"Thank you."

"You know I got you." *Always.*

Chapter Two

FAIRY TALES

Demi

The Past

$\mathcal{E}$verything was so loud. The rain against the hood of the car, the whistling of the wind, the jazz booming through the speakers... and my father. He'd been yelling for twenty minutes straight about the weather, my schoolwork, dinner, my choice of outfit, the holiday, my attitude, traffic, my performance during the swim meet. The rampage had started at the event and—actually, it started the day my mother moved out six years ago. That was the day he'd made *my* existence *his* problem.

Life was hard being the daughter of Allan Strong, Esquire. *Heaven forbid I leave that part out.* And it was even harder being the daughter of the woman who'd left him.

My father had lorded his influence over my mom for years, threatened her with bitter consequences if she so much as got a pedicure without his approval. As a child, I was an eternal optimist with stars in my eyes. I absolutely believed in the fairytale, the knight in shining armor who would ride to our rescue and slay the dragon. That's not what happened, though.

On my eighth birthday, we had a party. Not for my birthday, but for Labor Day. My father liked to entertain his colleagues and his clients. There were so many people at our house and lots of food. Typically, I'd spend these parties alone in my room with a good book, my music, and my imagination. But I'd spent a good portion of the day outside with the other kids. On my way back inside, I'd stumbled on my mother talking in hushed tones to a man I hadn't seen before. Staying in a kid's place was something that had been drilled in my brain. I attempted to give them privacy but tripped over a basket of clothes on my way to my bedroom.

When she heard the commotion, she glanced over at me and smiled. At the time, my mother's smile was every-thing to me. This particular night, her golden skin seemed to glow under the dim light of the hallway. Even her white dress gave her an angelic appearance. Instead of chastising me, she'd held her finger up to her mouth, signaling that I needed to be quiet. Then, she told me to pack my bag because we were going on an adventure. Like the dutiful child I was, I completed my task and waited. And waited. I fell asleep atop of my suitcase and awoke to the sound of broken glass and my father's booming voice calling me downstairs. My world shattered when he informed me that my mother had taken my sister and left.

Time had done nothing to dull the ache I felt when I thought about that day. As a result, I avoided birthday celebrations. I didn't care to go outside on Labor Day. I definitely hated the idea of a barbecue with my father's colleagues, but he'd dragged me out to yet another gathering. Even though I'd begged him to let me go up north with my best friend, Dallas, and her family. Putting on a fake smile to people who hated my mother and only tolerated me wasn't my idea of a good time.

"I told you to play nice with my boss," my father grumbled. "That dour expression on your face did me no favors."

I glanced at him, noted his tight grip on the steering wheel. While my father had never punched me, I often wondered if one day he would. Ignoring him, I turned my attention to the scenery.

"Always embarrassing me," he spat, disgust in his tone. "You're useless. Just like your mother."

"I'm nothing like her," I murmured. That ethereal image of her six years ago had faded with the memory of her voice. In its place was resentment. Some days, I hated her. Mostly, I just didn't care. *At least, that's what I told myself.*

"I can't tell," he sneered, glaring at me out of the corner of his eye. "You're selfish, entitled, undisciplined, and disobedient."

"I'm not," I argued. "I told you I didn't want to go."

"What you want doesn't matter to me," he said through clenched teeth. "It never did."

I hate you. I wanted to scream it at the top of my lungs, but it would do nothing but make everything worse. Tears burned my eyes, and I swallowed past a hard lump in my throat. Praying had never really helped. *Is God even here?* Where was my deliverance? All those fairytales my mother read to me… Where was my happy ending? There was no horse drawn carriage waiting to whisk me away, no glass slippers that magically transformed me into a beautiful princess. There wasn't even a poisonous needle, or an apple, to put me out of my misery.

My father muttered a curse. "Now you're crying. Useless."

My vision blurred as he sped down US-23 toward Ann Arbor. "If you hate me so much, why didn't you let me go with Mom?"

"I've been shielding you from the reality long enough. You're old enough to know the truth now, Demita," he told me, almost gleefully. "Your mother didn't want you to go with her."

My stomach dropped and a chill shot through my body. "What truth?" I asked. "That you made her life so miserable that she left her own child to get away from you?"

The sting of his hand across my cheek took my breath away. My hand flew to my face, shielding it from him. But he didn't hit me again. At least not physically.

My father snickered. "Telling you to pack that suitcase was her way of keeping you preoccupied while she took my shit and left. When she filed for divorce, she was very clear." He launched into the details of the proceedings, even giving me a quick summary of the court-ordered alimony. "Your mother gave me full legal and physical custody and requested no parenting time."

To some teenagers, legal speak would probably go over their head. Since my father made his living as a divorce attorney, I knew exactly what he meant. Before today, I understood that my father was an abusive, cruel asshole. Now, I understood that my mother was a selfish, weak bitch.

Lightning cracked the sky ahead and the loud clap of thunder followed as the storm intensified. I turned away from him and wrapped my arms around myself. The tears finally fell then, but I wouldn't give my father the satisfaction of seeing them. I blocked out the music, the insults, and him to concentrate on a survival plan. Four more years of living under his roof. Four more years of pain. Four. More. Years. *I can't do it.*

Several minutes later, my father pulled over to get gas. I scanned the area. The gas station was less than a mile away from Dallas' house. I knew this because we'd walked there several times. I peered up at the sky. The rain was coming down hard and fast now. I could barely see the traffic light on the corner. But I did see the faint green circle. The sign was clear. *Run.*

Sucking in a deep breath, I opened the car door.

My father glared at me. "Get back in the car."

"I have to use the restroom," I lied. I ran into the small store and hurried to the bathroom. The torrential down-pour was evident even from inside the small stall and I started to rethink my plan. The Youngs were on vacation and the house was probably locked up. Although they lived close, their massive property was hidden behind a wall of trees at the end of a private, dirt road. I remembered where Dallas said they kept the spare key, but... *What if they moved it?* Biting down on my thumbnail, I struggled to think of another option. It was either now or never.

"God, I know you probably won't even hear me," I cried. "But please help me."

I blew my nose, washed my hands, and stuffed my palms into my pockets. I made my way to the door. My father was now seated inside the car, so I bolted out of the store and ran. By the time I made it to the dirt road, I was out of breath but determined to get there. I jogged a few steps and fell face first when the strap of my flip flop broke. I lay there for a moment before pushing myself to my feet. I walked the rest of the way, shivering from the nonstop rain and the slight drop in temperature.

The moment I caught a glimpse of the house, I sobbed. Because there were lights on. Someone was home. I made it all the way to the paved driveway and then stepped on something sharp, crying out as pain shot up my left leg. Bending down, I checked the bottom of my foot for metal. My eyes zeroed in on a nail lying on the ground and I cursed it to hell. But I kept walking.

Finally, I made it to the door and pressed the doorbell. A moment later, no one had opened the door, so I raised my hand to knock. With all of my remaining strength, I used my fist to pound on the wood.

Seconds later, Dallas' brother, Tristan, opened the door. He frowned. "Demi?"

"I ran away," I offered. "Can I come in?"

He pulled me inside. Stepping back, he assessed me. "From?"

"Everything."

Dallas had seven siblings, but I was glad that it was Tristan who opened the door. He was the oldest. He would definitely know what to do.

"Tristan," a voice called from the kitchen. I realized it was Duke Young. Dallas, Duke, and Dexter were triplets, and I knew Duke well. "Is it the pizza?" Duke walked into the foyer. "What's going on?" He rushed over to me. "Are you okay, Demi?"

I shook my head. "No."

"Did someone do something to you?" Tristan asked, tilting his head to look at me. He was tall. Tall and fine. I'd daydreamed about him many times since I met him. He touched my cheek where my father had slapped me. "Who hurt you?"

I swallowed. "My father hit me."

Tristan's eyes narrowed and his mouth formed a thin line. "Does he hit you often?"

"No," I whispered. "He just makes me feel like shit every day."

"Where did you come from?" Duke asked.

"We stopped at the gas station," I explained. "And I ran."

Sighing, Tristan said, "he's going to be looking for you. Most likely, he'll figure out you ran here."

I grabbed his hand. "Please don't tell him I'm here. I can't go back there."

Tears spilled down my cheeks and I rushed to wipe them away, but Duke stopped me. "It's okay. You're okay." He searched my eyes. "We won't tell him you're here."

"I'm scared," I admitted. Duke hugged me. He didn't seem to care that I was muddy and wet, he just held me. From behind me, I heard Tristan talking to his parents about the situation. Eventually, Duke pulled away and I stared at the mud on his white t-shirt. "I'm sorry about your shirt." I looked down at my bare foot and cursed myself for tracking blood and mud onto the hardwood floor. "And the mess."

He waved me off. "Don't worry about it." He took off his slippers and handed them to me. "We'll clean it up. Put these on so you don't stain the carpet upstairs. Dallas has clothes that you can change into." He held out a hand. "Come on."

Tristan approached us before Duke could lead me up the stairs. "Mom and Dad told me to keep you here. They're heading home now. They will handle your father."

For some reason, that made me cry harder. "Thank you," I whispered.

"We'll take care of you," Tristan said, squeezing my shoulder. "Get cleaned up and I'll get you something to eat."

The doorbell rang, and I tensed. "It's him."

"It could be the pizza." Tristan walked to the door and peered through the peephole. His shoulders fell, confirming my initial thought.

"It's him," I repeated. "He won't stop."

The pounding came next, followed by shouting from the other side of the door. "I know you're in there!"

Motioning for us to go upstairs, Tristan called, "Who is it?"

"Allan Strong," my father answered. "Open the door and send my daughter out."

"Who is your daughter?" Tristan asked.

"You know who my daughter is," my father yelled. "Demita Hope."

As Duke led me up the stairs, I glanced back at Tristan. He stood at the door, fists clenched. Ready to fight. *My hero.* "Is he going to be okay?" I asked Duke.

In my ear, he whispered, "Don't worry. He'll handle it." Once we rounded the corner toward the long hallway, I heard a commotion downstairs as Tristan and my father started arguing. I attempted to run back, but Duke wrapped his arm around my waist to hold me. "Demi, stop. Tristan is fine."

In my fourteen-year-old mind, I couldn't reconcile that Tristan would be a formidable match for my father. He was only three years older than me. My father was in his forties and lifted weights every day after his morning three-mile run. "He's going to get hurt," I murmured.

"He won't," Duke assured me.

"I should just go home with him."

"No." He grabbed a towel from the linen closet. "I'll get you some clothes and you can take a shower." Duke found me an outfit from Dallas' drawer and started the shower. "I'll be back to check on you."

"You're going down there?"

"Just for a little bit. I'll be right back. Hurry up."

Duke backed out of the bathroom, closing the door behind me. I didn't get in the shower, though. I took my clothes off, climbed in the tub, and sat there, letting the water fall on me. My mind raced, thinking of everything I did wrong. I leaned my head against the wall and cried. Then, I fell asleep.

Fluffy fabric against my chest startled me, and I opened my eyes to find Duke standing above me. Seconds later, I was in his arms as he carried me to Dallas' room. He set me on my feet, turned his back to me, and ordered me to dry off.

With shaky hands, I did as I was told and waited for him to turn around. "How long was I in there?"

"Too long," he said.

"Is my father gone?"

"Long gone," he replied.

"Is Tristan okay?"

"Ask him yourself," he answered, motioning at Tristan, who was standing in the doorway.

Tristan smiled. "You scared us."

Immediately, I noticed the dried blood on his lip. "He hurt you?"

"I'm fine," Tristan assured. "He won't come back here again."

"That's because you knocked him the fuck out," Duke chimed in. "He deserved it, though."

Approaching me, Tristan tipped my chin up so that I could meet his gaze. "You can rest now."

I climbed onto the bed, and he covered me with the comforter. "Really?"

"Promise."

Closing my eyes, I let sleep pull me into a sweet dream about my own, personal dark-skinned Knight who saved me from a dastardly King with an uppercut to the chin.

Present Day

My alarm blared at the exact time it was supposed to the next morning. Which sucked because I didn't want to get up. Typically, I'd start my day with a swim. Today... *I need coffee.*

Sighing, I tapped at the screen of my phone. The annoying chimes didn't stop. I hit it again. And again. Until I felt a hand brush against mine, snatching it from my grasp. I screamed, rolling over and toppling onto the floor with a thud. I struggled to recall the events of last night. Eating alone at the hotel restaurant, waiting for Tristan to join me, drinking with Duke, flirting with the waiter ... I peeked over the edge of the mattress, praying it was Duke and not the waiter in my room.

Duke stared at me as if I had grown another head from the other side of the bed. "What the hell is wrong with you?"

I sighed and climbed back up on the mattress. "I didn't know if you were the waiter from last night." I fell back against the bed and covered my head with a pillow. "Everything hurts."

"Your leg?" he asked.

"Yeah."

"Your left foot?"

I frowned. "Yep."

"Your left wrist and arm."

I lifted the pillow and glanced at him. "Yes. How did you…?"

Duke raised a brow. "Because your ass fell in the damn elevator for no reason at all. Just tripped over nothing. I had to carry you to the room."

"Stop lying."

"I don't lie to you," he said through clenched teeth. "I'm going to tell you the truth even if that shit hurts."

Duke was absolutely a person in my life who didn't pull punches. It was a "Young" thing most people didn't understand. Ma and Pop, as I called them, encouraged transparency, integrity, and excellence among other things. But they also acknowledged that life was different for everyone and treated all of us as individuals with a mind of our own. Moving in with them had transformed my entire life and I would be forever grateful for their influence.

"Okay, tell me the truth," I whispered, not sure I wanted to hear about my harsh reality right now.

Duke let out a curse-filled groan. "You already know the truth." Seconds later, he was gone, and I felt… alone.

I sighed heavily, sat up, and finally looked at my phone. I had several missed messages and texts from more people than I cared to talk to.

Dallas: *I'm not going to threaten you. But yo' ass better call me back as soon as you wake up.*

Dallas: *Where the hell are you?*

Mom: *I need to borrow some money.*

Everly: *Call mom. She's getting evicted from her house.*

Everly: *I'm coming to LA next week. Can I stay with you?*

Dorian: *We need to talk.*

Dorian: *When are you coming home?*

Tristan: *Sorry about last night. Something came up.*

The sting of last night was right beneath the surface. Tristan's text had only pulled the scab off the wound. After

I moved in with the Young family, I focused on living my life. Went to school, graduated, went to law school, graduated, worked as a staff attorney, quit my job, then opened my own practice. In that time, I'd dated. Some men were memorable, some were forgettable. I'd learned lessons from all of them, especially my current soon-to-be permanent ex, Dorian. But none of them were Tristan.

Admittedly, I'd had stars in my eyes and happily ever afters in my heart since he'd assaulted my father to protect me. When the police knocked on the door early the next morning to arrest Tristan, my young self knew we were meant to be. He would've gone to jail if Pop hadn't issued a threat of his own to my father. I still didn't know what Pop had on my father, but it worked, and the charges were dropped before sunset. Victory was short-lived, though, because Tristan came home from jail and then promptly enlisted in the Marines.

Another text alert flashed across my screen, and I seethed as I read the message.

Dorian: *Are you going to pay the electric bill?*

Finally, I responded: *I will when you get the hell out of my house, muthafucka.*

Okay, so my personal life left much to be desired. *Maybe I'm being punished for agreeing to meet with Tristan while still in an entanglement?* A sexless relationship wasn't a damn entanglement. My pussy hadn't hugged a real dick in years. Why? Because my man suddenly found God and chose to be celibate without consulting me first. It wasn't all his fault, though. I could've ended it a long time ago, but I didn't. Companionship had propelled me to stay. While Paityn and Rissa lived in Cali too, both of them were happily married. I was pretty lonely out there, no matter how many surprise visits my bestie made to see me. Which made my recent decision to move so easy. I still hadn't decided on Atlanta or Michigan, but either would bring me closer to my family. Because the Youngs *were* my family. That included all of them plus their extended circle.

Dorian: *I'm not leaving until you talk to me. I want us to pray together.*

To avoid feeling like a heathen, I chose my words carefully: *Pray the Lord leads you to a new dwelling.*

Dorian: *Demi, please.*

Me: *Get out.*

I blocked his number and dialed Dallas.

She picked up on the first ring and immediately switched the call to FaceTime. "Girl, you—" She frowned. "What are you going through? You look a hot-ass mess."

I smiled at my bestie and patted the mound of crunchy hair on top of my head. "This is the first time I'm seeing the damage."

"Hurry up and get in the shower."

"I will. Just moving slow." I asked where my goddaughter was. "Is Preston still doing the victory dance?" A couple of days ago, she'd recorded Dominique calling for "Da" and I had to console my poor friend.

"You know he is. Punk." She rolled her eyes. "I need to go back in time and make him push her out of his dick."

Cracking up, I fell back on the mattress. "You're too much. While you're at it, bless him with that stretch mark you were complaining about the other day too."

"I'm sayin'," she agreed. "All that work, months of waddling and strong ass contractions. Then she turns around and says his name first."

"Tragic," I said.

"Enough about me," she said. "Where the hell have you been? I've been blowing your phone up. I almost sent Duke to the hotel to check on you."

"He just left," I told her.

"Good. We've talked about this before. I don't care what you're doing, answer the damn phone when I call."

Everyone knew Dallas hated to be ignored. She gave us all hell for not returning calls. "I know, sis. I just couldn't look at my phone after everything."

Her brows pulled together in a frown. "What happened?"

I shrugged. "He didn't show up."

"Again?"

"Yeah."

Dallas bit down on her lip. Although Tristan was her brother, she'd never pulled any punches with me. She'd told me time and again that it was time to close the chapter on that crazy-ass fantasy. "So…?"

"I know what you're going to say." It was the same thing *I* would say to another woman in my position. But there was something about Tristan and our past that made it hard to let go.

"If you know what I'm going to say, why not just do it?"

"I will," I promised. "I'm done."

"Like you were *done* with Dorian?" she tossed back.

That was different. But the same. *I'm just fucked up.* "I'm done with him too." I'd already filed *and* served the Sixty-Day Notice to Quit. Which he completely ignored, assuming I'd change my mind like I'd done so many times before. "His time is up soon."

"Good. 'Bout time." Her expression softened. "Are you okay?"

Someone once told me that God always sent angels to live among us. For the longest time, I felt like I'd met an angel the day I met Dallas Young. From the moment our eyes locked in fencing class, I knew I'd found a sister. And despite her huge family, she'd treated me as if I'd shared a womb with her. We weren't connected by biology, but she'd taught me that we didn't have to be blood to be family. Our bond had only grown stronger over the years.

I cursed the fresh tears that had formed and willed them not to fall. If it were anyone else, I would've given my patented "I'm fine" response, but since it was her, I said, "I'm not. But I will be."

"Need me to come see you?"

I shook my head. "No, girl. I'll see you next week." Due to a work conflict, I would miss Ma's potato salad and Thanksgiving with the family. But I would make it to *Young'Uns Weekend*. Every year, we went on an agenda-free trip after the holiday. This time, we'd rented an Airbnb in Aspen. "Don't let them eat all of the pancakes."

"I promise."

We chatted for a few minutes about the holiday, Secret Santa, and Blake's wedding date drama. When I hung up, I set my phone down and scooted off the bed. I walked toward the huge window and stretched, lifting my arms toward the ceiling, then reaching toward my toes.

A throat cleared behind me. This time I didn't scream, though, because I knew who it was. I glanced at Duke over my shoulder. He held up a bag. "Breakfast."

I grinned and walked toward him. "I knew you'd come back."

"Only because you need to eat."

I hugged him. "Thank you." Taking the bag, I groaned as the smell of sweet mango and granola wafted to my nose. He handed me a cup of orange juice and I giggled with glee. "You know me so well." On most days, I didn't have time for breakfast. Fresh fruit and yogurt was my go-to morning meal. I pulled the yogurt parfait out of the bag and ate my first bite. "This is good. Not as good as pancakes, though. And bacon."

Duke snorted. "You should go home and make some."

"Ha ha," I mumbled around a mouthful of granola. I sipped my juice. "I'll get some Thanksgiving weekend."

"Whatever." He eyed me warily. "You good?"

I paused, cup to my lips. "Yeah," I lied. "I'll be fine. You can go."

"What time does your plane leave?"

"Around two."

He glanced at his watch. "I have a meeting at Pure Talent, then I'm on a flight to Detroit. I'll drive you to the airport."

"Thank you."

He placed a hand on my shoulder, squeezing gently. "You asked me to tell you the truth."

Oh shit. "Like you said, I already know what it is."

"You're better than this." He searched my eyes, his light brown eyes all-knowing but soft. "Take care of your shit at home and focus on you. Not Tristan."

I swallowed. "I know." I thought about home and stopped him before he walked out of the room. "But… I could use a favor."

Chapter Three

KING OF SORROW

Duke

$\mathcal{I}$ never had to work hard to fuck. That reality was probably why my mother made my father sit me and Dex down to talk about the mechanics of safe sex at an early age. I lost my virginity to the babysitter on my twelfth birthday. At seventeen, I was getting my dick sucked by the babysitter's mother. By the time I was twenty, I'd mastered the art of seduction while simultaneously avoiding committed relationships. It was simple. I liked pussy, but I loved women. I'd spent a lot of time observing them. Nine times out of ten, they just wanted to be respected—for their time, for their contribution, for their mind, for their body, and for their heart. In my experience, they preferred cold-heart truth over flowers and candy any day. Which meant I didn't have to pretend to want forever just to get down. If I wanted someone, I told them. At that point, the decision to move forward was theirs alone. And then there was…

I knocked on the heavy wood door and waited. Seconds later, it swung open. An elderly woman, grey hair and grey eyes, opened the door. "Hi, Mr. Young. Thank you for coming. She's excited to see you. I'm Ola." She held out her hand. "Great to finally meet you."

Shaking her hand, I said, "You too. To be honest, though, I'm not convinced this is a good idea."

"I understand." The woman let out a sigh. "Before you come in, I feel the need to let you know——"

A familiar voice called out, "Duke?" Carolyn Fuller walked toward me. "You're here." She smiled. "You look good."

"You called." I stepped inside. "I came."

To some, Carolyn was a woman who lived a quiet existence in her high-rise apartment overlooking the Detroit River. To many, she was a businesswoman, the founder of one of the largest black-owned businesses in the Country. To others, she was the former owner of one of the largest escort services in the metro Detroit area and the gateway to their forbidden pleasures. To me, she used to be everything.

She pulled me into a hug. "You are a sight for sore, tired eyes."

I ran a hand down her cheek. The years had been kind to her. While the slight droop in her eyelids was noticeable to someone who'd studied her face for hours, her brown eyes were bright and expressive as always. *Not what I expected*. There were more fine lines on her face, but her skin was soft. Her dark-brown hair had turned grey, but it was still thick and long. "You look beautiful," I whispered, brushing my lips against her forehead.

She smirked. "You have to do better than that." There

was a time when I would've given her more than a fore-head kiss. A long time ago, I would've carried her upstairs and had my way with her petite frame, to her delight. But things had changed between us. *I'd* changed.

"You know that's not where we're at," I said truthfully.

Carolyn's smile fell. "Fine." She glanced at Ola. "Is everything set up?"

Ola flashed a warm smile. "Yes, Carolyn."

Glancing at me, Carolyn took my hand and led me further into her house, straight to the kitchen. On the countertop, there were three pans and a turkey.

Ola gave me a tour of the kitchen. "If you need anything, Mr. Young, I'll be in the study." After she made sure Carolyn was situated on her stool, Ola excused herself.

"Thanks for fitting me into your schedule," Carolyn said.

Since I'd started cooking, I'd studied under some of the most talented master chefs in the industry, working my way up from dishwasher and kitchen porter to junior chef followed by station chef, then sous chef. I'd competed and won an ill-fated reality show and spent a year working as a head chef for one of the judges. Sometime after that, I partnered with a friend of mine and opened a restaurant where I was the executive chef. Now, I made a very comfortable living doing à la carte work, meaning I did what I wanted for *who* I wanted. Whether it was catering events, teaching a cooking class, or working as a personal or private chef for wealthy clients.

I opened my bag and pulled out my tools of the trade. I always brought my own ingredients, cooking utensils and equipment. As I sanitized the workspace, I asked, "How many people are you expecting?"

Carolyn watched me curiously over the rim of her

coffee mug. "Maybe ten? Trinity told me she was bringing her new boyfriend."

I froze at the mention of her daughter. The comment seemed innocent enough, but it was the first indication that something wasn't right. "Okay." When she didn't speak for a while, I peered up at her. "Something you want to ask me?"

She shrugged as tears filled her eyes. "No, I'm just sitting here admiring you." I knew her well enough to know that she never just *sat* there. She didn't become a millionaire by just watching things happen. She *made* shit happen. Carolyn was a shrewd businesswoman who'd been a force to be reckoned with, despite her unassuming appearance. "Trinity's getting engaged."

"Good." I opened the refrigerator to make sure she'd purchased the cheese I hadn't been able to secure on such short notice. When I spotted it, I gathered it. On the other side of the island, she was still staring at me. "I'm happy for her," I added.

Carolyn arched a finely shaped brow. "Are you really?"

I busied myself with the task at hand, filling a saucepan with water. "Yes," I answered finally. "She deserves a full life."

The conversation had taken a turn I wasn't comfortable with, but I rolled with it. For many reasons, Trinity Fuller was a stark reminder of my wayward past. She was always a good girl. Although we dated for a short time, we'd never been intimate, never took it beyond a few dinners and museum visits. Unfortunately, she'd met me at a crazy time in my life, which was the downfall of our relationship.

I fell on hard times shortly after we ended things, lost a lot of money due to heavy drinking and heavy gambling. I didn't go to my parents because... Yeah, that just wasn't an option for me at the time. Carolyn convinced me to work for her as an escort. It was an easy out to my debt problems. The choice was clear. I started small, a few dates here or there with random, rich women. Sex wasn't required, so I didn't engage. Until I did. Not with a client, though. But with Carolyn herself.

Our affair was hot and heavy. I thought I loved her. In hindsight, though, I realized it wasn't anything like true love. Obsession, maybe. Lust, definitely. But not love. My life spiraled out of control with her. It took Trinity finding out to snap me out of the trance. In her rage, Trinity not only exposed the affair to her father, she told my parents too. My actions devastated my family and fractured the trust they'd always had in me. I'd worked hard to get it back. To extricate myself from Carolyn and the fallout, I had to practically disappear. The best decision I made was traveling to Paris to study, not only for my career but for my sanity, for my life. Because I came back a changed man. That didn't mean I didn't fuck up every now and then, because I absolutely did, but I didn't gamble away my money and I stopped drinking to excess.

"I miss you," Carolyn said after a few moments of silence.

Sighing, I went to work on the turkey. "How's retirement?" I asked, changing the subject. The last thing I wanted to talk about was me and her.

Carolyn caught the hint. "It's going. I hate..." she trailed off, staring out the kitchen window. "The sun is shining."

I didn't press her to continue the conversation about her business. "It's warm outside too. Nothing like a regular November in Michigan."

Carolyn had formed The Fuller Group, a top HR Consultant firm. When her husband filed for divorce, he'd been relentless in his quest for revenge. By the time he was done, he'd taken mostly everything—the house, the cars, and half of her business. What once was a huge company had faltered under the weight of the scandal and had recently been sold to a larger corporation.

"Are you still painting?" I asked.

She met my gaze then, a pained expression on her face. "No. I stopped doing it right around the time you left."

Avoiding her stare, I tried to focus on grating the cheddar cheese as the heavy feeling in my gut intensified. "Maybe you can pick it back up one day," I suggested.

Over the years, I'd felt many things when I thought of Carolyn. Regret. Anger. Sadness. Shame. But mostly I felt guilty. Because I hadn't really lost anything, and she... Not only had she lost control of The Fuller Group, but the scandal of our relationship had ultimately exposed her underground business and opened her up for criminal charges. And through it all, she'd protected me. She'd prevented everyone, including my parents, from discovering my role in her organization—even when her own world was crumbling around her. For that, I was forever grateful.

Ola returned to the kitchen and whispered something in Carolyn's ear. Standing, she announced, "I have to take care of something."

Once they disappeared around the corner, I started preparing the candied yams. When she'd called last week, she'd requested a traditional Thanksgiving dinner with all the trimmings. My menu consisted of the usual holiday fare with a few surprises. By the time Carolyn had returned an hour later, the turkey and yams were in the oven, the greens were on the stove, and the mac and cheese was ready to bake.

She slid onto a barstool. "You're fast."

"You know I don't play when it comes to food."

I slid the mac and cheese into the convection oven on the wall while Carolyn poured herself a glass of champagne. "Should you be drinking that?" I asked.

"It's just one glass. Won't hurt." She held up the bottle. "Join me?"

I shook my head. "Not today. I still have a lot to do at home."

"Ah, spending the day with your family. Nice. How *is* your mother?"

I stiffened. "Off limits," I warned.

Carolyn raised her arms. "Okay. Sorry, baby. I almost forgot things were different. It feels normal to have you in my kitchen."

I didn't speak to that. I simply cleaned the dirty pots and started on the cornbread. Normally, I wouldn't make dishes ahead of time. Since I knew Carolyn, and this was last minute, I'd prepared the potato salad, homemade cranberry sauce, cornbread dressing, and pound cake at Bliss' house last night.

"Are you seeing someone?" Carolyn asked.

"Why?"

"Just curious."

"Is that why I'm here?"

"Maybe. I told you… I miss you. I miss us."

"If that's why you called me, you're wasting your time. And mine."

"I do love your cooking."

"You could've hired anyone to make your dinner."

"And you could've turned me down." Carolyn walked around the island and wrapped her arms around my neck. "Don't be like this." She kissed me. "I know you came here because you missed me too."

Despite our past and everything I knew to be true

55

about Carolyn, this side of her, the side that could dish it *and* take it, made me smile. Still, I had no desire to travel back down that road with her. I removed her arms and took a step back. "Carolyn, you know this is not what I came here for." I tried to keep my voice calm, even through my own inner turmoil.

"Why *did* you come here?" She folded her arms over her chest as fresh tears spilled down her cheeks. "I know you don't need the money."

That part was true. I didn't need her money *or* her. But I *did* need to see for myself that she was okay. *One last time.* "Are you good?"

Her smile faltered. "What do you mean?"

"Are you happy?" I clarified.

She hunched a shoulder and brushed a thumb over my collar. "Why do you care?"

"How could I not? Especially after everything we've been through."

My phone dinged several times in a row, and I figured the family thread had exploded with commentary about something I didn't care about at the moment. I'd been in town for less than forty-eight hours and that text thread had been jumping since I'd arrived. Last night, Paityn had surprised everyone with a pregnancy announcement during Game Night at my parent's house. Since then, my sisters had gone crazy texting about baby showers and Dallas' crazy ass waddling before she was out of her first trimester. Then, the conversation had evolved into which sibling would have a baby next.

After about the thirtieth ding, Carolyn grabbed my phone. "Don't you think you should get this?"

I dried my hands and took the offered phone. The first text was from the sweet sister.

Bliss: *Can someone please tell Dad that we can't play softball in this weather?*

From there, everybody had something to say. I didn't bother reading every text, but a few stuck out.

Blake: *Can a person get some dick in peace? Chill out on the damn messages.*

Asa: *Be like Dex and don't answer.*

Paityn: *Dexter is newly engaged. Leave him alone.*

Bliss: *Tell Charlye we said Hi!*

Charlye Burke had made my brother the happiest I'd seen him. If Dex wanted to get some morning sex with his fiancée, I saluted him. But I didn't dare enter the fray because Dallas was like a heat-seeking missile on a target. She'd probably badgered Bliss all morning with questions about my whereabouts.

Asa: *Where's Duke?*

Dallas: *Making dumb ass mistakes. But, Dex, it's on sight when I see you.*

I should've known I wouldn't be able to keep this visit a secret from them. Privacy was a rare occurrence among my siblings, even though our parents had encouraged us to mind our own damn business.

Bliss: *You officially talk too much, Sissy.*

I didn't blame Bliss for telling her, though. Dallas had probably badgered her all morning with questions about my whereabouts. And Bliss had probably tried to lie and tell her she didn't know, until she couldn't anymore.

That one text from Dallas unleashed another round of messages from everyone, *including* Dex and Blake, asking for details. I chose peace, not violence, and closed the thread. To my surprise another text came through.

Demi: *Look at this shit.*

A picture of a seemingly half-baked turkey with no seasoning popped up.

Demi: *They're trying to kill me. Save me some turkey, please.*

Thanksgiving was a whole vibe in our house, and Demi had been part of it since the day she came to live with us. And maybe even before. When she'd mentioned she wouldn't be there this year, it felt odd to not have her with us.

Me: *Where are you?*

Demi: *Pray for me.*

Another pic came through. This time of macaroni and cheese that looked more like buttered noodles. The next one she sent was a little harder to make out. But I finally figured out it was green bean casserole.

Demi: *I need some cornbread too.*

Demi: *Just make me a whole plate.*

Demi: *I wonder if you can get it on the plane.*

I couldn't help but imagine her face in the moment. The *bitch, please* look she'd perfected long ago.

Me: *Eat dinner rolls with butter to get full. Don't touch that turkey. Not done.*

Demi: *OMG!*

I frowned and replied: *What?*

Demi: *She's sprinkling raisins in the mac and cheese.*

I chuckled, almost forgetting where I was. I glanced up at Carolyn, who was watching me intently. Clearing my throat, I texted: *I got you on the plate.*

A second later, she responded: *Save pancakes too. At the cabin.*

I responded with a thumbs up emoji and tucked my phone in my pocket. Without acknowledging Carolyn's questioning gaze, I finished beating the sweet potatoes. A little while later, I set the sweet potato pie in the refrigerator. "Once the yams are done, I'll put the pie in the oven. Then, I'll be on my way. I'll leave instructions on how to finish the rest."

"Who is she?" Carolyn asked.

I frowned. "What?"

"The woman on the phone."

"It was Demi."

She sat back in her seat, eyes on mine. "Really?"

I raised a brow. "Really."

"Ah." She took a deep breath. "Does she know you're here?"

If she didn't know now, she would before the end of the day. Dallas would definitely share with her. "Probably."

"Hmph."

"What is that?" I asked. "*Hmph*?"

"Nothing. I just… I know that smile, that look in your eyes. You used to be that way with me. I can't help but wonder how long it'll take for you to realize that you're in love with her."

Carolyn comparing herself to Demi felt wrong. And talking about my feelings for Demi to her wasn't about to happen. "She's family," I told her.

I continued my work in silence while Carolyn watched. Once the pie was in the oven, I cleaned up and packed my bag. When Ola walked back into the kitchen, I gave her instructions on how to reheat the food.

Wringing her hands, Carolyn asked, "Can you stay?" Her eyes darted back and forth between me and Ola. "Please," she begged. "Trinity will be here any minute."

I glanced at Ola, then back at Carolyn. "I can't stay."

"She'll want to see you," she cried. "Maybe you two can talk things out."

"Why don't you go lie down?" Ola smoothed a hand over Carolyn's back. "Remember what the doctor said about your blood pressure? Try to stay calm."

Gripping my sleeve, Carolyn pleaded, "You can't go. You have to wait for Trinity."

Ola attempted to steer Carolyn away, but she clung to me like a lifeline. I tried to comfort her, but she was inconsolable as she called for Trinity over and again. As Ola grabbed her medical bag and pulled out a syringe, I choked back my own tears because I knew Trinity wasn't coming. There would be no talking things out. Trinity wouldn't be at Thanksgiving dinner, Trinity wasn't getting engaged, Trinity would never get married... *Because Trinity is dead.*

Chapter Four

DON'T WASTE MY TIME

Demi

*W*hen I'd decided to go to law school, I had one goal. To be better than my father. For years, he'd earned a reputation for being the worst divorce attorney a woman could hire. And I wanted to be the best attorney for women married to assholes like him. Period. So when I graduated with my Juris Doctorate, I immediately went to work at one of the best family law firms in Washtenaw County, Michigan.

I'd worked long, hard days and nights to earn my nickname, The Divorce Whisperer. And I dared any man to come into court with me unprepared because they thought I was unqualified. The first case I won against my father had been the most memorable. The moment he'd entered the courtroom like he owned it had been seared on my brain. He'd underestimated me when I was a teenager, and he'd underestimated me that day too. And I'd beat him, getting my client a seven-figure settlement from her philandering husband. That wasn't the only time I'd bested him in court. He hated to see me coming, and I liked it that way.

Moving to California hadn't changed that. I still regularly worked in Michigan, representing my clients' best interests in divorce court. But my decision was made based on two things—attracting more celebrity clientele and building a relationship with my mother and sister. Mom had moved to Los Angeles with the same man I'd seen her with at our house the day she'd left. Two more husbands later, she was still there. She was also still a liar, still manipulative, and still selfish. Upon my arrival in California, she'd promptly asked me for money and a car. I'd quickly distanced myself from her, but she was my mother. Despite how much she'd hurt me, there was a part of me that would probably always want her in my life. Even if she was full of shit.

Lately, she'd been calling me, begging me for another chance to be a good mother. I wasn't sure when the change of heart happened—or *if* she even had a heart—but I was pretty sure she was working an angle. The last time we'd spoken hadn't been a good experience for me and had essentially devolved into an argument about how *I'd* been awful to her since I was a kid. *Me.* When she'd left me like yesterday's trash with my abusive father.

Even with the past between us, and against my better judgment, I'd accepted an invitation to Thanksgiving "dinner." I'd regretted it from the moment I arrived. It was more like brunch, though, because it would be served at noon. *Who the fuck does that?* Her reasoning was because she had another event to attend. Which meant I'd be hungry by actual dinnertime.

Walking in the door that morning, I'd been greeted by a strange man with a wandering eye who'd promptly made me extremely uncomfortable when he suggested I call him Daddy. Then, my sister's boyfriend leered at me while my sister doted on him. And let's not get started on the food. The meal was already done. Well, the turkey looked under-cooked. The rest of the sides were in serving dishes, ready to go out on the table. In other words, everything would be cold as hell when we ate. *I guess it's up to us to warm our own plate up.*

As a kid, I didn't remember seeing my mother in the kitchen. I recalled a housekeeper coming to the house to cook sometimes and my grandmother making chicken one day. But that's it. My father had once told me he married my mother for her beauty, because she looked good on his arm, not because she was a great homemaker. He'd told me that when he'd forced me to make his dinner three times a week so that I didn't end up like her.

"Demi, please check on the ambrosia in the fridge," my mother instructed, re-entering the kitchen after she'd excused herself to shower. Her sandy, blonde hair was pulled back in a ponytail, and she wore a pair of black jeans with a green silk blouse. She once told me that green was her color, so she rarely dressed without incorporating it into her outfits. Even the smoky eyeshadow she wore drew attention to her green eyes. And she donned tear-drop emerald earrings. "I want to be sure it's set."

My mother was biracial and was raised by her white mother. Before I got there, she'd been so excited to share her mother's recipes with me for the first time. But when I saw that turkey? All I could do was think about how Ma was probably making the shit out of her homemade rolls. And that potato salad... *Lawd, I miss my family*. The thought was sobering, that I was actually with my *biological* family while simultaneously wishing I was with my *real* family.

While my mother sang an old school R&B jam I didn't recognize, I opened the fridge to check the ambrosia. *Yuck.* I studied the contents of the bowl. Marshmallows, cherries, oranges, pineapples. Coconut? *Are those pecans?* "I think it's..." *Disgusting?* I frowned as I eyed the dessert again. "...ready. Do you have pound cake?" The desperate tone in my voice surprised even me.

My mother frowned. "No. I'm not a fan. But I did buy a delicious pumpkin pie at the grocery store for another dessert option."

"Oh," I mumbled, making my way back over to the dining room table.

There were always plenty of desserts at home on Thanksgiving. Ma handled the pound cake, Paityn usually took care of the peach cobbler, while Duke slayed the sweet potato pies. *He probably made about five of them mugs too.* The house probably smelled like a mixture of nutmeg, cinnamon, and everything else that was good. My stomach growled. *Shit.*

Everly set a bowl of wet-ass mashed potatoes on the table. They weren't fluffy like Blake's. Or even mine. I made great potato dishes. My specialty was fried with onions. I peeked in the bowl and was surprised there was no evidence of butter, not even a small pat. *I should've offered to bring something.* "Did you make these?" I asked my sister.

Everly was my mother's daughter from her first husband. Fortunately for her, her father was actually a stand-up guy who honored his visitation agreement. Which was why I don't have many memories of my sister in the summer because she'd always spent that time with *her* dad.

"Mom did," she told me before she disappeared into the kitchen again.

"Sure did," my mother said, as she walked the ham over to the table. "I can send you the recipe. I got it from your grandma." She leaned in and smelled the ham. "Smells good."

Confused, I leaned in too and all I smelled was cold pork. Because there was nothing else to it. It was just a hunk of meat, no pineapples, no brown sugar. Nothing. Duke's ham was probably warm and tender. If I thought about it really hard, I could taste his special glaze. He was so good in the kitchen my mouth was watering just thinking about his candied yams too.

The last thing set on the table was fried chicken. And I silently thanked God for seasoning that I could smell. I wanted to dip my head and take it all in. Everly must have made this because her grandmother could throw down in the kitchen. I knew this because when Everly graduated from college, I went to the celebration with Dallas. We smashed that day.

Everly sat down next to me and nudged me with her elbow. "I'm glad you're here."

I forced myself to smile, then promptly told a bite-sized lie. "Me too."

"Mom is really grateful," she whispered. "She talks about you all the time."

That's doubtful. My sister wasn't as nice as she was acting today. She was more like my mother than even she probably cared to admit. They even looked alike. The only difference was skin color, because Everly's father was Black too. But to be polite, I said, "Thanks for telling me that."

"Seriously. We were talking about it, and both of us want to be closer to you."

Yeah right. "Sounds nice."

"I need my sister," she continued, oblivious to my inner torment. "I hate that things are strained."

I needed a sister too. And God gave me one when I met Dallas all those years ago, then he blessed me with three more when *she* introduced me to her sisters. "Me too," I repeated.

I took more pics of all the dishes that were set out and sent them out to Dallas. *And Duke.* Earlier, Duke had warned me not to eat the turkey because it wasn't done. Luckily, my mother had put it in the oven for a little bit after I'd sent the pic. Instead of looking pale and under-cooked, it now looked pale and dry.

By the time dinner was served, I was longing for a way out and a flight to Michigan. But I wouldn't leave. It had been a while since I'd been in the room with my mother *and* my sister. So, I was determined to make the best of it.

We ate in silence—well, *they* ate—which was absolutely not how Thanksgiving was back home. Dinner probably wouldn't be ready until about four, maybe five. But there'd be lots of people, sports on the television, cards on the table, and a house full of love.

"Did you ever get my message?" my mother asked.

I buttered a roll and tried to imagine it was homemade and not the brown-and-serve type. "Huh?"

"The text I sent," she clarified. "I told you I needed a favor."

I scanned the faces around the table, a little embarrassed that she'd essentially forced me to address this in front of people. But I would. "I did."

"Well?"

"I don't have it," I told her, taking a bite of a crunchy green bean. I set my fork down and drained my glass wine. Everly poured me another, and I thanked her.

"I don't believe you," Mom said. "You own your practice. You work."

You could too. "I also have bills to pay. Why do you need it?"

She glanced at her boyfriend. "Desmond owes back child support. In order to get his passport so we can travel, he has to pay the balance. You'd be doing us a favor."

"So you're not getting evicted?" I glared at my lying sister, then met the waiting gaze of the man in question. "How much child support do you owe?"

Desmond stammered a bit, then finally said, "About ten thousand."

"Hmm. Isn't that something? You're perfect for each other. Neither of you take care of your children."

"*I* asked for the money to help him," my mother interjected. "He didn't put me up to it, so don't talk about him like that because you don't know him."

I pushed my plate away. "Okay, then. Why would you think that I'd give a man I barely know money to pay his child support?"

"You're not giving it to him. You're giving it to me."

"Why should I give *you* money?" I tossed back.

My mother set her glass down on the table hard, rattling the plates near her. "Because I gave birth to you. I fed you. I read you stories. I fostered your imagination. *I* inspired you to become an attorney."

Before I could even stop myself, I laughed. She was right, though. My parents did inspire me. Because they treated me like shit. "In some ways," I agreed. "But it was sheer will and hard work that got me to where I am today. But you wouldn't know anything about that, would you? Because you don't know *me*, and you don't know how to work. Real talk? If I had waited for you and my father to do shit, I wouldn't be doing anything."

"Hey, now," Desmond chimed in. "Don't talk to her like that. This is our house."

"*Her* house," I corrected. "I know because I helped her get the loan modification a few years ago."

"Demi!" Mom shouted.

"Is that why I'm here?" I asked, dropping my napkin on the table.

Everly sighed. "This isn't the time to talk about this."

"Answer me," I commanded. "Did you invite me here to ask for money?"

My mother had the decency to shift in her chair. Because she *should* be uncomfortable with my question. "Partly," she admitted.

"Ah," I took another deep breath. Then let out another humorless chuckle. The room was quiet for a moment while I gathered my thoughts. Any hope that I had for my relationship with this family evaporated. "This is bullshit." I stood. "How dare you ask me for anything!"

"Watch your tone in my house," she warned. "Show me some respect. I'm still your mother."

"You gave birth to me. Then, you left me and stayed gone. You don't have the right to claim to be my mother. My *mother* is 2,200 miles away, probably making the shit out of some chicken and dumplings right now. With love. My mother *and* father paid cash for my tuition to Hampton University every year because you couldn't be bothered to support me in my education. Then, they paid for law school so I could graduate debt free. They didn't ask me for anything in return. They didn't even ask me if it was okay to do it. They just did it because they care about me." I grabbed my purse. "My *mother* held me when you didn't bring your ass to my graduation party. My *mother* called me this morning just to tell me she loved me and wished I was there. *You* are not my fuckin' mother. That honor goes to Victoria Young. *She* is my mother. *She* did the job you couldn't." I pulled out my wallet, grabbed all the cash I had and tossed it on the table. "There's your money. Two hundred dollars. Do whatever, but don't call me again. Fuck you."

Then, I snatched a couple of pieces of chicken, wrapped them up in a napkin, and stormed out.

Chapter Five

MR. WRONG

Demi

"*Where* are you going?" Dorian walked up behind me. "Don't you think we should talk?"

As far as I was concerned, I was done talking. I'd met Dorian in law school. We were two of seven Black students in our Critical Race Theory class. I was immediately attracted to him because he was smart as hell. He could break a subject down with finesse, leaving every woman in class transfixed. He asked me out once class ended and our relationship blossomed from there, even after he dropped out of law school to study philosophy. He'd been a huge support when I'd made the decision to go into private practice. And decided to move with me to California. That's when things started to unravel.

Now, I couldn't stand him. I never expected marriage, but I did expect him to pay some damn bills in the house.

There was always an excuse, a reason why he didn't get the job. Sometimes it was a feeling he got in the interview. But when that nigga came home and said he turned down a job because the company's mission didn't align with his belief system, I lost it. And just like I'd done with my mother yesterday, I was way past ready to cut him out of my life.

"Demi," Dorian called.

"Get out," I ordered. "You know how eviction works. Don't make me throw your shit out on the sidewalk."

"I don't think you realize what you're doing."

He reached out to touch my face and I flinched, smacking his hand away. "Don't touch me."

He held up his hands, placating me. "Sorry."

"And don't try to counsel me like I'm a parishioner at your Bedside Baptist Church." Last year, Dorian surprised the hell out of me by starting his own online church. To date, he only had five members, all of them women vying for a spot on the pastor's dick.

"Let's get married."

I snickered. "You tried it. "I don't want to marry you. I don't want to talk to you. I just want you gone."

"You never did pray with me."

I rolled my eyes. He'd attempted to bring God into our disagreements time and again. I was tired of it. "Give it up, Dorian. If you believe in God, then you should believe that He didn't create you to be a bum. All you do is sit on my couch all day and eat my food. Get a damn job."

"I hear you. I even have an interview next week."

"Good for you. But that doesn't change anything between us." I packed several outfits into my suitcase, then walked into the bathroom to gather my toiletries. He followed me. "Why are you in here?" I'd kicked him out of my bedroom months ago, hoping he'd get the hint and leave. But… *He's still here.*

"Where are you going?"

"Where do I always go after Thanksgiving?" I tossed back.

"You moved here to be closer to your mother. Why are you still spending so much time with the Youngs?"

Dorian couldn't stand the family, probably because they'd seen through him on the first meeting. While Dallas had known him from law school, she'd told me he wasn't worthy from the beginning. The rest of the family fell in line, with everyone from Raven to Pop warning me about him. And, once again, I didn't listen thinking I knew what was best for me.

I checked my watch. My flight was scheduled to depart in three hours. With LA traffic, I needed to get on the road right away. I finished packing while he stood there watching me, hoisted my suitcase, and brushed past him.

I pulled my winter coat and boots out of the front closet and hurriedly stuffed them into my carryon, along with snacks, a change of clothes in case my luggage was lost, and a couple of books. At the front door, I glanced at my phone. My rideshare was outside.

"I don't get a hug?" Dorian asked.

I frowned at him. "Man, please. Take your ass in your room, pack your shit up, and be gone before I get back."

L ater, Dallas called as the car pulled up to the lodge. Instead of answering, I texted her to let her know I was there. The driver helped me unload my luggage and even walked it to the front door for me, where Dallas was waiting with a big grin. She pulled me into a tight hug, and I let her. That's when I cried, right there on the porch. I didn't care that it was cold as hell outside. I didn't care that the driver was still standing there. I just wanted the comfort my sister was giving me.

"Thanks for getting her here safely," she said to the driver.

Without looking at him, I mumbled my thanks and rested my head on her shoulder again.

"Come on, boo." Dallas led me inside the house, then grabbed my luggage.

To avoid being seen with tears in my eyes, I asked Dallas to take me to my room first so I could get myself together. "I don't want them to see me like this," I added.

Dallas and I each took a bag to the second floor. We were lucky enough to find a luxury lodge with eight King master suites, each with its own bathroom, and a flex space with additional beds.

In my room, which I'd share with Bliss, there was a desk and a walk-out balcony. There was also a mini fridge so that we wouldn't have to trek all the way down to the kitchen for snacks or drinks.

"This is gorgeous," I whispered, walking around the space.

"I'll give you the full tour later," Dallas told me, setting my suitcase on a chair in the corner. "Duke is in heaven with that kitchen. You should've seen him and Paityn in there doing their thing this morning."

Plopping down on the bed, I fell back on the mattress and sighed. "I'm so tired, sis."

Dallas joined me, lying down next to me. "I'm glad you're here."

I glanced at her. "Yesterday was horrible." I'd told Dallas about Thanksgiving with my mother last night, but it was still bothering me this morning. "And today wasn't any better. I got into with Dorian before I left, got stopped at TSA… I'm just done."

Dallas turned to face me. "You're going to be okay, Demi."

I placed a hand on my forehead. "I feel like such an idiot. Wanting a relationship with her after everything."

"She's your mother."

I shook my head. "No, she's not."

Dallas hugged me. I sobbed again while she rubbed my hair. "It's perfectly normal to desire that connection, Demi. Stop being so hard on yourself for that."

"What about Dorian?"

She muttered a curse. "We've all done it. Been with no-good ninjas."

"I've been with more dirtbags than you."

"Yeah, you're pretty attracted to lost causes. Remember Marco?"

I laughed. "Ugh. Marco was a mistake not worth mentioning again."

"Girl, I saw him at the grocery store a couple of weeks ago. He is busted. I don't know what you saw in him."

Shrugging, I said, "It was high school."

"And college," she corrected. "With his trifling no-teeth-having ass."

I snorted as I cracked up, remembering how Duke and Dex blazed me for getting with someone who looked and sounds like he could be Mike Tyson's twin. "He had a good heart."

Giggling, she asked, "Could he *spell* heart?"

Nudging her, I said, "Shut up."

"Anyway, you're still fire. You are one of the best people I know. Talented, smart, funny, and gorgeous. You don't need Dorian or his whack-ass dick."

I bit down on my lip. There wasn't much I hadn't

shared with Dallas, but the fact that I'd essentially been celibate right along with Dorian wasn't something I wanted to tell anyone. The only person who knew was Duke, and that was because I'd slipped up and admitted it to him one day. "I have a confession to make."

She frowned. "What?"

"Dorian and I haven't had sex in years."

Dallas blinked. "Huh?"

"When he gave himself to the Lord, he gave up on fucking me," I explained.

"Shit," she mumbled. "For real?"

"I'm so serious."

"Years?"

I nodded.

My bestie didn't say anything for a moment, but I could see the wheels turning in her head. "So you let that fool stay in your house, and he wasn't even giving you the "D"? And you didn't tell me?"

I stood and paced the room. "I was embarrassed."

"Giirrrlllll!" Dallas shook her head and let out a deep sigh. "This is crazy as hell. The whole time I've been thinking you were having underwhelming sex when you weren't getting any at all." She smacked her legs and stood. "Well, I guess you know what you have to do now that you're essentially free." She approached me and brushed a finger over my cheek. "It's time for you to get fucked."

My mouth fell open. "Dallas!"

"I'm just sayin'."

I covered my ears and walked into the bathroom to wash my face. "I'm done with this conversation."

"No. Not really. I distinctly remember you twerking when you found out I was doing Preston *and* encouraging me to keep doing it."

"But you knew Preston for years before you did it. I'm

not having sex with a random person, Dallas." I splashed water on my face and dried it with a towel.

"Maybe he won't be a stranger." She gasped. "You should let Bliss hook you up."

I sliced a hand in the air. "No. I don't need a matchmaker. I just need a break. I'm going to take this time to focus on myself, figure out where I want to be."

Dallas tilted her head and studied me. "Okay, I won't push. But the minute you complain to me about being lonely or horny, I'm going to remind you of this conversation."

"Deal."

"Now, let's go. Time to get the day started. We're pulling names for Secret Santa."

The game room was in the back of the house. Before we walked in, Dallas asked me was I good. When I nodded, she took my hand and pulled me into the room. "Look who I found. She pulled up right as I was calling her."

I took my time greeting everyone in the room. When I got to Duke, I punched him. "That's for not saving me any pancakes."

"Shit," he grumbled, rubbing his shoulder.

"They slapped too," Blake added.

"That's why I'm about to give this short stack I hid for you to Harp's greedy ass."

I gasped. "You saved me some?" I jumped into his arms and planted a kiss to his cheek. "Thank you."

Duke led me to the kitchen to retrieve my breakfast. He stayed with me while I ate. "This is exactly what I needed," I mumbled around the food in my mouth.

He leaned against the counter and smirked. "I bet."

"Are you going to tell me where you were?"

I paused, fork midair. Swallowing, I said, "I don't really want to talk about it."

He placed a hand on mine. "Are you okay?"

I drank the rest of my orange juice and ate a piece of bacon, chewing slowly to stall the conversation. Duke wasn't deterred, though. He just watched me. "I was at my mother's house."

His eyes widened. "Again... Are you okay?"

It was Duke's way to not be concerned about the details. He only ever wanted to know if I was good. "Not really." I explained the dinner scene briefly, then told him about Dorian. "So that was my holiday."

"I guess it's a good thing I brought you a plate, then." He winked. "So you can make your turkey sandwich today."

I grinned. Every year, I looked forward to the Day After Thanksgiving Turkey Sandwich. And Duke made it extra good. I pressed my palms together and bowed to him. "Bless you."

He barked out a laugh. "Greedy."

"I've been through a traumatic experience. I need good food to make it all better."

Smiling, he searched my eyes. "I got you."

"You do, don't you?"

"You never have to ask."

We stared at each other for a moment longer than normal. But it didn't feel awkward. It felt... nice. It wasn't even surprising because Duke had always been a constant for me. But it was also something more than nice, something I couldn't name.

I blew out a breath and took another bite. "I'm getting full."

"Stop eating then," he said with a smirk.

My stomach did an odd flip, and I braced my hand

there. "I will when I get done." Deciding to change the subject, I said, "Dallas told me about *your* Thanksgiving."

"I had no doubt that she would."

"Well…?" I motioned for him to continue. "What made you go there?"

"Closure."

Duke's history with Carolyn had been a touchy subject with everybody, especially him. After everything had gone down between the two of them, and the subsequent fall-out, he'd never mentioned her again. "Is that it?" I moved the food around my plate. "You made her dinner for closure?"

"Pretty much."

I figured that was all he would give me, so I said, "Okay. I'll take your word for it."

"Thank you."

After I ate, we went back to the game room. As we played games, talked shit, and just chilled, I marveled at how easy everything was with them. I never wanted to give that up.

Right on time, Dallas stood and announced the Secret Santa drawing. She gave her big spiel for Charlye's family, who'd joined us this year. Then, she threatened Asa with bodily harm if he failed to buy his gift on time.

When Harper asked where Tristan was, he unknow-ingly put a damper on the room. Tristan hadn't been to a *Young'Uns' Weekend* yet, and real talk, he wasn't really missed by most of the siblings. All the sisters knew about the Atlanta incident, but as far as I knew, Dexter and Asa had no idea what had happened. And Duke… I avoided his annoyed stare because I knew he was still pissed about everything.

Paityn finally cleared her throat and answered, "He's busy."

Lennox placed a finger over Blake's mouth before she could interject, shaking his head at her and silently letting her know not to say anything. Much to her chagrin. Off to the side, I noticed Charlye and Dex whispered to one another and wondered if someone had told him.

"Dallas, come on," Asa said, breaking the awkward silence. "We're ready."

Dallas jumped into action, and everyone picked their names from the box. I'd just looked at the name when I heard Bliss gasp. I followed her gaze to the door. Tristan stood there, hands in his pockets.

I scanned the room, noting the varying expressions on each of his siblings' faces. Only two of them looked happy to see him, but that didn't stop him from entering the room. "What's up?" he greeted. "Am I too late to draw a name?"

My heart dropped, and I let the small piece of paper I'd pulled fall on the floor. Feeling a need to escape, I left the room. I wasn't sure where I was going, but I needed some air. I veered off down a hallway and exited through a glass door.

Chapter Six

WRONG IDEA

Duke

*a**m I too late to draw a name?*

When Demi bolted out of the room, Dallas attempted to follow her, but I stopped her. My sister glared at me and opened her mouth to protest. "Let her go," I ordered. "She just needs time."

"But—"

"He's right," Paityn interjected. "She'll be fine. We need to talk."

Without prompting, Charlye herded her family out of the room, followed by Preston and Bishop. But before Preston walked out, he told Dallas, "I'll find her."

Am I too late to draw a name?

The more those words played on a loop in my mind, the angrier I became. As siblings, we'd traveled together often because it was important to us to maintain our tight bond. Long gone were the days where we all lived in close proximity, so we made it a point to schedule sibling time without our parents. The weekend after Thanksgiving was just one of those trips. We vacationed in the summer together, and sometimes in the spring. And we also managed to carve out small group time. My sisters took girls trips while my brothers and I went camping several times a year.

Yet, in all those instances, at every single function, Tristan was never there. That big-head muthafucka never showed up for anything. And the fact that he just magically appeared at the lodge today was some bullshit. Because he had a motive. *Demi.*

Blake lit into him first, "What the hell is your problem, Tristan? You just walked in here like you didn't fuck shit up with Demi last week."

"I don't have a problem," Tristan grumbled.

"It's the audacity for me," Dallas chimed in, shaking her head. "To show up unannounced."

"Ruining the entire vibe," Blake added.

"You haven't called," Dallas continued. "You didn't RSVP. You didn't pay shit on this house and you, what? Figured it was time to catch up after being gone for months with no communication?" Dallas' reaction was indicative of her unconditional love for Demi. Usually, she would've defended Tristan against an onslaught of criticism, but it had been a long time and he'd missed out on several pivotal moments in *her* life. "I can't even tell you how fucked up this is. I had a fucking baby that you've never met."

Tristan glanced at Paityn. "You want a shot at me?"

My older sister shook her head. "I don't have anything to say, Tristan."

His gaze dropped to my sister's growing belly and smiled. "You're pregnant?"

Like all of us, Tristan was well aware of my sister's trouble conceiving. I didn't doubt that he was happy for her and Bishop because he knew how long they'd been trying.

"I am." Paityn brushed her hand over his cheek. "I'm so happy to see your face. I've missed you."

"You're angry with me. I get it."

"I feel like you're being disingenuous right now," Paityn admitted. "You have a motive for being here that doesn't involve simply spending time with us. That hurts."

I heard a soft sniffle from behind me and craned my neck. Bliss dashed tears from her cheeks and stood. "I hate to say this because you know I love you with everything in me. But I hate that you came here. All I can feel is the tension in the room when you're around. It's like you're a dark cloud casting a shadow on a sunny day. It's a tragedy to me because…" She sucked in a shaky breath and took the Kleenex Dexter offered. "…you have so much to give. I remember feeling invincible, free when you were around. Now I'm just heavy."

Blake muttered a curse because Bliss was the heart of our group. And judging by the tears in my sisters', and even Asa's eyes, the fact that Bliss had shed tears had affected everybody in the room. As for me, it made me even more angry.

"Listen, bruh," Dex said, "I don't know what's going on, but I don't like it."

Dexter had been preoccupied for the past several months. Not only was he planning a wedding, but he'd also made the decision to split his time between Michigan and Atlanta due to Charlye's job. And since he'd spent Thanksgiving in Atlanta with her family, he hadn't been privy to the latest drama.

"You don't have to like it," Tristan told Dex. "But

you're *my* brother. And you've always been fair. Shouldn't I have a chance to explain myself?"

"I think you should be able to speak your peace," Asa agreed. My youngest brother had the benefit of not being a twin, a Triple, or the oldest. He'd pretty much been able to live his life under the radar, without much pushback from the family because of his age and general no fucks given attitude. But he was closer to Tristan than most of us, so his opinion didn't surprise me.

Tristan sat, resting his elbows on his knees. "I didn't mean to hurt Demi."

"This time?" I asked, unable to keep silent any longer. He waved me off, but I wasn't deterred. "What are you doing here?"

"I thought I could come and try to mend some relationships."

Blake scoffed. "You could've come to Thanksgiving dinner. Mom was waiting for you to show up, after you told her you would. And you didn't."

"I know I'm not your favorite person, lil sister," Tristan said, "but I do care."

"If you care, do something about it other than spout lame-ass excuses." Blake glanced at Dallas. "When was the Mediterranean Cruise for Mom and Dad's anniversary?"

"Last year," Dallas answered.

"Right. Aside from your cameo appearance at Dallas' wedding for twenty minutes, that was the last time we saw you. And, honestly, I'm tired of your blatant disrespect of Mom and Dad."

"I do miss y'all." Tristan met my gaze finally and I caught a glint of something in his eyes. It wasn't regret. It wasn't shame. But I couldn't put my finger on it just yet. "I want to be here. But I need to talk to Demi first."

"No." I shoot my head, drawing seven pairs of

surprised eyes to me. I didn't care. My urge to protect her was stronger than his desire to gaslight the family into giving him what he wanted. And I didn't want to think about *why*. I just knew I had to make sure she was good. "That's not going to happen today. You've done enough."

Bliss squeezed my arm. "Duke, it's okay."

Ignoring my sister, I leveled a hard glare on my brother. "Why do you want to see her? So you can lead her on a little more? String her along for a couple more years? Nah, nigga, she's good." I caught Dexter's curious glance out of the corner of my eye, but I kept going. "She's reconciled the fact that you and her are not a thing. Oh, and that happened after you stood her up. Again."

"When did you start speaking for Demi?" He snickered. "Because last time I checked, she was capable of making her own choices. Despite what you may think, I do care about her.."

"That's never been in question, Tristan. She knows you care about her. I mean, she's part of the family. What she doesn't know is that you don't want her. You never did."

"How would you know?" Tristan challenged.

"Man, shut the hell up," I blared. "You know as well as I do that if you wanted her, your ass would be here. With her. You never wanted her like that. Which is fine. But don't make it seem like there could be something when we all know there won't be anything."

Paityn stood in front of me. "Baby brother, I think we all just need a break right now. Especially you."

"I'm fine," I assured her. "He came and inserted himself into the weekend. He can hear what I have to say."

"Demi is good for me," Tristan said.

"No, she's just a good person," I shot back.

"I'm just not that good for her right now," he continued.

Rolling her eyes, Blake asked, "So you're playing the martyr now? Falling on your valiant sword?"

Tristan eyed her warily. "You don't understand."

"I definitely do," she said. "And just so you know... if Demi was one of *my* clients, I would've told her to leave your ass alone a long time ago."

"This anger can't just be about Demi," Tristan mused.

"It's not," Dallas confirmed. "It's about you."

"Well, let's hear it." Tristan stretched his legs. "Tell me what I can do so that we can move past this."

"You could actually spend real time with all of us," Asa suggested.

"And be engaged during that time," Bliss added.

Tristan nodded. "Okay."

The conversation had taken an unexpected turn. If I were to believe everything my brother was saying, he'd seemingly realized the error of his ways and was ready to confront his past to build a relationship with us. I wasn't sure who he thought he was talking to but none of us were stupid. Even Asa was eyeing him suspiciously. After all, we'd been raised by two of the best bullshit detectors I'd ever met. My parents had perfected the art of spotting a lie before it was even released into the atmosphere.

"You know the reason why we're not close anymore?" I asked.

He let out a heavy sigh. "I'm sure you're going to tell me."

"Because you're comfortable in your lies."

"And this sudden change of heart is giving..." Blake placed a hand on her hip. "...You think we're dumb as fuck."

I pointed at my little sister. Blake was essentially me in a pair of yoga pants and a long ponytail. Of all my siblings, she was the most like me in her ability to not give a fuck about anybody's feelings. "That part."

Tristan's jaw ticked. "Whatever."

"Here's another truth for you," I offered. "You don't want Demi because you've been fucking Sasha for years."

"Whoa!" Asa shouted.

Paityn gasped. "What?"

Dallas' eyes widened, but she recovered quickly. "Seriously?"

Tristan's eyes flashed to mine. "What the fuck are you talking about?"

"Didn't think I knew about that, huh?" I'd known about it all along because Sasha told me herself. She'd also sworn me to secrecy which was why I hadn't told anyone else. Until today. "Here's another fact. I saw you with *her* while Demi was waiting for *you* alone at the damn hotel bar."

Tristan stood. "Sasha has nothing to do with this."

"So why hide it?" I asked.

"I'm not the only one hiding shit, Duke." Tristan approached me. "You have some skeletons too."

Backing down wasn't my thing. Never had been. "But they're not hidden. You're just not asking the right questions."

"Does the family know about your past?"

I folded my arms across my chest. "If they did, I wouldn't care."

"I'm curious now." Tristan glanced at everyone, then back at me. "Doesn't anyone want to know why Duke is so protective over Demi?"

"I always assumed it was because she's one of us," Dallas mused. "Kind of how you're supposed to be."

"Demi is a grown woman," he argued.

I shrugged. "And? Woman and men do things all the

time that are against their best interests. Hell, Bliss is accomplished, beautiful, intelligent… but she still ended up with Tyler's secret-family-having ass.

Bliss smacked me. "Hey!" she snapped. "This isn't about me."

My eyes softened. "I'm sorry, but I'm trying to prove a point."

She rolled her eyes." Whatever. Go ahead."

"And what did you do when you found out he hit her?" I continued. "You were ready to wear his ass out. If this was Demi and anyone else, you would want to do the same. Why shouldn't I kick the shit out of you right now?"

Dexter clasped my shoulder. "Alright, now. We're not fighting here."

I appreciated my brother's calm demeanor. He was like Pop in that way. And I knew what he was trying to do, but I wasn't trying to hear it today.

Apparently, Tristan wasn't either because he stepped to me like I was a stranger on the street. "You could try."

I snickered. "We're not kids anymore, *brotha*. I wouldn't have to try."

His nose flared in anger. "Why do you care so much?"

"Why *don't* you care as much?"

"It's always you," Tristan shook his head. "Why do you have a problem with me?"

"Maybe if I had time, or cared enough, I might sit down and give you all the reasons why I think you're full of shit. But since we're in a house full of people who are not Youngs, and I have shit to do, I'll just go with my main problem."

"Which is?"

"You never sit in your own shit. When we were young, I thought you were the coolest, the baddest cat. There was nothing you could've done that would've knocked you off that pedestal. But you jumped off that mug in one of your crazy rages. Up until that point, we had no idea you weren't mom and dad's biological son. Even after we found out, we didn't care."

"He's right," Dex agreed. "It never mattered to us."

Tristan's mother was my father's little sister. When she died, my parents took him in and raised him as their own. Although Tristan knew the truth, our parents had never told us the details. Mostly, because it never mattered to them. Tristan had been theirs since he was two years old, and even before that. My mother was in the delivery room when he was born and had even named him. And because Aunt Sara had struggled with a long-term illness, Ma had stepped in to provide constant care to both of them during that time.

"We didn't tell people you were our adopted brother," Paityn said.

"You were just our big brother," Dex added.

"You made it *us* against *you*," I continued. "And *you* used that to alienate yourself from us."

Paityn hugged Tristan. "I just want you to be okay."

"In the meantime," Dallas approached him, "I need you to leave."

Chapter Seven

I CAN'T MAKE YOU LOVE ME

Demi

The setting sun provided a beautiful backdrop as I took the scenery in. Closing my eyes, I thought about everything that had happened to me yesterday and today. Part of me was happy that Tristan was there. Despite what happened between us, I wished he'd mend his relationships with his siblings. But the selfish part of me, the part that hated the thought of being around him right now, wanted him to leave. *Can I tell him that?*

I heard a rustle behind me but didn't turn around. I didn't have to, though, because Tristan walked up to me and stood beside me. Peering out at the mountain, he said, "I'm sorry."

I swallowed. "What for?"

"For not being what you need."

"Tristan, what is this? Why are you here?"

"I had to see you, to apologize for not showing up the other night."

"Why didn't you?"

"I wasn't ready to have this conversation with you."

"Obviously you're still not ready because you're not saying shit." I walked away from him, then whirled around to face him again. "I don't understand you," I shouted. "Why did you call and tell me you wanted to see me if you were just going to stand me up again?" When he didn't answer, I shook my head. "Never mind. You know what? I've decided that your excuses don't matter to me."

"There are some things you need to know."

"What is it? Are you sick or something?"

He frowned. "No, but—"

"Okay, then. There is nothing you can tell me that will make this better for me. This isn't the first time you've done it. And I won't give you another chance to hurt me. As a matter of fact, I'm now convinced that you're here because I didn't call you, because I didn't hunt you down to beg you to talk to me."

"That's not it."

I held up a hand. "Stop! Stop playing me. I don't deserve it. Especially when I've done nothing but support you."

He dropped his head. "You're right."

"I know I'm right. Go home, Tristan."

I started to walk past him, but he grabbed my arm. "I don't want to lose you." There was a desperation in his voice that I hadn't heard before and my heart skipped a beat, right before my brain screamed *fuck him*.

"Why?" I asked, folding my arms over my chest. "Why don't you want to lose me?"

His tongue darted out to moisten his lips. "Because… I need you."

Tristan stepped closer, so close I could feel the heat of his body against mine, so close that I could smell the soap on his skin. He was so tall, so male, it was overwhelming. He brushed the back of his hand down the column of my neck, and damn-it, my eyes fluttered closed. It wasn't the first time he'd touched me, but it was the first time he'd touched me like *this*. The soft caress almost made me forget why I couldn't stand him right now. Because I'd dreamed of similar moments with him. I wanted it for so long. *But…*

What I didn't want was the roller coaster ride he would inevitably take me on. Steeling myself, I pulled away from his touch. "Back up," I warned.

"Demi, I want you to know how much I…" He leaned forward, almost like he was going to kiss me. Yet, for the first time in a long time, I didn't care.

I took a full step away from him. Wrapping my arms around myself, I said, "I'm not doing this with you. Not today. Not anymore. I'm done."

Tristan's shoulders fell. "You don't mean that."

Nodding, I said, "I do. I really do." Turning my back on him, I waited until I heard him leave to slump into one of the chairs. I counted to ten and opened my eyes. Duke was standing there, arms folded over his chest.

He handed me a blanket, then took a seat next to me, but he didn't say anything. He just pulled out a blunt from his pocket, lit it, and took a long pull. Then, he hit it again before holding it out for me. "You need this."

I took a hit and leaned back against the chair, wrapping the thick fabric around me. "Thanks for this. It's cold out here."

"Hence the blanket." He blew out the smoke. "You alright?"

"Yeah."

"Good, because you just let that nigga run you out of the house and *you're* the one that was invited. Not him."

"Seriously, Duke. What is your thing with Tristan?" I'd seen the brothers fight many times over the years, but I didn't know why there was so much tension between them. That dynamic predated my time with them. "Why can't you stand him?"

"I love my brother. Maybe that's why I can recognize that he's full of shit." He sighed, shifting to face me. "The real question is why *can* you stand him? It's not like he's consistent. He makes every gathering, every event, hard. He doesn't show up for you."

My feelings for Tristan had consumed my life for so long, I didn't even remember all the reasons. Just the major ones. "He was the first person to stand up to my father. For me. His life changed because of that."

"His life changed because of him," Duke countered. "He was already going to the military. That incident just moved the date up."

I didn't know that. "Even so... He didn't have to put his freedom on the line for me."

"And you didn't have to place him on a pedestal because he did the right thing at the right time."

She sighed. "You just won't let me have this, will you?"

"He doesn't deserve this blind loyalty you have for him."

"I guess I could see something in him that nobody else could see, ya know?"

"Are you sure you're not just making up shit in your head to justify this decades-long crush you've had on him?"

Damn. Rubbing the back of my head, I muttered, "That's rough."

"This isn't just about Tristan either. For some reason, you've entered these relationships with fuckin' idiots, like

Dorian, because you know they don't measure up. Maybe subconsciously you think that you're going to end up with Tristan? Either way, you refuse to see the situation for what it is."

"What is it?"

"He doesn't want you." That cold truth stung as if he'd slapped me on my face. "If he did, he'd be with you. If he did, you wouldn't be here with me smoking this weed."

I rested my head on his shoulder. "I don't know why I'm like this."

He kissed the top of my head. "The good news is you can choose not to be that woman anymore."

I wrapped my arms around his waist. "You always show up for me."

"And you always do some crazy shit like marching yo' ass outside like it's summer and we're not in the mountains."

"Shut up," I said, shoving him away.

"Shoulda seen your butt…" He stood and stomped back into the house. Then, back out. "Dropping your Secret Santa name on the floor and shit. Now we have to go through that entire process again."

I dissolved into a fit of giggles at Duke's antics. "I was upset."

"Next time be upset *and* make good choices."

"I'll remember to keep my emotions in check."

"Trust me." He hit the blunt again. "If you don't learn anything from me, remember that life goes on after someone pisses you off. You have to decide if you're going to roll with it or stop living because of it."

It was way past time for me to get my shit together. I counseled women on the verge of leaving their significant others every day. I've held hands and Kleenex, gave hugs, threatened abusive husbands… I'd even stepped in front of a few of them to keep them from hitting a client. *Several times*. None of that stopped me from doing my job. But when it came to my personal life? I'd twisted myself into knots trying to appear like I had it together. When, in reality, I didn't lose control. I gave it away. First to Tristan because I'd made him the hero in my story. Then to Dorian because I'd become complacent in my own life. *No more*.

Decision made, I gave Duke a sidelong glance. "I think I'ma roll with it."

He gave me a fist bump. "You really have no choice."

"I just need you to stop knowing shit."

A smirk formed on his lips. "I can only be me."

We sat there in comfortable silence for a few minutes. "Duke?"

"What's up?"

"I have to stop getting high with you. I thought that tree was a bear for a minute."

He cracked up. "You're silly for that." He stood and pulled me to my feet. "We should probably go inside before you try to talk to that pole over there."

I hugged him, reveling in how safe I felt with his arms around me. "Maybe I should go to bed."

"Nah," he wrapped an arm around my neck as we walked into the house, "that's not a good plan."

Pausing mid-stride, I turned to him. "Why?"

"Because if I have to deal with Dallas, so do you."

Chapter Eight

IT WAS A GOOD DAY

Duke

"Uncle Duke, you have to smile! *And* talk." Raven peered over the camera and motioned for me to say something. "The people want to hear your voice."

"For you?" Paityn handed me the olive oil and plastered a smile on her face. "Is that good, Raven?" she asked between clenched teeth.

"You're trying too hard, Sissy," Blake said, from her spot at the kitchen table.

My family had decided to spend Christmas in Cali with Paityn and Bishop. It was my mother's bright idea because she wanted to limit Paityn's air travel due to the baby. I still wasn't sure why it was harmful for Big Sis to travel this early in her pregnancy, but I didn't question Ma.

Paityn and Bishop lived in Santa Monica, right on the beach. The five-bedroom home was perfect for both of them because they loved to host guests. For this trip, my parents rented an Airbnb a few blocks away. The ladies stayed with Paityn while me and my brothers stayed at the rental.

The days leading up to Christmas had always been jam-packed full of activities for the family. Ma liked to keep us busy. Today was Cookie Day, as we called it. When we were kids, all of us played a role in making sure we had several types of cookies for the holiday. As we grew into adulthood, Paityn and I led the charge while Ma barked orders from her chair.

The plan was to order pizza from one of Bishop's favorite restaurants. However, Tyn had begged me to make my spicy honey garlic salmon bites—for the baby—so Raven suggested we film.

I'd taken Skye's advice and hired my niece to manage my social media and my followers had already responded positively to the change. Right away, Raven had created a calendar to keep track of my content and brought in a few friends to help with vlog production. It was a win-win for all of us because they needed the experience, and I needed the help.

Ma breezed into the kitchen looking well-rested after a trip to the spa, probably on our dime. We'd been funding her beauty appointments since she brought in the Cussing Jar, and Thanksgiving had been a particularly raunchy day for us.

"Hey, babe." She kissed my cheek, then moved on to greet my sisters and Raven. "What's going on?" She took a seat next to Blake.

While Raven gave my mother a brief rundown, I argued with Paityn about the apron she'd given me to wear. I balled up the fabric and passed it to her. "I'm not wearing this."

Tyn pushed it back to me. "Duke, I don't see a problem with the apron. It'll work for today."

"It's bright yellow and says 'Queen Bee' on the front."

My sister shrugged. "Put it on backwards, duh." She attempted to tie the thing around my waist, but I spun away from her. "Duke, you're trippin'."

I held my hands up. "I don't need it. Let's get this show on the road."

It took a few minutes for Raven to get the camera ready again, but when she yelled "Go" I started with a quick overview of the recipe. Off to the side, Blake and Ma watched with interest as I did my introduction.

"What's up? I'm in the kitchen with Big Sis today, teaching her to make one of my favorite recipes." I glanced at her. "And judging by the way she's holding that knife like she wants to stab me, she'll need a lot of help."

"Boy, I know you lyin'." Tyn shoved me playfully with her free hand, and I cracked up. "I taught *you* how to hold a knife."

I pulled her into a side hug. "Just playin' y'all." I planted a kiss on her cheek. "Big Sis was a huge part of my food journey growing up. I used to watch her do her thing all the time."

I enjoyed cooking with Paityn because she was skilled in the kitchen. And I'd never told her this, but her dessert expertise surpassed mine every day of the week. She'd taught me the difference between a chef knife and a butcher knife, showed me how to season a cast iron skillet, and even put me up on how butter could transform any dish. The lessons hadn't stopped there, either. Every early recipe I'd tried had been with her by my side. She'd always been there for me, encouraging me, rooting for me. When I wanted to pursue culinary arts instead of medicine, she offered strong support during that conversation with our parents. She'd been there for every career milestone I'd had since then.

"Her blueberry muffins? And her peach cobbler?" I continued. "Fire."

Tyn grinned and took a bow. "That's right. Put some respect on my name."

"Maybe she'll bless us one day with a demonstration. For now, though, we gon' get these salmon bites sizzling so she can eat. 'Cause, ya know, she's ready."

"And is!" Paityn agreed.

I looked at the camera. "She's greedy," I whisper-yelled.

She wrapped her hands around my neck and mimicked a choking gesture. "You might be a lowkey celebrity, but I'll still whoop your a—"

"Alright, now," Ma chimed in, "Don't embarrass me on the YouTube."

I motioned for Raven to follow me as I walked over to my mother. "This is Ma." I kissed her cheek. "She is the original Chef Young."

My mother waved at the camera. "Hey y'all. Just so you know, don't be sliding into his TMs trying to go out with him."

"TMs?" Blake asked.

"Ma," I chided. Behind me, Raven was giggling, and Paityn was in tears behind the island. "Don't be embarrassing me like that. If you're going to speak new lingo, at least get it right."

"It's DMs, Nana," Raven explained.

Confused, Ma looked to Blake. "TM stands for text message, right?"

Blake smirked. "No, Mom. The actual saying is slidin' into the *DMs*. Direct messages."

Ma's mouth fell open. "Oh, okay. That makes sense. Carry on."

I made my way back over to the kitchen island, where Paityn was wiping her face with a napkin. I demonstrated how I cleaned and cut the salmon. Then, I allowed Tyn to douse the salmon with olive oil, instructing her to go hard. Next, I gave a brief explanation of each seasoning and why I used it as I coated the fish with it. And more was better.

"What is this again?" She studied one of the bottles, then sniffed it. "Smells good."

"It's my special blend," I told her, concentrating on the task at hand.

"Duke?" Paityn smacked my shoulder.

I blinked.

"You've been holding out on me, brotha. I need some of this. Are you selling it?" Her chin trembled. "I'm so proud of you."

The first tear caught me by surprise. I eyed the camera, then looked at Tyn. "Stop crying." I looked at the camera again. "She's emotional." I moved on, but she shocked me yet again with a tight hug. When she wouldn't let go, I grumbled, "Come on, now. Pull it together, Big Sis."

That seemed to snap her out of her state, and she backed away, sucked in a deep breath and gestured for me to continue. Which I did. Several minutes later, the salmon was done, and we were making the sauce.

Once complete, I poured the sauce over the salmon. "Look at that shit," I mumbled. "You definitely want to keep this recipe in your back pocket for that quick weeknight meal. I like to serve it as an appetizer myself."

Paityn tasted a piece and groaned. "So good."

Blake leaned over the counter and snagged a piece as well. "Slappin'," she said.

I put a few salmon bites on a plate and took it to my mother, who sampled it and gave me a thumbs up.

Back in front of the camera, I forked one of the salmon bites and held it up for the camera. "You already know. Perfectly cooked, full of flavor, with a kick. You need to make this at home, and when you do, tag me." I gave Paityn the opportunity to share her social media handles, which she did proudly. She also offered viewers a special promo code to shop at her naughty toy store. Then I ended the video by asking them to like and share, throwin' up the deuces, and saying, "It's a wrap. Peace out."

Raven announced. "Done." She set the camera down and dug into the salmon. "Uncle Duke." She hummed. "You did good. You should've seen the comments coming in."

Paityn nodded. "I agree. You're amazing in front of the camera."

"Maybe we can incorporate some of the comments into the video," Raven suggested. "We can flash a few across the screen and respond in real time to your fans."

"That's a great idea." Blake joined us at the kitchen island. "But don't get too friendly with them people. I don't want to have to fuck some crazy woman up for overstepping."

Ma coughed, holding out her hand. "You know what it is."

Blake groaned and pulled a twenty out of her pocket. "That should cover my next few, right?"

Ma snapped the bill in front of her and inspected it. "I'm considering a penalty increase this week. I want to go to London with the book club in the Spring."

Paityn laughed, still tearing the food up. "Maybe it's time for y'all to stop cussing so much."

I checked my phone. "That's not going to work," I mumbled as I scrolled through my IG account.

"Oh shoot," Ma said. "I forgot to call Demi to let her know what time we'd be starting. That baby has been working so hard. I wish she would've opted to stay here with us for the whole week."

I pretended not to listen as my mother and sisters discussed the latest news about Demi and her pending move to Atlanta. For the longest time, we'd all assumed she'd find her way back to Michigan, but she'd swiveled last week and announced she'd soon make Georgia her home.

Paityn pouted. "I don't want her to go. I loved her being close."

"Good thing Rissa is still here," Blake said. "Besides, Demi will still have clients here. And Zara, X, and Skye spend a lot of time in Cali. Duke too."

Pure Talent and Skye Light PR had offices in Los Angeles, so they traveled back and forth often. I tended to work where I was needed. A huge bulk of my clientele resided in California as well. Over the last year, I'd spent so much time on the west coast, I'd considered investing in a property.

"Everyone will be in Atlanta before long," Raven mused. "My dad is thinking of buying a house down there. He wants me to help him pick a place."

"Really?" Ma said, a hint of sadness in her voice. That alone made me want to beat the shit out of my brother. "I pray he does finally put down roots soon. It can't be easy never having a place to call home."

"Because he damn sure doesn't consider Michigan home," Blake murmured, taking another bite of salmon."

"Blake," Paityn chided. "Not here."

Ma sighed. "I've been waiting for one of you to tell me

what happened between you all in Colorado." After Tristan left the lodge, he'd disappeared yet again. I knew from Bliss that Ma had been trying to contact him in the hopes he'd make an appearance for Christmas, to no avail. Dad had made several unanswered calls too. "Maybe that's something we'll put on the agenda this week."

"No need, Mom," Blake said.

Paityn placed her hand on Ma's and squeezed. "What Blake means is you taught us to communicate honestly. We did that, and Tristan responded how he did."

"How he always does," Blake added, with a hard roll of her eyes. "I'll be glad when he finally owns his shit." She muttered a curse, pulled out two twenty-dollar bills, and handed them to my mother's waiting hand. "I'm sorry, Mom."

"Can someone tell me what's going on?" Raven asked, her big, brown eyes filling with tears. "I think I deserve to know what happened. You're talking about *my* dad."

We'd tried to keep certain things from Raven because Tristan was her father. Despite being witness to several fucked up events in her short life, including the back-and-forth drama between her parents, she'd still maintained a good relationship with Tristan. He was still her hero. And no matter what *I* felt about my brother, I wanted it to stay that way.

I smiled at my niece. "It's nothing to concern yourself with, baby girl. You know how I am. I talk a lot of shit. And you know how your father is. We just don't get along."

Blake frowned at my attempt to take the blame for how things transpired. "Don't do that," she warned.

Ignoring Blake, I mussed my niece's curls. "Don't worry about it. The Youngs are gonna Young." Which was the truth, but real talk, that conversation in Aspen had only scratched the surface. Our issues were deeper than his treatment of Demi.

Raven seemed to accept my response and shared more of her conversation with her father. I cracked my knuckles as Raven told us that he'd been offered a job with the government. The day my brother accepted a nine-to-five job was the day I'd propose to whatever chick was in my bed. It would never happen. We were alike in that way. My brother had worked for himself since he left the military. He made his living as a private investigator. His line of work allowed him the freedom to drop off the face of the earth with no contact because he could always blame his lack of communication on a job. I had to hand it to that muthafucka. He'd successfully created a positive narrative for himself, that he was trying to be a better person. At least to his daughter, who'd passed that information along to my mother. *Well played, brotha.* And the fact that he was *considering* a move to Atlanta, *after* Demi had settled on her destination, wasn't lost on me.

Raven confirmed my thoughts herself when she mentioned, "I think he's trying to move closer to Demi." She smiled wistfully. "I think he likes her."

I could feel Blake's eyes on me. When I finally looked at her, she lifted an eyebrow, silently letting me know that she had questions. I shook my head letting *her* know she'd be waiting forever for the answers. I could admit Blake wasn't totally off the mark, though. Tristan's words had replayed in my mind several times over the past month, and I'd been forced to ask myself... Why *do* I care so much?

Ma squeezed my knee. The gesture wasn't abnormal, but it was clear she'd sensed something. And I wasn't sure I wanted to know what she'd picked up from the conversation, from what hadn't been said. I took her hand and kissed her palm. "Love you," I murmured.

My mother patted my cheek. "You too, son." Changing the subject, she said, "Demi has a lot on her plate right now, Sweetie. I'm sure romance isn't a priority for her. But I'll be glad when that Dorian is finally out of the picture."

Although Demi had done her due diligence on the eviction, Dorian had decided to dig in his heels and take her to court. Since she didn't want to leave him alone in the house for too long, she'd decided to work and sleep at home, only spending a few hours with us in the evenings.

"The hearing was this morning," Blake informed. According to Dallas, Demi had been able to call in a favor and get on the docket before the courthouse closed for the holiday."

Speaking of Demi, a message notification flashed across my screen.

Demi: *It's time. Calling in that favor now.*

An hour later, Blake and I entered Demi's place, with Dallas on FaceTime.

Demi held up a piece of paper and grinned. "Court order. He's out of here." She glanced at Blake's phone and spoke to Dallas, "Sis, I'm so excited."

"Told you," Dallas said. "Give her a high five, Blake."

Blake held up her hand and Demi slapped it before they both did a little twerk. "Yas, boo. Bliss and Paityn wanted to join us, but Mom needed their assistance on something."

Demi smiled, her deep dimples on display. I couldn't help but smile too. Her energy, her excitement was contagious. "It's cool. I'll see y'all later," she told Dallas. "Then, we can celebrate." She squeezed my arm. "Dex and Asa are coming, right?"

I stared at her hand on my arm, unsure why the contact made me question everything that used to make sense. Swallowing, I forced my gaze and my mind away from her soft touch—and the warmth that had accompanied it. "Yeah." I noticed the smirk forming on Blake's lips. "Let's get to it."

Dorian emerged from the back of the condo, a frown on his face. "Demi, I think we should…" He narrowed his eyes on me. "What are you doing here?"

I shrugged. "It's moving day."

Dorian looked at Demi. "We need to discuss this. You can't move out."

"She's not moving, muthafucka," Blake said, a wicked gleam in her eyes. "*You* are."

"Meaning it's time to get the hell out," Dallas shouted through the phone.

Demi kicked an empty box his way. "Since you thought I wasn't serious, and skipped the court hearing today, the judge granted this." She waved the Order and smacked the piece of paper against his chest. "Read it."

Dorian made no move to pick up the box and set the piece of paper down on a table. "We spent years together. I think you owe me a conversation."

"Did he…?" Dallas said. "I know he didn't just say that."

"He sure did, Sissy," Blake acknowledged.

Demi dropped a pile of books into an empty box. "I'm done talking. But I did do you a solid. I got you a truck and movers. It's time to pack your shit and leave."

"The way I see it," I slid on a pair of work gloves, "you have two options. We can do this the nice way, meaning I'll drop your belongings off at the place of your choosing. Or

I can drop your shit in the harbor." Dorian reached for Demi, and I stepped in between them. "I think you need to pray about your next step, Pastor. Because if you do anything other than show her some respect, I *will* send you straight to hell."

"And you better hope the Lord intercepts you on your way down," Blake taunted.

We stood there for a moment, while Dorian weighed his options. I knew he wasn't stupid, though, because he picked up a box and started packing. Several minutes later, Dex and Asa arrived with the truck, and we made quick work of removing him and his shit from Demi's condo.

Later, Asa and Bliss played with Naija on the beach. Demi sat near them, holding Dominique. This particular view, seeing my niece experience the beach in December and watching Demi with my other niece was at the top of my favorite Christmas memories. Hearing Naija's delighted screams as my brother chased her and listening to Demi sing silly songs to Nique was a close second.

Ma joined me on the patio and hooked an arm around mine. "It's beautiful."

My eyes raked over Demi, from her thick curls swaying in the breeze to her bright eyes and sun-kissed brown skin to her full lips and long legs to her bare feet. "So beautiful."

"The weather," Ma clarified. The mild weather in California beat the snowstorm currently happening in Michigan every day of the week. She glanced at me out of the corner of her eye. "Demi is too."

I shifted to face her and shrugged. "She's alright."

Mom shot me a knowing glance because even my best attempt to appear unaffected never worked on her. "Boy, bye."

"Is there something you want to ask me, Ma?"

She stared out at the scene unfolding on the beach, a soft smile on her lips. "Not right now. I'll wait until you're ready to talk."

"You could be waiting forever."

Ma tapped her chin with her forefinger. "No," she said simply. "It won't take that long." She ran a finger over my cheek. That gesture had been a lifesaver more times than not. "My baby boy. You're my genius. You know a lot about everything. So talented. So confident. So smart. So gifted. I'm pretty sure I've told you this before, but I need you to know that there's nothing…" When I averted my gaze, she turned my head back to face her. "*Nothing* you could ever do that would make me turn my back on you. Nothing."

I leaned into her palm as unexpected tears filled my eyes. "You don't know everything."

"It doesn't matter. I don't need or want to know everything about my children. Part of life is making mistakes, choosing the wrong woman, taking crazy risks even when you know better. Despite what you *think* you've done that is so unforgivable, I love you regardless. Your faults, your bad decisions don't define you. When you realize that, you'll be ready to have that conversation. Deep down, you already know this. Which is why you met with Carolyn last month." I frowned, but she rushed on, "You're not the only one that be knowing shit."

I barked out a laugh. "Ma, you just said *shit*."

She held out a hand. "But *you* shouldn't say it. Give me my money."

Chuckling, I handed her a hundred-dollar-bill. "We still have a whole night of movies. I'm sure I'll slip up some more."

Ma embraced me, providing me comfort I didn't know I needed. "I better head inside and wake your father up.

Let them know we'll start in fifteen. Bishop ordered the pizza half an hour ago."

I nodded. "Got it."

Before she walked into the house, she turned to me. "By the way, you know Demi is more than alright. Stop playin'."

Laughing, I told her, "She's none of my business."

Ma studied me for a moment. "That's where you're wrong. You'll see."

Chapter Nine

GO CRAZY

Demi

I grew up on guard, afraid to utter a word because it might have set my father off, scared to close my eyes for fear that I'd wake up to more heartbreak. As a result, silence was my home, my solace, my strength. The world around me was loud, but I was at my strongest when I was silent.

After Dorian moved out and the holidays were over, I settled into my new normal. The first few days were good. I had my work to keep me company. While I got a lot of shit done, I found myself missing the noise, the laughter. Being around everyone at Christmas had restored my soul in a way that made me feel invigorated. Which cemented my decision to move. I wanted to be around my family.

My assistant knocked on my office door. Stepping into the office, she grinned. "You have company."

Behind her, Duke poked his head in. "I'm hungry. Let's get lunch."

I smiled, grabbing my purse and slipping on my blazer. "What are you thinking?" On my way out of the office, I gave him a hug. *Did he always smell this good?* Like spices and dark wood, mixed with a hint of coffee.

Duke placed a hand on the small of my back and steered me out of my office. And *Damn*. Was that a spark? "Do you have a taste for something?" he asked.

"Not really. You choose."

The corners of his mouth quirked up. "I got you."

"Then, lead the way."

We settled on Korean cuisine at a restaurant on Santa Monica Boulevard. I loved dining out with Duke because he'd opened my mind and tastebuds to food I would've never tried before. And this Bulgogi I had was fire.

I moaned as I sampled the grilled beef. "This is delicious." I speared another piece with my fork and held it out to him.

He leaned forward and ate it, nodding. "Good shit."

"I'm telling you… every time I'm with you I gain five pounds. Or more."

Chuckling, he said, "That's the plan."

After I moved in with the Youngs, I'd lost so much weight that Ma spent months making cakes just so I could gain a few pounds. Stress made food the least of my concerns. Always had been that way, so my weight fluctuated a lot. I'd been under a tremendous amount of stress over the past year. Mostly, because I was unhappy. With my life, with my location, with my *non*-relationships. "I'm doing better," I said.

He searched my eyes the way he always did. Like he was seeing every part of me. It felt safe, but also strangely arousing. "Sure?"

Do I need to have no-strings-attached sex? Maybe Dallas was right. I let out a shaky breath and prayed my reaction to Duke was just a symptom of the underlying issue. *I'm just horny.* "Yeah." I twisted my napkin around my finger. "I'm going back and forth on whether to sell my place."

Leaning forward, he asked, "What if you let me buy it?"

"You want to move to California?" For some reason, the thought of him moving to LA while I moved to Atlanta didn't sit right. I'd chosen Georgia because I had family there. He was a huge part of my decision because I knew I'd have some support. "I—"

"No. I'm not moving here. I just think it's good business to have a place to land in Cali because I'm here a lot."

I set my fork down. "I can understand that."

He frowned. "You alright?"

Nodding, I told him I was fine. "I wasn't sure what your answer would be."

"You'd be upset if I moved here?"

I thought about lying, because it made absolutely no sense to be angry about him living his life. But he'd see right through it. "Maybe a tiny bit *disappointed.* I wouldn't begrudge you, though."

He flashed a sexy-as-fuck smile. Wait... *Sexy?* What the hell was wrong with me? His lips had been the same since I'd met him. Just regular, not *sexy.* I zeroed in on his mouth again, then chided myself for thinking outside of the set parameters of our relationship.

"Demi," he called, pulling me out of my thoughts. "What's up?"

"Nothing." I bit into one of the house-made pickles. "Yum." I took a sip of my lemonade. "I love it here."

He raised a questioning brow. "Really?"

The warm, low timbre of his voice made my stomach

do an odd flip. *Note to self. Get. Some.* But not with Duke. I pointed at him. "Stop."

"Stop what?" He folded his arms over his massive chest, and my eyes were laser-focused on the way his shirt fit just right, accentuating his ripped body.

What the fuck? We'd argued about him not closing the toilet. We'd fought over the last bowl of cereal. I was technically his sister. "Nothing." I gulped down the rest of my lemonade and asked the passing waiter for a refill. *I need to go to sleep and start over tomorrow.*

"Anyway," he said, "What do you think?"

I blinked. "About…?"

"Buying your condo?"

"Oh."

"Or you could let me buy half and we share the expenses?" He stared at me with those light eyes. The same ones that had *never* ignited a fire deep in my belly—until now. "Since you'll still represent clients in the area."

I'm losing my damn mind. Panic rose inside of me as I fanned myself with the menu. Luckily, the waiter arrived, dropping off a fresh drink just in time. "It's hot in here," I croaked.

"Okay," he grumbled. "Whatever, Demi. If you don't like the idea, just say it."

Again, the voice. It was like a warm embrace. *Oh God.* I sighed. "Why are you doing this?"

He eyed me warily. "What am I doing? You're trippin' the fuck out for some mysterious reason."

I motioned toward is face. "You're flirting with me," I blurted out.

Duke leaned back in his seat, a soft smile forming on his beautiful lips. *Why am I looking at his mouth again?* "I'm not flirting with you."

I snorted. "You definitely are."

He laughed, peering up at the ceiling. *Even his neck is hot.* He took a deep breath, then pinned me with a heated gaze. *Or did I just imagine that?* "What are you going through today?"

I slumped in my chair. "Don't look at me like that."

Raising his arms at his sides, he asked, "Like what?"

"Like you want to…" I grumbled a curse. "I don't know. Do something to me?"

"Like take you over my knee and spank you?"

I choked on my lemonade. Embarrassed, I wiped my mouth with a paper napkin. "This is dumb."

He laughed. *Punk.* "I'm just playin' with you." I didn't like it. "You're acting crazy as hell. I can't look at you now?"

"Not like that."

"Whatever you say," he said.

We ate in silence for a few minutes. It was uncomfortable when it had always been comfortable. I didn't know what to do to turn things around, and it bothered me that I'd made it this way. "I'm sorry."

He eyed me over the rim of his glass. "For what?"

"For everything. I'm just tired. And a little bit stressed."

"How can I help?"

The question was innocent, but it felt loaded. To me. And the irritating part? I was pretty sure it wasn't that deep for him.

"I'll be fine." I ran my finger over the edge of the bowl. "I've been working really hard lately."

"You need a massage."

"From you?"

Duke's eyes flashed to mine. "From a massage therapist."

Oh.

"I'm not sure what's going on with you," he said, "but you know you can talk to me. Is it your mom?"

I shook my head.

"Your dad?"

"No."

"Dorian?"

"Hell no. That fool disa-muthafuckin-ppeared after you threatened to throw his stuff in the harbor."

He laughed. "Well, he knew what to do."

I let out a soft sigh of relief. That laugh seemed to break the ice, and I was able to focus on food, and not Duke's body.

A few seconds later, he said, "I did ask you a question, though. You didn't answer me. And you hate when I do that to you."

"Now I understand why you do it." I shrugged.

"Listen, Demi." He leaned forward, and once again, I was transfixed by his mouth. *Damnit.*

I stood up abruptly. "I have to go."

"You're not going to finish your food at least?"

I ate another piece of beef. "No. I'm good. I was going to blow off a meeting, but I just decided not to do that. I'll call you later and we can discuss the… um… The house."

I rushed out of the restaurant like a fuckin' scaredy cat. But before I left, I peeked in the window. Duke was just sitting there, his brows furrowed. I spent a few seconds studying his profile and wondered why he looked so good and why everything was different. *Do I want things to change?* He must have sensed me looking at him because he turned and caught me staring. And because I seemed to be comfortable acting like a lil' bitch today… I waved, then left.

My stomach growled about an hour later, which basically confirmed that I'd let my wayward thoughts get in the way of sustenance. I searched my desk drawer for snacks and found one granola bar.

Several minutes later, my phone buzzed. I smiled when I glanced at my screen, and accepted the call, putting Dallas on speakerphone. "Hey, boo."

"You got me on speaker?" Dallas asked.

"Of course. I'm finishing up a complaint."

"Me too, sis."

I bit into my granola bar. "What's going on?"

"So, Duke called."

I froze. "Oh?" I tried to mask my voice, to pretend that the mere mention of his name wasn't giving me fits. "What is he talking about?" I'd asked the question because I was genuinely curious to know if he'd told my bestie about that awkward lunch.

I heard chewing on the other end of the phone and my stomach growled again. "He mentioned coming to see you when he got there today," Dallas explained. "I told him to talk to you about buying your condo."

I sighed with relief that Dallas still had no idea how crazy I'd acted earlier. "I saw him today," I told her. "He mentioned the house when he took me to lunch."

"Well…?" she prodded. "I think it's a great idea."

"Yeah," I said. "I guess."

"Wait, are you changing your mind about selling?"

"Sorta." After I'd basically ran out of the restaurant like a teenager with a crush, I'd taken some time to think about his proposal. It made sense to keep the condo since I'd continue to handle business in LA. Having Duke buy an ownership share would be a big help for both of us. It would also save us a fortune in the long run and provide potential passive income if we decided to venture into short-term rentals during times when the house was empty.

"It's just good business for both of us," I added after explaining the details of his offer.

"True story," Dallas agreed. "While you're thinking about that, consider buying Dex's place here in Ann Arbor. You both spend time here and Bliss might want her spare bedroom back."

Either way, I'd essentially be tied to Duke. Which would have been okay yesterday. Now, I wasn't sure I could trust myself around him. It was no secret I had a bad history with choosing the right men. *Hello, Dorian. Hey, Tristan.* Whether that was purposeful or not, I never wanted to do anything to jeopardize my relationship with Duke. He'd been a constant for me, a light in my sometimes-dark life. I couldn't risk fucking it up.

"Sis," Dallas called. "You still there?"

I blinked, surprised that I had zoned out on the call. Clearing my throat, I said, "I'm here. Just thinking."

"I'm worried about you."

"Why?"

"Is your mother still calling you?"

"Every damn day." Although I'd told my mother to fuck off, she'd continued to call me. Sometimes twice a day. Her messages teetered between endearing and threatening, and everything in between. As if that wasn't bad enough, somehow, my father had been made aware of the conflict. He'd called me yesterday to tell me *I* was wrong. *The fucking audacity.* After he'd spent the better part of a decade hauling her into court with frivolous motions just to torture her. "I blocked her and my father."

"I'm sorry, sis," Dallas said.

My office phone rang, and I was grateful for the interruption. I did not want to spend my afternoon talking about my parents. "I better get this."

"Okay, boo. I'll call you later."

An hour later, after trying to finish work, I gave up and decided to leave. The best thing to do was to put the day behind me, but before I went home, I had a stop to make.

Duke

I'd just put a pan of pasta on when the doorbell rang. When I opened the door, I was surprised, and maybe a little too happy, to see Demi. "Hey."

She leaned against the door jam. "Hey. Can I come in?"

Stepping aside, I let her enter and locked up. "What's up?"

"Are you sure you're not busy?" She walked around the living room of the Airbnb. Instead of staying at a hotel, I'd opted for a house because I needed the kitchen to prepare for an event I was catering.

"I'm good." I motioned toward the back of the house. "Come to the kitchen."

Demi followed me and took a seat at the breakfast bar. "You're cooking this late?"

I turned off the stove and spooned the hard-boiled eggs into a bowl of ice water. "Just making tuna macaroni salad for Tyn. She's craving it. Bishop will be here within the hour to pick it up."

"Aw, that's so sweet."

I peered at her as I cut a white onion. "You're out late."

"Actually, I had intended to come here earlier, but I wasn't sure it was wise."

Frowning, I set the knife down. "Why wouldn't it be wise?"

Demi nibbled on her bottom lip as a blush worked its way up her neck to her cheeks. "What happened at lunch was pretty awkward, right?"

Awkward was a word. Admittedly, I'd stayed at the restaurant for another twenty minutes, in case she returned and admitted she was punking me. And since then, I'd wracked my brain trying to figure out why she'd flipped out on me today. "You were on one today."

"I don't know why either. Well, that's not entirely true."

Earlier, Demi had ordered me to stop flirting with her. For years, I'd gone to painful lengths to keep my relationship with her genuine and pure. She'd been through so much, and I needed to be a strong support for her. It was a vow I'd made to myself the moment she'd shown up on our doorstep that fateful night. That meant no flirting, no innuendo, and absolutely no exchanging of bodily fluids. Yet, lately, it seemed that everything I'd done before to stay close but distant wasn't working anymore. Because I *wanted* to be near her in a way that was new for me. Hell, I was mulling my options now, looking for a way to erase the distance between us.

"I don't really want to talk about the reasons," she continued. "I just want to forget it happened."

I stared at her. While I wanted to delve into what happened, I needed to respect her wishes. "Did you eat dinner?"

"I got a sandwich from McDonald's and threw it away."

"That was your first mistake," I told her. I picked up a pair of latex gloves and held them out to her. "Help me peel these eggs. Then, I'll make you something for dinner."

She grinned. "Deal."

We worked in silence, her on the eggs and me on every-thing else. By the time the pasta was done, I had already diced the onion, green pepper, and celery. Meanwhile, Demi was struggling with her task, cursing the eggs to hell and back as she painstakingly peeled them.

Once I poured the noodles in the strainer and ran cool water over them, I turned my attention to her egg prob-lem. I walked over to her and picked up an egg. "It's not that hard, Demi." I inspected the egg. "Keep on and there won't be any egg left to put in the salad."

She elbowed me. "Oh, shut up. They're defective."

Chuckling, I peeled three eggs while she was still *trying* to finish the one. "Give me that shit." I snatched it away from her. "Can you grab the relish out of the fridge?"

Demi shuffled over to the refrigerator and peered in. "Damn. There's so much food in here. Ooo, you have blueberries?" She pulled out a jar of sweet relish and handed it to me. "Do you have an extra strainer?"

I told her to look in my case, which was sitting on a bench near the kitchen table. "While you're at it, can you wash the strawberries too?"

"I've been thinking about your proposal." She dumped the blueberries into a strainer and rinsed them off. "I say we do it."

Eyeing her, I asked, "Why the change of heart?"

"It's not a change. I thought it was a good idea when you asked earlier. I was just going through something."

I chopped up the eggs and swept them into the bowl with the tuna, noodles, and the vegetables. "Still don't want to talk about it?"

"Nope," she chirped. "Not at all."

I added mayo and yellow mustard to the bowl. "So how do you want to do this?"

She turned to look at me, resting her hip on the edge

of the counter. "I wanted to talk to you about something else, though."

Curious, I stopped mixing the salad. "What is it?"

"Are you open to renting the house out several times a year? Because I think we can go into business with a few rental properties. Just a suggestion."

"Hmm." The idea didn't suck, and passive income was always a bonus. "I see where you're going. Start with your place and then expand to other locations?"

She snapped her fingers. "Exactly. We could buy Dex's house." She shrugged. "Just sayin'. It wouldn't hurt. And we'd have a place to land in Ann Arbor."

"I like it." I held up a fist and she bumped it with hers. "Let's bring our lawyers into it."

"Sounds like a plan."

Demi popped a blueberry in her mouth and did a cute little dance, while I tried not to think about her ass as she swayed to the music. I scooted past her to grab another jar of mayo and was hit with her scent. It was unmistakably Demi, like fresh flowers and mandarins with a hint of vanilla. I found myself leaning in. And for some very strange reason I wanted to bite her. *Softly, of course.* I wanted to take her earlobe into my mouth, to brush my mouth over her pulse point, to press my lips against the tattoo on the back of her neck.

To make matters worse, Demi kind of slumped against me. She didn't speak, she didn't even move, and I wondered what she wanted from me in that moment. Did she want me to do those things? If I did what I wanted to do, would she flip out again?

Before I could ask, she stiffened and whirled around, her eyes wide. "You *were* flirting!"

My gaze dropped to her mouth, then dipped down to her...

She punched my arm. "I knew it."

I gripped her wrist to prevent her from hitting me again. Not because it hurt, but because it felt right to have her hand on my body. Even if it was a playful smack. "Demi, I'm not flirting with you." *Wanting to kiss someone is not the same as flirting.* I would die on that mountain. "You're in my space, and I'm trying to get this damn salad done."

"You're so full of shit. You made me question myself earlier. All those half-smiles and those intense stares. Your tone of voice. The non-verbal cues? Of all people, you should know how important it is to pay attention to what isn't said."

My parents had made all of us—Demi included— aware of the ways that people communicate. A person's body language could tell you everything you needed to know about their state of mind. "That's true."

"It's all in your body language."

I swiped my thumb over the pulse point on her wrist and held if there, enjoying her sharp intake of breath. "Really now?"

Demi stared at my hand around her wrist and met my gaze with hooded eyes. Swallowing visibly, she whispered, "You're doing it again."

"That's true." I leaned in. "But I'm not the only one whose body language is telling a story."

"My body isn't telling you anything." She breathed a curse when I stepped closer to her, still unsure how far I would take this. The stakes were pretty high, but she was also so damn irresistible I wanted to see something.

"It's the way your breath catches when I move closer to you," I murmured. "The way your pulse speeds up when I brush my finger over your wrist. The way your eyes seem to always be focused on my mouth."

"Meanwhile *you're* looking at *my* lips," she tossed back,

letting out a nervous giggle. I liked it. "And the lean... It's very flirtatious." She grabbed a handful of blueberries.

I circled her nose with mine. "I think you want me to flirt with you."

A couple of the berries fell to the floor. "Oh, shit." Neither of us attempted to pick them up. She planted her hands on my chest but made no move to push me away. "I think... You should probably finish that tuna salad before Bishop gets here."

I searched her eyes. "Is that what you really want me to do?"

"I don't know," she confessed. "But I'm like two seconds from flipping out because... What the hell is happening here?"

Unable to help myself any longer, I nipped at her jaw line, then trailed a line of kisses down her neck to her collarbone, enjoying her sharp intake of air. More blueberries tumbled to the floor. "We're paying attention to our non-verbal cues," I whispered as I kissed my way back up to her mouth. I stopped short of brushing my lips to hers because... Partly because I respected her. Mostly because I instinctively knew that if I kissed Demi... *I won't want to stop at her mouth.*

Demi let out a strangled giggle. "You're stupid for that." The low rasp of her voice went straight to my dick.

I moistened my lips, tempted to close the distance between us, tempted to kiss the shit out of her. *Everywhere.* "I'm very serious."

The air changed around us again and I leaned in even closer. So close I could feel her sweet breath on my mouth. We were at the point of no return. Whatever we decided would have a lasting effect on our relationship. This was the point I should pull back, apologize, and pretend this didn't happen. But I wasn't ready to walk away, and I wasn't sorry. Even though, I'd perfected the art of *not* giving a fuck, I knew that I'd never be able to act like I hadn't been this close to her, this ready to kiss her. *To do more than kiss her*.

I kissed the corners of her lips before pressing my mouth to hers. And... *Damn*. I was right. I didn't want to stop. Not when she tossed the container of blueberries on the floor, not when she groaned my name against my lips, and certainly not when she finally kissed me back.

Unfortunately, the doorbell rang signaling Bishop had arrived. Demi jerked back, dropping to her knees to pick up the blueberries. I took a deep breath and went to answer the door. Yet, while I made my way to the front of the house, I also made the decision to not let this be the end of this conversation—or the last time I felt her lips against mine.

Chapter Ten

THE NEARNESS OF YOU

Duke

I should've just walked away. I'd let my lonely dick convince me that I could sleep with a random woman I'd met at my homeboy, Rashaad's, rehearsal dinner. And because the wedding planner—who also happened to be a friend of Bliss'—asked me to seduce a bridesmaid for information. And because Demi had essentially ghosted my ass after that interlude with her last month, except for the businesslike texts about our pending property transactions. And because I was still salty as hell about it... *That was my play*!

The past couple of months been the longest stretch of time without new pussy since I was twelve years old. I'd had several offers from beautiful women too. Maybe Granny was right when she told me my "dingaling" would betray me one day. At the time, I thought she was just high off that good weed she'd been smoking. But now…

Marley—aka Short Bridesmaid—leaned in, placed a wet kiss on my mouth and brushed her palm over my dick. I looked down and waited. *Nothing.* Truth was that things hadn't been the same since Christmas. Hell, even before that. Sometime around Thanksgiving. I knew why, but I didn't want to accept that Demi had unknowingly hijacked my sex life. Because damnit… every woman I'd met paled in comparison to her. No one had her sense of humor or her intellect. No one made me rethink my plans for life like she did. No one made me want to kiss them until they surrendered everything to me. Not even my mother. *Crazy, right?*

Marley cursed, pulling my attention back to her and away from the conundrum I'd found myself in concerning Demi. "This bitch," she mumbled, dropping her phone onto the sofa. "I'm sick of her shit. I quit. I'm not standing up with her at that wedding" She folded her arms over her chests. "No. Meri is being ridiculous. She just texted me to tell me that I was forbidden from getting some tonight because she couldn't get some. Who the fuck does that?"

By all accounts, the bride was a piece of work. Apparently, half of the wedding party quit because she was a Bridezilla from hell. And Rashaad's entire family hated the thought of him marrying the lady. Normally, I'd stay away from this type of drama, but I welcomed the distraction.

Scooting closer to the frustrated bridesmaid, I wrapped my arm around her. "Maybe I can help."

Marley smiled, then she frowned. "Shit," she hissed, snatching her buzzing phone from the couch. A few seconds later, she let out a piercing scream.

"Calm yo' ass down," I said. "I'm not trying to be content for the next police brutality video."

Marley's shoulder slumped and tears spilled from her eyes. "I just… I hate her. I'm only in this wedding because my mother made me." Then, she proceeded to spill her guts, telling me all the shit that could ruin this damn wedding. And when she was done, she jumped on my lap and kissed me. I immediately picked her up and deposited her back on the couch. "What's wrong?" she asked. "Don't you want to?"

This situation had me fucked up. Because I *didn't* want her. It was a waste of time to pretend otherwise. "No, I don't," I admitted.

Her chin trembled. "Is it because I complained about Meri? I know you're connected to Rashaad. I'm sorry that I—"

"It's not that," I told her. "This isn't going to work."

"Not even for one night?"

I shook my head. "Not even for a night." I stood and made my way toward the door. "But you should come clean about Meri. Rashaad needs to know that she's been cheating on him for months."

Marley hugged her pillow and dashed fresh tears from her cheeks. "You're right. He doesn't deserve this."

"I should probably get going." I squeezed her shoulder. "Take care."

On the way to my parents' house, I cursed my dick and my mind for not cooperating with my game. But I also decided it was time to think about what I wanted. Instead of making the turn down my parents' driveway, I did a U-turn and headed in the opposite direction, toward Dex's house.

Dex opened the door. "What's up?" I followed him into

the kitchen. "It's late. I thought you were going home with Short Bridesmaid?"

"That didn't end well," I admitted.

He pulled two mugs out of the cabinet. "I put coffee on when you called. Figured you might need some."

I glanced around the room, noting the wedding shit on the kitchen table and the moving boxes on the far side of the room. While Dex and Charlye would split their time between Michigan and Georgia, they'd both agreed that Michigan would be their home base and had recently closed on a new house with a big yard for their future kids.

Picking up the acrylic card box, I turned it over in my hands. Next week, Dex would be married, and I would be... *probably still not fucking Demi or anybody else.* I set the box down and lifted the silver knife set. "I'm surprised Bliss isn't pitching a fit about this. No bling."

Dex chuckled. "She bought it." Bliss' profession as a matchmaker made her extremely invested in our happy endings. Paityn had doused her little flame when she'd decided on a quickie backyard wedding at our parents' house. Dallas destroyed her plans by getting hitched at the courthouse right before she went into labor. And Blake had yet to set a date for her nuptials, much to my sister's chagrin. "She quickly realized I wasn't going to give her a big wedding when Charlye decided she didn't want to get married at the family church," he explained. "I did promise we'd jump the broom, though."

Charlye was the perfect match for my twin because she kept everything simple. Neither of them wanted a huge wedding party. She'd only chosen two bridesmaids—her sister and Dallas. Dex had asked me and Justus, his best friend and Charlye's brother, to stand up with him.

I took a seat at the kitchen table. The thing about Dex

was he'd always been steadfast. He was the family counselor, and I needed his counsel tonight.

Dex joined me and handed me the mug of coffee. "You good?"

"I am," I admitted.

He eyed me over the rim of his mug. "What's bothering you?"

When we were younger, I'd deemed myself as my brother's keeper. I didn't care who it was, I was ready to fight if anyone said something out of pocket to him or any of my siblings. Dex was different, though. He was the level head to my hot head, the reserved twin while I was more outgoing. The experts called it compensating personalities. I just called it our life.

Around third grade, though, I started to appreciate Dex's calm presence in my life. As kids, he was my sounding board; someone I could talk to about pretty much anything. He'd often talked me out of making bad decisions. As we got older, Dex had never changed. *But I did.* Staying close but distant became a necessity because I was doing things that I wasn't proud of, things that I knew would be a disappointment to them. Although Dex had never turned his back on me, my experiences made me more cautious about the things I shared.

I leaned forward, clasping my hands together. "I hesitated about coming here. You know how I am about talking about my shit." The people closest to me knew *some* things but nobody knew *everything*. And I preferred it that way.

"Circle tight, mouth shut," Dex said, repeating something I'd told him years ago. I knew my brother understood the sentiment very well, since he'd lived his life the same way.

"Exactly." Yet, if I wanted to tell anybody my business, it would be Dex. Xavier would be a close second choice.

"But you're here. You obviously need to talk about something."

"Demi," I admitted.

Dex frowned, setting his mug down. "*Our* Demi?"

My Demi. "Yeah."

"You're not changing your mind about the house, are you?"

"Nah, man," I assured him. Demi and I would finalize the purchase of his home within the next couple of weeks. "Everything is all set on that front."

"What is it?"

"*It*'s just her."

Leaning back in his chair, Dex smiled. "I thought I saw something at Christmas."

"What did you see?"

"Even before that," he added. "A look. The way you are with her. Attentive. Protective."

I waved him off. "I'm like that with all of my sisters."

"Demi's not your sister," Dex tossed back. "At least, not in the way that would prevent you from having feelings for her." I stared at him, trying to communicate with eyes that my *feelings* were the problem. He seemed to get it, because he said, "How long have you felt this way?"

Shrugging, I mumbled, "Shit if I know. One day I just looked at her and wanted to…" I scratched the side of my face. "She's beautiful."

"No doubt," he agreed.

"And smart."

"Absolutely."

"Sexy."

Dex glanced back at the door, presumably to make sure Charlye wasn't close by. He lowered his voice, "Definitely."

When I frowned, he rushed on, "Not that I'm trying to hide it, but Charlye is convinced I had the biggest crush on Demi in high school."

Curious, I leaned in. "She knows your gaze was squarely on *her* back then, right?" Dex had been #Team-Charlye since we were little kids. I'd never even seen him look twice at Demi.

"My fault," he explained. "I made the mistake of telling her that Demi could sing me to sleep any night."

"Ah." She didn't do it often, but when Demi sang, it almost made time stand still. Her voice was soft and sultry, regal yet vulnerable. Even her speaking voice had a lullaby tone to it. It had often soothed the coarse parts of my soul and had even brought me back to consciousness when I was bleeding to death in the hot New Orleans heat. "That sound…" Of all the things I remembered about that night, what stood out the most was the relief, the hope that surged through me once I knew she was there. Although my parents had always offered us a safe place to land, Demi had provided a safe haven for me that night. But it wasn't the only time she'd done it. I felt that way often when she was around, and that realization hit me like a punch to the gut. I'd never been the guy dreaming of a future with *one* woman and maybe some kids running around the house, but the thought that I could have that every day for the rest of my life… I blinked myself out of the memory and looked at Dex. "I want her."

Dex observed my quietly before he asked, "Do you want the idea of her?"

Shaking my head, I replied, "Nah. I just want her."

"What about Tristan?"

The fact that he'd brought up Tristan irritated the hell out of me. "He doesn't deserve her." That would've been true even if I didn't want Demi for myself. Tristan had done nothing but treat her like an afterthought, an option that he *might* choose eventually.

"You do know that this could present a problem that you two may not be able to come back from."

"Why?" I challenged.

"You know how it is. People sleep until something—or *someone*—wakes them up."

"I can't worry about that."

"But *I* can worry about you. I've never seen you so resolute about a woman."

"She's not just any woman," I argued.

"Exactly." Dex clasped my shoulder. "When your heart is in it, there's always a risk."

In the past, I'd done my share of dirt, hurt a lot of feelings. It would be karma if I threw all my cards on the table only to have Tristan swoop in with a royal flush and break me. Yet, even if a determined Tristan joined the game, in the end, it would still be up to Demi to call the play. The safe option would be to ignore everything, find another woman to fuck, and keep it moving. But I'd never been one to take the safe route. Which meant one thing. Time to raise the stakes.

"Isn't that what life is all about, bruh?" I asked.

Dex smirked. "Well, Dad always taught us to step up to bat. What are you going to do?"

"Hit that shit out of the park."

I nstead of staying at Bliss' last night, I went to my parents' house. Against my better judgment, I'd let Ma convince me to make a huge breakfast for her newly arrived houseguests. Wedding Week was in full swing, and my mother had opened their home to several people. This included her former pastor and his family, who'd moved to Memphis years ago. And Chastity.

Last night, I'd managed to avoid my recently divorced prom date by sneaking through the back door and up the private staircase straight to my bedroom. And I'd been hiding from them ever since. At least until my father knocked on the door.

"What's up, son?" Pop stepped into my room. "Hmm." He shoved his hands into his pocket and spun around, taking in the newly decorated space. "Your mother told me it was a small remodel."

Stretching, I chuckled. "She wasn't playin' around. You should see the other rooms."

Luckily, my mother hadn't forced any of us to relive our childhood when we returned to the house. While we could always stay there, she'd transformed each of the bedrooms into small hotel-like suites with upgraded amenities. Even with fresh paint, new furniture, and plush carpet, it still felt like *my* room. Having visited all of us several times, she'd taken elements of our own homes to create the space. For me, I preferred clean and comfortable. And Ma delivered with dark wood furniture, metal and glass accents, soft leather chairs, dim lighting, and different shades of grey and blue. The small refrigerator was filled with my favorite drinks. An accent cabinet hid snacks, and a box of Frosted Flakes. The one thing she didn't get rid of from my childhood was the hot plate I'd purchased years ago.

My father studied the hot plate, rubbing his palm over the top. "It's you, though."

"Right."

Pop sat down on one of the leather chairs, crossing one leg over his knee. "How are you? I feel like we haven't talked in a while."

I grabbed a bottle of water from the fridge. "Work's been busy."

"Are you really buying Dex's house?"

Nodding, I told him the plan Demi and I had come up with. "I think it's a good investment."

Pop clasped his hands together. "I agree. I have to say, I'm glad that you're thinking about your future."

There was a time when I could care less about planning. I was living just enough for the next day. When I decided to get myself together, I'd been intentional about taking care of business. "Can't be forty and doing the same fucked up shit." My father had never been concerned with why, when, where, or how we talked. He simply kept the door open. And he preferred transparency over anything else, in words and in deed. "Have to make sure I'm setting myself up for easy living later."

He stared at me. "I just want you to know that I've noticed. You might live by that keep-shit-quiet code, but I'm still your father. I know you. I've seen the positive changes."

For a moment, I considered telling Pop about my feelings for Demi. But decided against it. "Thanks."

"I'm proud of you."

I paused, meeting his waiting gaze. It wasn't the first time he'd told me that, but it felt like it. Swallowing past a lump in my throat, I nodded. "Thanks." I cleared my throat. "Means a lot to me."

Pop stood and embraced me. After a few seconds, I hugged him back. When he pulled away, he smiled. "Be careful when you come downstairs. Ms. Chastity has you on the brain."

I cracked up. "That ship sailed a long time ago."

"That's what I told your mother."

"Keep Ma away from Bliss. They'll matchmake me to death if I let them."

Tilting his head, Pop assessed me. "I don't think that'll be necessary." He walked to the door. "See you downstairs. Your siblings are on their way, so you should probably get started on breakfast."

Again, I was torn between letting Pop know about my plan with Demi and keeping it to myself. In the end, though, I let him go.

After I showered and shaved, I stepped into my bedroom. "Oh shit!" I clutched at my towel as Chastity sauntered over to me. "What the hell are you doing in here?"

Chastity opened her robe and let it fall to the floor, revealing her naked body. "I figured I'd wake you with a nice surprise."

I gripped her wrist when she grabbed my towel. "Chastity, nah." Normally, a glimpse of pussy would be enough to make me change my day, but not *this* pussy. And not *this* woman. "You gotta get up out of here."

Chastity reached for my dick. I did a spin move, veering out of her way. "Come on, now." I pushed her hand away. "Stop."

She pouted. "Duke," she wrapped her arms around my waist from behind and bit down on my back. "Before my divorce," she licked my neck, "my husband shut me out of the bedroom."

I maneuvered out of her hold, but she was like a magnet. Everywhere I turned, she was there, pawing at me. I grabbed a pair of pants out of a drawer, but she hopped on the dresser.

Wrapping her legs around me, she whispered, "It's been years since I've felt passion." I swatted her hands away, eyeing the open bathroom door. "And those damn kids… I help with homework, I drive to extra-curricular activities. It's time for me to do something for me," she whined, tugging at the towel.

"I agree. But not with me." I yanked a shirt out of the dresser.

"Your mother told me you were single."

"I am." I picked her up and dropped her on the bed. "But this isn't going to happen."

Chastity's shoulders fell on a sigh. "Are you serious?"

"Very." I tossed her robe at her. "Put that on."

She quickly slipped the robe on and tied it. Averting her gaze, she breathed, "I'm sorry. I must look crazy. I don't know what's wrong with me. I just haven't felt like myself since the divorce."

"That's understandable."

"Please don't tell anyone I did this."

"I won't say anything," I promised.

Chastity nodded. "Thank you." She pointed at my towel. "I'll let you get dressed." She shuffled to the door. "See you at breakfast?"

"I'm cooking, so yes."

She apologized three more times before she opened the door.

Outside in the hallway, Dallas whispered, "Oh shit," as Chastity breezed past her with her head down. My sister glanced at me. "What the hell?"

And she wasn't alone either. Before my sister could badger me about this latest turn of events, before I could slam the door in her face, she was joined by Bliss, Blake, *and* Demi. *Shit.*

Dallas started first, yelling at me about fucking with Pastor's niece again. Blake chided me for being a dumb-ass. Bliss was next. My sweet sister mused about potential second-chance love.

Blake snorted. "Aht Aht. Duke doesn't want that messy-ass bitch."

"He better not," Dallas said. "Mom told me Chastity nearly ran her husband over with her car when he asked for a divorce."

As my sisters gossiped about Chastity and her marriage, I looked over at Demi, who'd remained quiet.

Demi's green eyes darkened as her gaze dropped from my bare chest to my... towel. When she met my eyes again, she let out a disgusted growl. "Really?"

"Demi," I called softly. "It's not what you think."

Bliss gasped. "Oh."

"Wow," Blake whispered.

Dallas slipped Demi a curious glance before she asked me, "Well, what the hell is it then?"

I glared at my sisters. "None of your business." I turned to Demi again. "Can we talk?"

Shaking her head, Demi said, "No. What you need to do is get dressed and flip them pancakes."

This was the part of the story when I would normally tell all of them to get the fuck out of my face. But... I couldn't let her go. Not yet. "Get yo' ass in here." I grabbed Demi's hand and tugged her forward, slamming the door before my sisters could barge in too.

Demi turned the doorknob, but my hand against the door prevented her from opening it. "What do you want?"

"We need to talk," I told her.

"Fine." Demi bolted to the other side of the room and immediately turned to face the window. Not me. "Seriously. Can you get dressed?" She tossed my shirt behind her head, and it floated to the floor right in front of me.

I stepped over it and walked toward her. "We're better than this."

Demi whirled around. The fury in her eyes was

replaced by something else as she looked me up and down. She swallowed visibly. "I can't talk to you like this." Scanning the room, she picked up the duvet on the bed and pushed it against my chest. "Cover up. You're a hazard." She brushed past me, back toward the door.

Letting the cover fall to the floor, I scooped my joggers off the dresser and slid them on, before approaching her. "Is this better?"

With her eyes squeezed shut, Demi turned slowly. Soon, her gaze locked on mine. Then, she walked away from me. Again. "This is so stupid," she said under her breath. "What do you want?"

I'd never really felt the need to explain myself to anyone, but I needed to make sure Demi understood exactly what I wanted. And it wasn't Chastity. "To finish what we started back in LA," I muttered against her ear before taking the lobe in my mouth. She shuddered but made no move to push me away. "Nothing happened today."

"I don't care." Her voice was a low whimper. "It doesn't matter."

"Actually, it does," I countered.

Demi blew out a deep breath and turned to face me. "Why?"

Unable to resist her, I leaned in, brushing her chin with my nose and kissing the corner of her mouth. "You matter to me."

She placed her palms on my chest. "Duke, this... I don't think." She blinked. Hard. "This isn't a good idea."

"Why?" My goal was clear. I just needed her to sign off.

"Because you're you." She jabbed her finger into my chest. "And I'm me." She searched my eyes. "We've been family forever, living in the same house, sleeping in the same bed sometimes, helping each other through some crazy bullshit. And nothing. Now, you're flirting with me, you're explaining yourself to me, you're touching me, you're sneaking into my dreams with that smirk on your lips, you're looking like you want to kiss me. Again."

"I do." I squeezed her hips and pulled her closer. This time, my dick didn't betray me, and I wanted her to know how she affected me. "Are you going to let me?"

Her gaze dropped to my mouth and she nodded. "Yes," she whispered hoarsely.

And I did, trailing my tongue over her bottom lip before sucking it into my mouth. Demi melted into me as I tilted her head back and deepened the kiss. The feel of her body against mine, the sound of her soft moans, and her scent were driving me crazy with need. It was no secret that I'd fucked coast to coast and abroad, but the mere act of kissing her, of holding her in my arms felt like the first time. Which was scary *and* right at the same time. I wanted to devour her, claim her as mine, climb inside her and never come back out.

My alarm went off and Demi jumped back like I'd burned her, nearly falling on her ass. Fortunately, I was able to catch her. "You should be more careful," I said, kissing her brow, then her full lips again.

With dazed eyes, she peered up at me. "Not again. Ugh!" She held her palm against her mouth. "What am I thinking?"

I hit the button on my phone, silencing it. "The same thing I'm thinking?" *Us. Her pussy. My dick.*

Demi shook her head frantically. "No. Obviously, I'm not thinking with my brain." Her gaze softened on me, right before she stood on the tips of her toes and kissed me again. Tangling my fingers in her hair, I let her take control of the kiss.

I backed her against the dresser, slid my hands up her thighs to the waistband of her jeans and unbuttoned them, and slipped my hand into her panties. "Just like I thought," I murmured against her mouth. "So hot, so wet for me."

She gasped when I flicked her clit with my finger, rolling it between my fingers. "I'm probably going to hell," she breathed. "Don't stop, though."

I wanted to drop to my knees and press my face to her pussy just to get a taste. So, hell nah. Stopping wasn't an option. "Don't worry. I won't," I assured her as I dipped one finger inside. Then, two.

Demi's mouth fell open. "Oh shit."

"Take your shirt off," I commanded.

"Now?" she asked, her eyes glazed over, dark with desire.

I bit down on her shoulder. "I didn't stutter."

That muthafuckin' alarm went off again and Demi snatched my hand out of her pants. She gasped. "Oh my God." She frantically buttoned her jeans and straightened her twisted shirt. "See. I did it again. It's so wrong. I need to go."

"Wait."

She rushed to the door, but I was too late to stop her from opening it. Within seconds, Blake, Bliss, and Dallas tumbled inside.

Demi stared down at them, then back at me. "Unbelievable." Then, she bolted.

And I glared at my sisters, who scrambled to get up. "Really?" I asked once they were all on their feet.

"Dallas held her head high. "Really. But you—"

Instead of allowing my sisters to grill me about what had just happened, I just closed the door.

Chapter Eleven

GOING OUT OF MY HEAD

Duke

*D*emi ignored me when I entered the kitchen. She continued to avoid eye contact as I prepared the food. Unfortunately, I wasn't as lucky with my sisters, who'd taken turns trying to get information out of me. While I scrambled the eggs, Dallas pretended to help. Pretend, because she hadn't even picked up a spatula. Bliss, on the other hand, grabbed the butter from the fridge and brought it to me. As I beat the pancake batter, she beat around the bush, asking every question except for the one that mattered.

When Blake approached me with the champagne, she popped the cork and turned to me. Lowering her voice, she said, "Are you fucking Chastity or Demi?"

Asa choked on his orange juice as he passed by. He glanced at me, then at Demi, before shaking his head and mumbling, "It's too early for this shit." He grabbed a piece of bacon and disappeared around the corner.

I glared at Blake. "Shut. Up," I grumbled, through clenched teeth.

My sister shrugged. "If I was a betting woman, I'd say Demi. Especially after she walked out of your room with her hair looking a hot-ass mess."

"Go somewhere," I warned.

"Why are you acting like this?" Blake asked. "What's up with you?"

"Don't you still have to choose a wedding date?" I sliced a tomato. "Maybe you need to worry about that, and not who I'm fucking."

She smacked my shoulder. "Whatever. Fuck this wedding," she snapped. The pastor and his wife glanced over at us. "Sorry, Pastor." Blake mouthed an apology to my mother and Lennox before turning to me. "I'm done talking about it. No amount of forced meetings, stupid bridal checklists, and Bliss' sad eyes will change that."

I snickered, satisfied that I managed to distract Blake from my business. "Right. Because everyone's wrong for wanting you to actually set a date and make it happen," I teased. "Do you even want to get married? I mean, because you definitely don't act like a blushing bride-to-be."

"Because I'm not," she shot back. "I want to be Lennox's wife. I don't care about the wedding. And fuck —" Blake tugged at her shirt. "*Forget* you." She stalked off, grumbling curses all the way to the living room.

Breakfast was served sometime around ten, after a twenty-minute grace-slash-sermon from the Pastor. Like every meal at the house, chatter was loud and lively. Aside from the unfortunate incident that morning and the continued silent treatment from Demi, I enjoyed being with my family. In less than a week's time, Charlye would officially be my sister. And watching how happy she made my brother, made all the wedding insanity worth it.

While Pastor grilled all of us about the status of our relationship with God, I tried to focus on my food, not Demi. But I couldn't stop myself from looking at her. For all intents and purposes, she seemed normal. She laughed at all of Asa's jokes, smiled at all the right points in the conversation, and gave everybody her undivided attention when they spoke to her directly. Yet, she still hadn't even acknowledged my presence. And she didn't even eat my pancakes.

Chastity leaned over and whispered to me, "I'm so sorry about earlier."

I squeezed her hand. "Stop apologizing. We're good."

On the other side of the table, Demi tossed back her mimosa and slammed the glass on the table.

"Sis, are you okay?" Dallas asked.

"I'm fine," Demi told her, biting into her biscuit.

"Maybe we could talk?" Chastity asked me. "I really could use an ear."

Demi finally met my gaze. *A hard glare is better than nothing*. I smirked. Because it was clear to me now. Demi was jealous.

"Are you busy this afternoon?" Chastity asked, oblivious to everything around her. "We could go for coffee?"

Clearing her throat, Demi poured another glass of champagne—no orange juice—and drained it.

Blake shot her a concerned look. "What are you going through, Demi?"

Demi gripped her butter knife. "Nothing."

"I'll take this, sis." Dallas tugged the knife out of Demi's palm and handed her a spoon. "Try the yogurt."

When the pastor pulled out his Bible and launched into a Sunday School lesson, Pop cleared his throat.

Ma stood, catching the signal. "Breakfast was good as always, Duke. Thank you." She squeezed my shoulder. "Pastor, it's an honor to have you here. If there's anything you need, don't hesitate to let me know." She glanced at her watch. "Unfortunately, we'll have to cut the lesson short, because we have scheduled a family meeting in the—"

"Family meeting?" Asa asked. "What for?"

"Because I said so." Ma flashed her patented you-better-not-interrupt-me-again-in-front-of-company smile. "In your father's study."

Pop excused himself, grabbed another piece of bacon and exited the room. Blake practically sprinted out of the room before she remembered Lennox was there. She peeked her head around the corner and beckoned him with her forefinger. The rest of us, followed my mother into the study.

Once we all crowded into the room, Ma glanced at Pop. "I wish you'd given me a little more notice, honey. What was that?"

Pop shrugged. "You know it was time, Bae."

"So, there's no meeting?" Asa asked.

Blake popped Asa in the back of his head. "No, fool. Are you hungover? You've been out of it all morning."

"Back up, Blake." Asa said, shoving Blake away from him and into Lennox's lap.

Across the room, Demi sat quietly. She'd done a fairly good job of pretending my hand wasn't touching her clit a few hours ago, but when our gazes met and that blush worked its way up her neck, I knew she wasn't as unaffected as she tried to be.

Dallas grabbed a piece of paper and fanned herself. "Are we done? It's hot in here."

Ma glared at Dallas. "We're not done. Since your father made this meeting possible, I'm going to use the time to tell you what I need from all of you this week."

Over the next few minutes, Ma spouted off a list of tasks to be completed before nine o'clock the night before the wedding. She also added in a request that we all stay overnight at the house the day before the rehearsal. "It would be nice to wake up together and have breakfast on the day before the wedding, before all hell breaks loose. Got it?" Everyone grumbled their acceptance of the proposal as if we had a choice. "Duke, let's plan a menu. I'm thinking ribs."

"Ma, it's twenty degrees outside," I argued.

Shrugging, Ma said, "So. You've done it before."

Bliss rubbed her stomach. "Naija's birthday party was a hit because of that food."

Yeah, and I had to practically bribe a little girl to save me one of the ribs I stood outside during a fuckin' cold front to grill. But I knew I wouldn't win a battle of wills against my mother, so I just agreed, "Sure, Ma. Whatever you need."

Ma kissed my cheek. "Thanks, baby."

Charlye raised her hand like she was in a classroom. "I hate to bring this up, Mama V, but can someone please talk to Pastor about the ceremony? I do not want to stand up there in those heels for three hours while he tells us all about everything that doesn't have to do with the wedding."

"I'm not even standing up there for an hour while he preaches the same sermon he did back in the day," Dex agreed.

Asa winced. "I could almost see Sister Pearl chewing

her dentures and beating that tambourine during Sunday Service when he broke out in song."

Pop barked out a laugh, then promptly shut up when Ma glared at him. Clearing his throat, he shrugged. "They have a point, Bae. I love the Lord."

"He heard your cry, Dad?" Blake added.

My father pointed at Blake. "That's right."

"Sing, Demi!" Dallas yelled.

Demi finished the verse, breaking out in a mesmerizing, yet unique rendition of Whitney Houston's song. I was laser-focused on her as she belted out the tune like it was second nature. When she finished the slow verse, Pop broke out in a fast congregational song. Demi followed along with him, putting him to shame with her vocal range. Then, Dallas, Blake, and even Bliss jumped up and started singing the chorus, while Ma happily clapped along.

When the song ended, Pop hugged Demi and kissed her cheek. "Thanks, baby girl. You know those are my favorite songs."

Demi smiled up at him. "I know. That's why I did it. For you."

"Love you," Pop told her.

She hugged him. "Love you too."

Pop took his seat. "Back to the meeting. The ceremony should be half an hour, if that."

Blake clapped. "Hallelujah. Dad said the magic words. Half-hour ceremony."

Dallas waved her hand in the air. "Can I get an Amen for the half-hour ceremony?"

"Fine," Ma relented. "I'll talk to him. Now, get out of here."

Demi's smile faded when she looked at me, then she slipped out quietly. I followed her. "Demi, wait."

She jogged up the stairs. "I have to go, Duke."

I pulled her into the linen closet. "Before you go, don't you think we should talk about this?"

Her shoulders fell. "I do think we should talk, but I can't do it right now."

"Why?"

"Because you're too close. I need some distance. I have to be able to think straight. And I can't with you standing there looking like you want to fuck me."

I barked out a laugh. "Whoa. That's not what this is about."

"And feeling like I want you to," she added, stepping closer to me. "I could get lost in this feeling. I need to figure out if it's just because I need some or because I just want you."

"Which do you prefer?"

Demi searched my eyes. "I prefer not to fuck this up. You're too important to me to act impulsively."

Demi rested her forehead on my chest. I wrapped my arms around her and kissed the top of her head. She was right. This was too important to fuck up. Although I knew what I wanted, I needed her to be sure of me. "Okay, baby."

She glanced up at me, a guarded look in her eyes. "You just called me baby."

I brushed my lips over her brow, then her lips. "Because you are my baby."

Demi frowned. "When did this change for you?"

"It hasn't," I admitted. "You've been my baby since the day you came to the house, muddy and wet and crying. I knew then that I would always do everything I could to protect you. I knew I would fight every damn body for you."

She smiled. "I know that. But that's what you do for your sisters."

I brushed my thumb down the column of her neck and her eyes fluttered closed. "Yes, but I don't want to see them naked."

"Stop." She laughed. "Seriously… have you always felt this way? And if so, why didn't you tell me?"

"That part is a little harder to explain."

"Please try," she whispered.

"What I will say is… I would never do anything that would place our relationship in jeopardy. And I would never come to you if I wasn't sure of my feelings. You're *that* important to me."

"It's not just a sex thing?"

It sounded like a trick question. Because I absolutely wanted her on my dick and in my bed. But I didn't *just* want to have sex with her. "I think it's pretty obvious I want that. You're already my family, you're my friend, and I want you to be my lover." I pushed a strand of hair from her face. "I just want you, even the parts that you think are too ugly to share. I want everything."

A tear fell from her eyes, and I brushed it away. "Duke… You don't commit. You're also a flirt. I don't want to kill anybody."

"I've never had someone I wanted to commit to," I told her honestly. "And I've been feeling pretty murderous around you too."

Demi cracked up. "I don't think I've ever seen you jealous."

"I've never *been* jealous—until *Young'Uns Weekend*."

"Tristan?"

"Oh yeah. I wanted to fuck him up."

"I love that about you." She hugged me. "You always make me feel safe."

"If you need some time, I'll give it to you. But I want you to come to me when you're ready to have a conversation. It doesn't matter if you tell me to fuck off. I just want to hear it from you."

"You say that now, but…"

"Have I ever lied to you?"

She shook her head. "Never," she croaked. "Please don't start."

I pulled back, cradling her face in my palms. I placed a gentle kiss to her mouth. "I'll be here when you're ready to talk."

Life was a series of decisions. Some good, some bad. Others hard, others easy. And right now, I was on the verge of making the hardest good decision I've ever had to make —letting her go. But I'd do it for three reasons. *One*, she needed time. I always gave her what she needed. *Two*, if she didn't leave, nothing would stop me from pushing her up against that wall over there and fucking the shit out of her. Everybody else and Ma's towels be damned. And the third reason? Call it intuition. Instinct. I knew women. I knew *this* woman. I'd spent a long time watching her, whether it was through the lens of a brother-like figure, a friend, a confidante, and a partner-in-crime. And she would come back. So, I kissed her again. "You should probably go."

Demi bit down on her bottom lip. "Are you mad at me?"

"No. But it's not a good idea for us to be in dark places together."

She let out a nervous laugh. "Right."

"And because I can't stop imagining your mouth around my dick."

"Oh," she gasped. "I should go then." She turned the doorknob. "I'll see you later."

Then, she left. And I let her go.

Demi

I spent the rest of the morning in hiding, away from Dallas and everyone else. Especially Duke. Although I'd been there for breakfast, I hadn't eaten much because I couldn't stop obsessing over how everything had changed between us, much to my stomach's dismay. Instead of enjoying his fluffy, buttery pancakes, I'd been forced to pick up fast food on the way back to my hotel room. Now, I was eating Chicken McNuggets while thinking about Duke McHotLips.

What the hell is wrong with me? It was just one kiss. *And a whole makeout session.* Okay, it was foreplay. *It was hot.* So hot, in fact, that I wanted him to put his talented mouth somewhere else. In my defense, though, he also had one very impressive, very hard dick imprint. *That I wouldn't mind sitting on any time.* It wasn't just the physical closeness, though. It was him. His words, that linen-closet confession, had replayed in my mind continuously.

For crying out loud, it was Duke. The same cocky asshole who'd once asked me to pretend I was his wife to get rid of one of his dates. The same muthafucka who'd forced me to watch cooking shows instead of *Divorce Court*.

In a few short weeks, he'd transformed into a man. A man who'd shown up every single time I needed him with no questions asked. A man who made me laugh even when I wanted to cry. A man who smelled like vanilla and cinnamon and leather and whisky and... sexy-ass male.

A soft knock pulled me out of my thoughts, and I sent up a silent prayer of thanks for the distraction.

"Hey, girl." Bliss held up two pizza boxes and pushed her way in.

Dallas followed seconds later with chicken wings. "You need to eat."

Blake brought in the rear, lifting a bottle of wine and a fifth of Don Julio 1942. "You also need a drink. Or three. No chaser."

I grinned as they set up for the impromptu pizza party. "Y'all are a trip. You just want me to tell you what happened with Duke."

"Yeah, pretty much," Bliss said, pulling out a speaker.

"Aht aht," Blake interjected. "I would've just called. I don't swap liquor for tea." She poured four shots in the shot glasses they'd brought with them and gave one to me.

Dallas hugged me. "I noticed you didn't eat a single pancake, which isn't like you. So, I figured you needed food."

Bliss glanced at her phone. "Tyn is mad she won't be here until tomorrow, so we'll FaceTime her in." Seconds later, we had music.

Holding up her shot glass, Blake commanded, "Drink up."

After my stomach was full and I had a sufficient buzz, I told them everything, from the moment I assumed Duke's feelings had changed to the first kiss at his Airbnb to Chastity walking out of his room. They listened intently, offering appropriate facial expressions and commentary at the right times.

Dallas blinked. "Sis, you better keep going. That's not the end of the story."

"I know that's right." Blake gave Dallas a hi-five. "You know we could hear some shit through the door."

Shrugging, Bliss added, "And your hair... Sis, it was obvious his hands were all up and through your curls."

I blew out a deep breath. "Fine." I paused because… *Can I really tell Duke's sisters that I almost let Duke fuck me in their parent's house?* I bit down on my thumbnail, considering my next words very carefully.

Dallas threw a pillow at me. "Stop overthinking it!"

"It's okay if you want to have sex with my brother," Bliss said with a shrug. "You're still a woman."

My mouth fell open, before I snapped it shut again. "I didn't…" I hugged the pillow. "We didn't do it."

"Oh, I know." Dallas waved a dismissive hand. "You weren't even in there that long."

"Shit," Blake snorted, "it doesn't take long to get down. Especially when you haven't had good dick in years. All he would have to do is touch it."

I hit Blake in the head with the pillow. "Girl!"

"I'm just sayin'." She giggled. "I don't know how you did it, chile. I could barely last six months."

Cracking up, I said, "That was self-imposed, ma'am." Blake had put herself on punishment from yak and dick a while ago. But then, she met Lennox and all bets were off. "And now you're happily engaged so it worked out."

"Engaged but not getting married any time soon," Bliss added with a hard glare toward Blake.

"We're not talking about me right now," Blake mumbled.

Dallas arched a brow. "Well…? Demi?"

"It was a mistake, but I did it on purpose."

"What?" They all said simultaneously.

"He told me that nothing happened between him and Chastity. Then, he kissed me again. I told him not to kiss me anymore, then I kissed him." I sighed heavily. "Then, he stuck his hand in my pants," I grumbled under my breath.

"I told you!" Dallas stood and held out her hand.

Bliss took off her earrings and gave them to Dallas. "Shoot. I love those earrings."

Dallas twerked. "I know my sis. Thanks for the earrings. They'll go good with my rehearsal outfit."

Bliss fumed in the corner. "I hate you."

"I love you," Dallas chirped. Turning to me, she said, "Okay, so the real issue here is not that Duke stuck his hand in your pants. It's that you *wanted* him to do it. Correct?"

I nodded. "I did. But I don't know why."

"Uh… he's fine?" Blake said. "He's my brother, but I know a fine-ass man when I see one."

"But he's Duke," I argued.

Blake rolled her eyes. "So. You spent years crushing on my ashy-mindset brother, Tristan."

Dallas barked out a laugh. "You're so wrong for that, Sissy."

"There's always another woman," I told them. "Did you see Chastity's ass at breakfast? All over him."

"And yo' ass was ready to climb over that table and stab her," Dallas giggled, "with a damn butter knife."

I couldn't even believe my own behavior. I'd never chosen violence in any of my relationships. "See! That's exactly what I'm talking about. A few hot makeout sessions and I'm ready to slice someone up."

"Even Ma noticed," Bliss admitted.

Mortified, I gasped. "What?"

Shaking her head, Bliss added, "It's okay, though. It was a good thing."

"Yeah." Blake took another shot. "Because *that* coupled with the whole Sunday School lesson thing threw her off her game. She didn't even make her goal with the cussing jar."

Dallas took over. "Totally forgot to collect our coins."

"Dad made it worse." Blake chuckled. "He coaxed her into booking the pastor and his family—"

"And all the other guests that had planned to stay with them," Bliss interrupted.

"—vacation homes or hotel rooms," Blake continued.

"They left right before we came here," Dallas explained. "So no more Chastity."

We all laughed. And it felt good to be with my sisters. "Oh, I needed that laugh," I said on a sigh. "Thank you."

"Okay, so back to the matter at hand." Dallas bit into another slice of pizza. "This pizza is good as hell. Anyway, how do you feel about Duke?"

A few months ago, my answer would've been a resounding "Nothing." Except, even that wouldn't have been true. I could never feel *nothing* for him. Because he was too important to me. "I've been thinking about it for a little while. For every life-changing event, he's been there." And not just with me physically but present in the moment with me, offering advice, pancakes, or even a joint. "I guess I never even considered that it could be more than what it always is between us. It's not like he can't have any woman he wants. There's always someone vying for his attention."

"He doesn't care about them hoes," Blake said matter-of-factly. "He *does* care about you, though."

"I know." I picked at the edge of my sweater. "I care about him too. Now that the switch has been flipped, I can't stop thinking about him. I can't stop wanting him."

Bliss smiled. "Aw, that's so beautiful."

"But what does that say about me?" I asked. "Last year, I was waiting for Tristan in a hotel bar."

"He didn't show up," Dallas said. "His loss."

I averted my gaze. "Now, I'm kissing his brother."

Blake smacked her lips. "Here's the deal. Before I finish, I need you to know that I charge a lot of money to clients for this same type of treatment. Ready? All of us knew that Tristan was never the man of your dreams. *You* just needed to realize that for yourself. That non-meeting at the hotel bar was necessary for you to remember that you don't need Tristan. You never did. He's not your hero, Demi. He's a flawed, asshole-ish man. I love him, but it's true."

"He's not that bad," I countered. "He's just tortured."

"He is," Blake agreed. "That's not your problem, though. You shouldn't accept his bullshit ass excuses because he's too damaged to do the work on himself. Sis, I love you. I will toss a grenade and blow some shit up for you. Tristan is my brother. I would cut a bitch for him too. But he's not for you. Dead ass."

Bliss turned sincere eyes on me. She squeezed my hand, offering the comfort only she provided. "From my perspective, it's not that surprising that you and Duke are discovering these feelings for each other. The way he was ready to kick Tristan's ass Thanksgiving weekend? I don't even think Dex would've been able to hold him back."

"That's sad," I said. "I don't want to be a source of conflict between them."

Bliss squeezed my hand again. "In a way, you are. But you're not. The issues they have with each other are deeper than you. They'll get it together. Like Blake said… not your problem. Duke is many things, but he's never been callous with your feelings. Or his. I can't see him risking your relationship to get his dick wet."

"Bliss!" Dallas shouted. "You said dick!"

Bliss smirked. "I like dicks. I just haven't sat on one in a while." After Naija was born, Bliss had put all her energy into her daughter. To the exclusion of any man. Not even the man she wanted.

Dallas took another shot. "Jace has a big one for you." Then, she cracked up. "Go sit on his."

Jace was a neighbor and close friend of the family. Him and his brothers spent a lot of time at the house when we were teenagers and he'd always had his eye on Bliss. But she'd been laser-focused on everything and everyone else.

"How do you know his dick is big?" Bliss asked. "Have you seen it?"

"We all did," Blake replied. "Don't tell Lennox. But remember when we went to the lake after the Fourth of July barbecue that year? He jumped in the water and somehow lost his swim trunks. Quite a sight."

"Damn, I missed it," Bliss exclaimed.

"You still have time," I told her. "I'm sure he'd be willing to show you that thing whenever you ask."

Bliss pouted. "You know I'm not asking."

"That's why we're different, Sissy," Blake said. "I need to see the goods."

Dallas changed the subject back to me. "So I guess it's my turn. I'll keep it short because I'm sleepy and ready for Preston to give me some. Okay… Duke is one of my favorite people in the world. Not just because we shared a womb but because of who he is. He's solid. I never have to question where he stands. He's gonna get my back even if I'm wrong. He'll tell me about myself later, but he's still #TeamMe. I'm gonna get mushy now. And I might even ugly cry. But you can't hold it against me."

"Oh God," Blake mumbled.

Dallas blew out a shaky breath. "You've been through so much, Sis." Tears filled her eyes, which in turned caused me to tear up. "Some people would've let that level of trauma kill them. But you let it make you better. You are a badass. Period. You deserve to be happy and feel loved. Duke is the same way. You heal each other. I've seen it when y'all think we're not paying attention. The way he always makes sure you eat. The way you two sit in silence together. I don't know all the particulars of your personal relationship with him, but I'll bet that you know things about him that we don't know. And you've probably told him things about you that you haven't told anyone. It's just the way you are with each other. It's innate."

"Stop crying," Blake commanded, grabbing a tissue. "You make me sick."

Bliss let out a watery laugh. "Right?"

Dallas placed a hand over her heart. "He protects you like I would. That's all I could ever ask. If you like him, I say tell him. Why deny yourself a chance at happiness?"

Bliss' phone dinged, and she gasped. "Oh no. We forgot to call Paityn." She pressed the screen. "Hey, Sissy."

"Are you crying?" Tyn asked. "What is going on over there?"

"It's Dallas' ass," Blake complained. "Always being heartfelt about Demi."

Paityn's laughter came through the speaker. "Let me talk to her." Bliss turned the phone so I could look at Paityn. "Hey, Sis."

I wiped my eyes with my sleeves. "Hey."

"I won't make you cry. I already know what happened. I'm just going to add my two cents." She sighed. "Duke has a soft heart under his hard exterior. But I personally would feel very secure knowing that you are holding it in your palm."

"Oh my God, Tyn," I cried. "You said you weren't going to make me cry."

"That wasn't something to cry about. The next thing I

was going to say… Be careful because I sent Duke a panty vibrator that he might want to try out on you." Paityn's naughty toy company had been changing our lives since she developed her first prototype. "Trust me, sis. It's something else."

"Give me that phone," Blake said. "You been holding out on me, Sissy."

We spent the next few hours laughing, drinking, and enjoying each other. By the time they'd left, I'd made a decision. The ladies had given me food for thought. In the end, it was Duke that had given me the biggest reason to take the next step with him—he was willing to wait for me.

Me: *I've thought about it.*
Duke: …
Duke: *That fast.*
Me: *Not that fast. You busy?*
Duke: *Not too busy for you.*

My heartbeat pounded in my ear as I typed out my message: *You said you kept imagining my mouth around your dick.*

Duke: *I did.*
Me: *Pull up.*

Oh shit, what did I just do? While I definitely wanted Duke, I wasn't sure if tonight was *the* night. Doubts swirled in my head as I contemplated sending another text. An *I'm-just-playin'* text. Ultimately, I decided to let things happen organically. If tonight was going to be the night, it would be. If we slowed things down, I'd be good with that too. As long as we were both on the same page.

I spent a few minutes straightening up the room before I jumped in the shower. And, just in case something naked happened, I shaved. When I heard the knock at the door, I took one last look at myself in the mirror, fluffing out my hair and applying fresh lip gloss. I turned to the side, poking my butt out a little bit. That thang was thangin' in my shorts and tank.

Finally, I opened the door, but it wasn't Duke. It wasn't even room service with the charcuterie board and wine I'd ordered. My mood turned sour because the unfriendly, unwelcome person staring back at me was my father.

Chapter Twelve

RUN TO YOU

Demi

"*D*emita Hope."

I hated when my father addressed me by my first and middle name. It always reminded me that my life before I left him felt hopeless. "What can I do for you?"

"Can I come in?" he asked.

"No."

He sighed. "We need to talk."

When I turned eighteen years old, I'd made it a point not to see my father. I didn't visit him, and I certainly didn't call him. The only time I saw him was when we faced each other in a court of law. The only reason anyone knew he was my father was because I was required to share any conflicts of interest to my clients. And, of course, most of the judicial staff knew our family connection. Other than that, I didn't refer to him as Dad. I called him Mr.

Strong in every single public interaction. "What would we have to talk about?"

"I would hate to do this in the hallway. May I come in?"

Although I felt a range of emotions when dealing with my father through the years, the only consistent feeling was dread. "I'll come out."

As we rode the elevator down to the lobby, we didn't speak. He didn't ask how I was doing or muse aloud about the weather. He simply stood there, eyes forward, head high. Like always. I stepped out of the elevator, and he followed me toward the hotel lounge.

On the way, I spotted Duke entering the hotel. He stopped, his gaze flitting from me to my father. I shook my head slightly, letting him know that I was good. Once inside the bar, I took a seat at a booth toward the back and waited.

My father ordered himself a gin and tonic. "She'll have a martini dry, up with a twist."

I wasn't surprised that my father had tried to order me a drink. It wasn't my type of cocktail, though, and only shined a dull light on the simple fact that he didn't know me. At all. "I'll have a water," I corrected.

The waiter excused himself and my father looked at me. "You're looking thin. That's good."

The dig hurt, especially since I was a little chunky in elementary school. Which was why he'd forced me to play sports, to help me lose the *baby weight* as he'd called it. The only good things to come out of that were fencing class, where I met Dallas, and swimming. I could escape from him in the pool because, oddly enough, he couldn't swim. It didn't stop him from making me feel like shit if I didn't compete at a level that he deemed sufficient—even though he'd failed to come to most of my competitions.

"You look beautiful," he said. "Like your mother."

That compliment also hurt. Because he had a habit of comparing me to my mother. Either I was too much like her or not enough like her.

My father droned on about work for a few minutes until the waiter arrived with our drinks. He glanced at me. "I hear you're planning a move."

I'd perfected the blank stare years ago, and I had no trouble using it on my father. That skillset had been learned through years of abuse.

"I saw one of your old cohorts in the courthouse and she mentioned you were relocating to Atlanta," he continued. "Are you staying in private practice, or will you join a firm?"

"Why do you care?" I asked, careful to keep my voice even but firm. Inside, I was anything but calm and collected. But I felt all the emotions, from curiosity to rage to fear to anguish. Because I had no idea what was coming next.

"Just making conversation. Demita, I realize that things haven't been pleasant between us in years."

"Is this your way of making it right?"

"I'd like to be able to converse with my daughter."

"Now, I'm your daughter?" I snorted. "'Cause, I remember you telling me that I was dead to you just a few years ago."

It was the first time I'd faced him in court. I presented my client's case effectively and efficiently, winning a sizable settlement from his client. He'd lost it in the hallway, scolding me like I was a child. The insult didn't land like he'd hoped it would, though. Especially after I thanked him for making my job easier by being a subpar attorney who only got as far as he did by using baseless, lawless, and childish tactics to defend his clients. The incident had caused quite a stir among his colleagues and, as a result, he'd lost a lot of credibility among his peers. And revenue when several of his clients' spouses sought me out for representation.

"I was angry. I didn't mean it."

I refused to tell him anything about my life or my career. "Why are you here? I'm not a ten-year-old girl fighting for Daddy's attention anymore. You can stop pretending to care."

"I need a favor."

I knew it. "What makes you think I'll help you do anything?"

"Because you love a challenge. You've devoted your life to besting me in court."

Raising a questioning eyebrow, I said, "I've already bested you in court. Several times. And, no, I devoted my life to helping women leave men like you without losing everything."

"Which is why I'm coming to you. Isabelle is getting a divorce."

My father married two times after my mother. Isabelle Porter was the child of his third wife, the one that he'd doted on after I left, the one that he had no trouble shelling out thousands of dollars for her tuition to Harvard University, the one who'd started and abandoned several businesses and was currently on her fifth career as a lifestyle vlogger. "Again, why should this concern me?"

My father shifted in his seat. "She's your sister."

"That's rich," I scoffed. "She's not my sister. I don't know her. I had no idea she was even married."

"She's your sister," he repeated.

"She's your third ex-wife's daughter. We never lived in the same house together. I don't have her phone number. I wouldn't be able to pick her out of a lineup." *Probably because of all the plastic surgery she's had.*

"She's *my* daughter."

I blinked. "What?"

"I am Isabelle's father."

Suddenly, the broken pieces of my childhood clicked together to form a picture I'd been too blind to see. "You cheated on Mom with Susan?"

"Yes, I had an affair."

"Is that why she left you?"

He had the nerve to look ashamed. Averting his gaze, he nodded. "One of the reasons."

"Yeah, well, there's always the undeniable fact that you're a narcissistic asshole."

"Don't talk to me like that," he warned, his voice low.

But I wasn't scared of him anymore. "Or what?" I challenged. "What are you going to do? Slap me?"

"Lower your voice," he commanded softly.

"Don't tell me what to do. You lost that right a long time ago."

"I should've known this was futile. Imagine how I feel, coming to my daughter to ask for help."

"I don't care how you feel. You're not my father." I shrugged. "You and my mother abandoned me because you're both selfish as fuck. And to make matters worse, both of you have the nerve to come to *me* and ask me for help."

"Demita Hope, you—"

"Don't call me that," I bit out between clenched teeth. "You can call me Ms. Strong."

"I named you Demita Hope and that's what I'll call you."

I snickered. "You know what. It doesn't matter because I'll never see you again after this." I laughed. "It's funny to me. I told Mom to fuck off last year, and now I get to tell you the same thing." I laughed again. This time louder and more obnoxious. "This is good because I feel like a weight has been lifted."

"Demita, calm down. You're embarrassing yourself."

"I'm not embarrassed." I called the waiter over and ordered a shot of Tequila. "Just being myself."

"I've told you time and again that you will respect me."

The waiter returned seconds later with my shot, and I took it, slamming the glass down on the table. "I don't owe you shit, *Dad*, not even respect. From the beginning, you made me feel like I was the reason Mother left, that I wasn't good enough for her to stay. And you continued to do that until I ran away from you. Now, it makes sense why you never even bothered to fight the guardianship. Because you had plans. You wanted to move your whore and her daughter—*your* daughter—into the house." The move was sudden, too. It seemed the minute the guardianship was finalized, he'd hurried to divorce his second wife so he could marry Susan.

"That's not true," he argued.

"I don't know why I'm shocked. I was always dispensable to you, just yesterday's trash. The reminder of your first failed marriage that you needed to put out on the street." I didn't realize I was crying until Duke appeared next to me, Kleenex in hand and a murderous look in his eyes. "Good thing I extricated myself from you before you could destroy me. Good thing I didn't need you to become who I am today." I stood, trying to hold myself together. But Duke's hand… He placed it firmly on my back, offering his strong support. Then, I melted into him, sobbing into his chest for a moment until I pulled myself together. Turning back to my father, I said, "Fuck you. And tell Isabelle to choke on a dick and fight her own battle."

My father stood and attempted to grab my hand, but Duke stepped between us. "No. I promise you... If you ever even look like you want to touch her again, I won't hesitate to beat the shit out of you."

"Ah," my father sneered. "You're the other brother. The thug."

Duke shook his head. "If that's what you need to tell yourself or your colleagues when I wear your ass out in this public bar, go for it. But we all know the truth. I saw a grown-ass man try to manhandle a woman. I defended her against a probable attack." He shrugged. "Sounds justifiable to me. Think your law firm will feel the same way?"

Swallowing, my father backed up. "You'll be sorry."

"I won't." Duke and I said in tandem.

Without another word, my father—*Mr. Strong*—left the hotel and my life for the final time.

I didn't feel safe in the hotel anymore, so Duke drove me to the house. Ma was in the kitchen cleaning up when we entered through the back door.

"Hey, Ma." Duke kissed her cheek.

"Hey, babe! You're back already?" Ma glanced over at me, and her smile fell. "What's going on?"

"Nothing," I lied. *Horribly*. "Just tired."

She eyed my suitcases. "Are you staying here tonight?"

Duke cut in, "Just for a couple of nights."

Ma's gaze stayed on me. "I'm glad. We haven't had a chance to catch up, so this will give us that time together. I want you to join me tomorrow at the spa." She folded up the dishrag. "Always remember your room is *only* yours. You can sleep in there anytime you want."

"I know," I nodded frantically. "I just hated that hotel."

"Babe, why don't you take Demi's bags upstairs and give us a minute?"

Duke squeezed my hand. "Okay." He tucked a strand of hair behind my ear, then kissed my brow.

My eyes widened at the tender display of affection in front of Ma. "Um," I croaked, unable to think of anything to say in that moment.

"Good night, Duke." Ma shoved him out of the room.

After he disappeared up the stairs, Ma filled up the tea kettle, set it on the stove, and turned on the burners. "Have a seat, love."

My throat burned as fresh tears filled my eyes. One of the first things I noticed after I moved in was that Ma called everyone babe—even when she was disappointed in us. But she also called me "Love". It was a term of endearment that nobody else had, which always made me feel special.

The kettle whistled, and she prepared our tea. Ma preferred black tea, while I enjoyed green tea. She worked in silence, putting just the right amount of sweetener in mine before she set the piping hot mug in front of me. Seconds later, she motioned for me to follow her to the kitchen table.

As we sipped our tea in silence, I thought about everything that had happened today. From the moment I'd seen Chastity walking out of Duke's room, it had been a rollercoaster ride with twists and turns, highs and lows. Yet, I couldn't say I'd had a bad day. Despite the confrontation with my father and the uncertainty surrounding Duke, I had moments of bliss. Time with my real family, singing and laughing, was at the top of my favorite things to do. Sister Time was the best and kissing Duke felt like the start of something great. All in all, I couldn't complain. *But...*

I still cried. Again. As the tears flowed down my face,

Ma just smoothed her hand over my back, whispering how proud she was of me, how blessed she felt to have me as a daughter, how much she loved me. Then, she pulled me in her arms, rocking me back and forth. Her scent, her voice made me feel safe and secure and wanted.

"Love, it's okay." She kissed my forehead. "You're okay."

I choked out another sob, before I started all over again. I cried for the little girl I was, the hopeful child of two selfish parents. I cried for the pain I'd felt for so long. I cried for the relationship I would never have with my biological family. And I cried because I felt happy to be with the woman who mothered me like she'd birthed me.

Eventually, I settled down. Ma didn't let go, though. She continued to hold me. "Don't you know that you are so special to me," she whispered, her voice shaky. "I love you so much, my sweet baby."

"I love you too," I mumbled.

"Do you want to tell me what happened?" she asked.

I cleared my throat and sipped my tea. "The man who I once called Dad came to see me today." I explained the interaction, the awkwardness between us, his attempt to pretend he wanted to have a relationship with me. "It was all bullshit, though. A guise so that he could ask me for a favor. Apparently, he fathered a child with another woman and passed her off as his stepdaughter. He wanted *me* to help her with her divorce."

Ma's eyes widened slightly. "Isabelle?"

I gaped. "You knew?"

"It wasn't hard to figure out. Just like it wasn't difficult to find out he'd been laundering money for some of his very wealthy clients."

"What?"

"Stew used that information to get him to sign the guardianship papers."

Well, damn. That was unexpected information. "Fraud, huh? Why didn't you turn him in?"

"We had to make a choice. Him losing his money and reputation, or your safety. Of course, we were prepared to fight to keep you with us, but there was always a chance that you'd have to move with your mother or some distant relative or even foster care. Honestly, I feared you wouldn't last in an environment like that. You'd already been through so much. You needed stability and love. And we wanted you here."

I'd always wondered what they'd done to convince my father to sign the petition. I knew he hated to lose, even though he didn't really want me. Now, I knew why. "Thank you," I whispered. "Thank you for accepting me into your home."

"*Our* home. This is your home, too, Love. You belong here."

"Sometimes I wondered what I'd done to deserve parents like them. Was I a bad kid? Hardheaded? Did I not listen when I was supposed to? Did I complain too much? Am I good enough?"

"Oh, Love. I'm so sorry you felt that way."

"For so long, I just wanted to escape." I sucked in a breath. "That night when I left, I didn't even care if I froze to death. I just knew I needed to run. I came here knowing you were out of town and prayed that the key would be where Dallas said it was. But Tristan and Duke were here. And my life changed that day for the better. I can't thank you enough for saving my life."

Ma hugged me again, squeezing me tight. "It's okay."

"I'm such a crybaby today," I sniffed, before pulled back. "I mean, it's like a faucet. Flowing freely."

"Crying isn't a sign of weakness, Love. It's a show of strength. You are stronger than you know. Stronger than most. So, go ahead and let it out."

I nibbled on my bottom lip. "Thank you for loving me, Ma."

She cradled my face in her palms. "You never have to thank me for that. I ride for mine."

"Ma!" I laughed. "You've been hanging out with Raven too much."

"Hey, I thought I was doing a good job."

"You are."

We drank our tea in silence for a moment. Until Ma asked, "Do you want to know why I call you Love?"

I wiped my nose with my sleeve and nodded. "Is it going to make me cry?"

"Maybe. But I think it's time for you to know."

"Okay."

"When you and Dallas became close, even though you were with your father, I knew you needed me. I was certain of it. I had no idea how things would transpire, but I'm so grateful that you came to us when you felt the need to escape that environment. It gave us the opportunity to love you the way you deserve to be loved. I decided in that moment to call you Love because I want to always affirm that you *are* loved. You are just as important as Tristan, Paityn, Duke, Dallas, Dex, Bliss, Blake, and Asa. I know I didn't give birth to you, but I *am* your mother. Never forget that."

I closed my eyes. "You are."

Ma brushed tears from my cheeks. "I'll always be that for you. Even if you marry my son."

I choked out a laugh. "Marry your son?"

"I do have eyes. I saw that kiss Duke gave you today. It

wasn't a kiss on the lips, but it told me all I needed to know."

"What's that?"

"I'm not sure what exactly is going on between you two, but I know he didn't even care I was there. His focus was solely on you. That looks like love to me."

I frowned. "Love? We haven't even gone on a date."

"Yes, you have. You've been dating for years. Just not in the conventional way."

"Ma, I—"

"What is a date? Spending one-on-one time with someone, getting to know them, growing close… You and Duke have *been* doing that."

"I hear what you're saying, but I don't think so."

"You bring out the best in him," she continued. "He pulls you out of your shell. You two complement each other. You paint between the lines. He prefers to use the entire canvas."

"How do you feel about it?" I asked tentatively, averting my eyes. "You know how I felt about Tristan."

Ma cupped my chin, bringing my gaze back to her. "He was a hero to you then. But not the hero *for* you now."

"You sound like Blake."

"My poor child. She's so wise, yet so stubborn. But she's right. It's hard to let go, but sometimes it's necessary."

"Don't you think it's too soon for Duke and me to get involved?"

"Not at all. I met Stew, hated him for a good three months, then loved him for forty-something years. And still counting." Their love story was something out of a book. I'd memorized all the details the moment they'd shared it with me. "Give it some time," she said. "You'll see. Like I told Duke back in December, it won't take long."

That comment made me curious. "Wait, you talked to Duke about *me*?"

"I sure did. Everyone always says that 'Duke be knowing shit.'" She cracked up. "Who do you think he got it from?"

I hugged her again. "I love you so much."

"Love you more." Ma stood, pulling me to my feet. "Now, get some rest. The Starks and the Reids are coming in tomorrow. You know how we get down."

I loved when the core families got together. It was always a good time. "Yes, ma'am. I'll see you in the morning." I rinsed out the mugs and loaded them into the dishwasher.

"Thanks, Love."

I made my way to the staircase. "Good night."

"By the way," Ma called. "Stop smoking weed with Duke."

I froze, whirling around. "Huh?"

Ma burst out into a fit of giggles. "I told you... I know things. Good night, Love."

I jogged up the stairs and turned down the hallway, but I didn't stop at my room. Instead, I ended up in front of Duke's door. I knocked softly. Duke opened the door, clad in a pair of low-riding shorts. That's it. That's all.

I hunched a shoulder. "I figured I could lay with you?"

He smirked, and without a word, he pulled me inside.

Chapter Thirteen

AFTER HOURS

Duke

The middle of the night was prime time for me. I was most creative after three a.m. If I was home, I'd probably be cooking, trying out a new dish, mixing seasonings, reading the latest trade magazines. I found inspiration in everything, from flowers to smells to flickering lights over cityscapes. Tonight, though, I found myself in a very different position.

Demi had come to me, asked if she could lay with me. The question was innocent, and nothing out of the ordinary. Yet, in light of everything that had happened between us, it felt impossible. Because I wanted more.

About an hour ago, I realized my attempt at normalcy between us had failed spectacularly. I didn't want to wake anyone else, so I didn't go to the kitchen. I also didn't want to disturb Demi, so I just stretched out on a chair. Staring at her sleeping form had become my obsession tonight. *I can lose myself in her*, I thought as I let my gaze trail over the ridge of her nose to her full lips. I could spend hours kissing her, tasting her. I wanted to consume her the way she'd consumed me.

Lost in my thoughts, a soft hitch of her breath drew my attention back to her face. Her eyes were open, focused on me. I expected to see hurt and pain there, but I only saw hunger. "You're up?" I asked.

A slow smile spread over her lips. "You are too."

"I couldn't sleep."

Demi kicked the blanket off, giving me a full view of her bare legs. Rolling onto her belly, she hugged a pillow. "I'm surprised you're not in the kitchen, concocting something delicious."

"I thought about it for a minute."

"What stopped you?"

"You."

She grinned. "What are you going to do about it?"

Demi had never been shy around me. I didn't expect that to change under the circumstances. When she'd told me to pull up earlier, though, I wasn't sure we would actually do more than have an earnest conversation about where we stood. But this... That was definitely a challenge. "If I come over there..." I let the rest of my sentence hang in the air because she knew what it was. In the past, I could lay with her and keep my hands to myself. Not anymore. Because my hands ached to touch her, my mouth wanted to explore her, and my dick... That muthafucka wanted to brand her.

"Duke?" She arched a brow. "I know. I'm good with that." She shifted onto her knees and crooked a finger at me, beckoning me closer.

As I walked over to the bed, she slipped her oversized shirt off and tossed it somewhere behind me. I stopped at the edge of the bed and dipped a finger into the waistband of her biker shorts, tugging her forward.

Demi crushed her lips to mine, biting down on my bottom lip before sucking it into her mouth. I gripped her chin, angling her head so that I could take full advantage of that mouth. Her low groans combined with her soft pleas almost did me in, but I wanted to drag this out, take my time with her.

I broke the kiss, chuckling at the exasperated pout that formed on her kiss-swollen lips. Brushing my finger over her mouth, I murmured, "Don't rush me." I tipped her chin up and kissed her again. "Turn around." She hesitated. "Now," I commanded softly.

Demi did what I asked and glanced back at me over her shoulder. Her mouth curved into a smile. "Don't think you can tell me what to do once we leave this room."

"Don't think you won't willingly give me control *after* we leave this room." I wrapped my hand around the base of her neck, turning her head to me and kissing her. Hard. I unhooked her bra and cupped her breasts in my palms, rolling her nipples between my fingers until she moaned. Sliding my hand under her shorts, I rested my forehead against the back of her neck as I ran my finger over her slick folds. *Shit.* She was so wet, so ready for me. I wanted nothing more than to bury myself inside her. But this time was about her. Hell, *every* time would be about her.

Demi spread her legs and I slipped one finger inside her, then two. She felt good, warm, wet. Slowly, I strummed her clit as I sunk my fingers deeper inside, pushing and pulling, until she let out a strangled cry and came. I'd miscalculated my need to actually *see* her face when she came, to lock eyes with her as she fell over. I wouldn't make the same mistake twice. I kissed her shoulder, biting down on the skin. "This pussy might kill me."

She slumped forward, lying flat on the mattress. "At least you'll die happy."

I pushed her shorts down, as I kissed my way down her neck, then her spine, licking and sucking her soft skin along the way. I tugged on the waistband of her panties with my teeth, letting it go with a snap against her waist. She lifted that beautiful ass, allowing me to pull them and the shorts off. I bit down softly on both of her cheeks, then dipped my tongue inside, licking her until she begged for mercy.

"Oh shit, Duke," she breathed. "Oh damn."

Again, I slipped my fingers into her sweet pussy, plying her again until she screamed her release into her pillow. "Shhh…" I whispered. "Thin walls."

"Okay," she whimpered into the pillow.

Chuckling, I flipped her over. My chest tightened as I took her in. Perfect. Everything about her was beautiful, stunning. Even the parts I knew she hated, I loved. I ran my finger over the beauty mark on her side, the mole on her knee, the stretch mark on her thigh. "Perfect," I whispered.

"Duke," Demi whispered. "You're making me nervous."

Which surprised me, because she'd never been nervous around me. *I love it.* "Just looking at you. All of you."

I lifted her leg and kissed the top of her foot. She pushed the other foot into my chest and slid it down to my dick. "I think it's time for you to take these off."

I slid my shorts off and climbed on the bed, kissing and nipping and licking her legs. Then, her knees. Then, the inside of her thighs. She gasped when I pressed my face to her pussy, trailing my tongue up her slit to her clit. Demi arched her back off the bed, but I held her still as I worked her, tasting her, teasing her, bringing her closer to another climax. She succumbed to her orgasm, writhing beneath me as I sucked on her clit until she pleaded with me to stop.

Before she could come down fully from her orgasm, though, I went in for more, circling her clit with my tongue and getting her close again. This time, I didn't let her come. Instead, I trailed the hard ridge of my dick up her leg, over her clit, as I brushed my mouth up her body to her mouth. I dipped my tongue inside and kissed her with everything I had to give.

I was always prepared to fuck. But now… staring down at Demi, skin to skin, with nothing stopping us from doing this, I felt woefully *unprepared*. I knew why too. Somewhere along the line, I realized that this was more. I could never *just* fuck Demi, because I already felt more for her than for any woman I'd ever been with. The stakes were high, and I was falling in love.

Demi rubbed her nose against mine. "Duke?"

I blinked my way out of that thought. "Hmm?"

"It's okay to fuck me."

I barked out a laugh. "What did you think I was going to do? I mean…" I pressed my dick against her opening. She gasped. "I'm right here."

Demi covered her face. "Oh God. That didn't come out right."

I placed a kiss on her mouth. "What did you mean?"

"I noticed that you were taking your time, being a little gentle. I just want you to know that I like it hard. And rough. So you can…do it that way."

I tipped my head toward the bedside table. "Grab a condom." I nipped her chin. "I told you… Don't rush me. I will fuck you the way I want to. This time."

She shuddered against me. "Well…" She reached over and pulled the box of condoms out of the drawer, wasting no time sliding it on my dick. She squeezed the base. "Okay."

With my eyes on hers, I inched inside her. *Shit.* I blew out a breath, closing my eyes against the rush of emotion that swelled inside me. I dropped my forehead on her shoulder, licked my way to her mouth, and fused my lips to hers. We stayed like that a moment, mouths together, bodies tangled—until Demi traced my jaw with her finger and bucked up against me.

It didn't take long for us to find a rhythm with each other. We were the perfect song and dance, pushing and pulling as if we were always meant to be this way with each other. We'd tripped over an invisible line and there was no turning back. There was no way I could stay close but distant from her. I wanted her with me every second, every hour, every day.

"Duke," she murmured against my mouth as we moved in sync. "Please don't hurt me."

Her words were so soft, so heartfelt, I opened my eyes to search hers. "I'll never hurt you." It was a promise I intended to keep, because hurting her would hurt me. "Never."

Demi opened her eyes then, her hooded gaze piercing something deep inside. Then, she shuddered around me as she came, stealing the tiny pieces of me that I'd kept hidden for so long, but giving me so much more in return. And I followed her over, growling her name into her neck. In that moment, I realized that I wasn't falling. *I already fell.*

W aking up with Demi's naked body pressed against mine was a surreal experience. I wasn't really one of those men who insisted on never sleeping over. Not because I wasn't an asshole, but because morning wood was a thing. Yet, instead of finding an excuse to leave or calling one of my sisters or Skye to barge in and cause a scene, I found myself wishing we could stay like this for a while.

The reality of our situation was that, in a matter of minutes, my mother and father would be up enjoying coffee together. Asa would be stomping through the house. Or any of my other siblings could pop up at any minute. And nobody really knocked at the house, except for Pop. Still, I wasn't ready to leave her—or see her go.

We would have a full house today and Ma had already commissioned me to prepare dinner. One of these days I would actually charge her to boss me around, but it definitely wouldn't be today. And I looked forward to seeing X, Zara, and Skye, and their families.

I nuzzled her cheek with my nose. "Demi?"

She groaned. "Don't wake me up."

"Better me than Ma."

Demi sat up, her curls wild and her eyes barely open. "Damn. I'm in your room." She pushed her hair back. "Oh God. Ma! She knows I was upset. She might try to check on me." Demi rolled over and fell off the bed. "Shit," she hissed.

I reached out and she grabbed my hand. I pulled her to her feet. "No need to panic." Demi turned in place, a frown on her face. She was unashamed of her nakedness, which was perfect, because I wanted her that way often. "Looking for something?"

She looked at me. "What did you do with my shorts?"

I shrugged. "I don't know."

"Ah." She walked to the chair and picked up her shorts. "Got 'em." She slid them on. "If you see my panties—"

"You won't be getting them back," I cut in.

The corner of her mouth quirked up. "What's with men always trying to steal panties?"

I didn't want to hear about her with any man. "I'm not even going to comment on that."

Demi did a fist pump when she found her shirt. She put it on and walked over to me. "I better go."

I hooked a finger in her pants and pulled her on top of me. "Or you could hop on my dick." She rolled her eyes, but she sat up, straddling my hips with her thighs. I slipped my hand in her shorts and brushed my thumb over her clit. She groaned. "You seem like you're ready to me."

She bent down and kissed me. "You're too much."

Smacking her thigh, I ordered, "You already know what to do."

Demi stood up and shimmied out of her pants, giving me an unfettered view of her freshly-waxed pussy. I took full advantage, pulling her closer, and licking her slit. Her legs buckled but I held her upright as I feasted on her until she came.

She dropped to her knees. "Like I said," she whispered, "too much."

I gripped her hips as she reached over, grabbed the condom, and slid it over my dick. She lowered herself on me. We made love hard and fast, our eyes locked on each other. It didn't take long, and soon she came, with my name on her lips. *Just the way it should always be.* And I was right behind her.

A moment passed before Demi met my gaze again. She brushed her finger down the bridge of my nose. "I could get used to this." She kissed me. "It's crazy, isn't it?"

I traced the line of her collarbone. "In a way."

"I never expected this to happen."

"I'm not sorry."

Demi studied me. "Me neither." She wrapped her arms around me. "I do have one question, though."

"What is it?"

She shifted. "Oh," she gasped. My dick was hard and ready. "You tryin' to hold me hostage? I have years to make up for."

"I'm with it."

"Oh boy," she rolled off me, glancing down at my erection. "Put that away." She covered me up. "I need a shower." She looked over at me. "Should we, um, talk or something?"

"What do you want to talk about?"

Demi hugged her legs, resting her chin on her knees. "Are we…? What are we to each other?"

I sat up. "What we've always been," I answered.

"Not really."

I nodded. "Yeah, we are."

"Explain."

Gripping her legs, I pulled her closer. "You've always been important. That hasn't changed."

"Of course, but we had good sex. And you like me." She closed her eyes as a grin formed on her lips. "A lot."

"I've always liked you a lot."

"No, you…" She nodded. "You want me."

"You're sure about that?" I teased.

"Duke!" She smacked my shoulder and jabbed a finger in my chest. "Don't play with me. I will kick your ass."

"I don't doubt it." I picked up her palm and kissed her wrist, right at the pulse point. "I do want you."

"Right. So what does that mean?"

"It means that I'm not trying to go back to last week, or even yesterday. I don't need time to *think* about it. I already know I want to spend my days and my nights with you. I want to take you out on dates. I want to cook for you. I want to make love to you."

"All night?"

"Every night."

She smiled. "I think I can get with that."

"I know it seems fast," I told her.

"Kinda," she agreed, entwining her fingers with mine. "But not really."

"I've never been one to avoid the truth of a situation. When I say I care, I do. When I say I want this to work, I mean it."

"Basically, what I hear you saying is that you want me to check a box."

I used to make fun of those damn notes people used to pass around in high school when it was time for Homecoming. But since she brought it up, I said, "Hell yeah. Do you want to be my girl? Check yes, maybe, or go to hell muthafucka."

She burst out in a fit of giggles. "You're stupid."

"Is that a yes?"

Demi nodded. "Hell yeah, muthafucka." She held up her hand and I gave her a high-five and a kiss.

I shoved her back gently and climbed on top of her. "Let's fuck to that."

An hour later, Demi was finally ready to leave my room. "I'll see you later. For real this time." She opened the door, but my hand around her wrist stopped her from leaving. Sighing, she lifted herself on the tips of her toes and kissed me. Once, twice, and one more time. "Okay, bye." She stumbled out of the room and froze.

"What is it?" I poked my head out of the door, expecting one of my parents to be standing there. But it wasn't either of them. Or Asa. It was Tristan.

Chapter Fourteen

FREE MIND

Demi

*W*hen I walked out of Duke's bedroom, I had no intention of pretending that what happened didn't happen. Yet, when faced with Tristan's glowering stare in the hallway... I wasn't sure if it was the best time to broadcast the change in my relationship with Duke. The only problem? While I hadn't seen myself in a mirror, I felt freshly fucked. *In a very good way*. Meaning... I was pretty sure I looked like I'd been doing more than *sleeping* in Duke's bed.

My feet were rooted to the plush carpet, but Duke's weren't. He'd emerged from the bedroom, with no shirt, looking hot as fuck. Over the years, I'd seen the two of them engage in physical battles. But I had no desire to relive those times. Especially since they would essentially be fighting over me. In their parents' house. While I was barely clothed.

Tristan approached Duke, but he didn't flinch. I didn't flinch either because I still couldn't move. The two brothers stood, toe-to-toe, glaring at each other.

"What the hell is going on here?" Tristan growled.

Duke folded his arms over his chest. The same chest I'd been licking mere minutes ago. "Minding our business. What are you doing here?"

Tristan's gaze flitted between Duke and I, finally landing on me. "I came to see you," he whispered. "Ma told me you had a rough night."

My cheeks burned as he looked me up and down. "Oh," I managed to say.

"She's fine," Duke said.

Tristan snickered. "I want her to tell me that."

"Does it look like she's having a hard time?" Duke countered. "The only person in this family that has ever treated her like shit is you."

"Don't do that," I told Duke, stepping between them. In the past, I would've spoken directly to Tristan. I would've pleaded with him to calm down. I would've centered *him* in the situation. This time, I turned to face Duke. "Can we please not do this here? Give us a minute."

Duke's eyes blazed with anger, but it wasn't directed at me. His focus was on Tristan. "No," he said without looking at me.

My shoulders fell. "Please?"

"No," he repeated, his eyes flashing to mine. "I'm not leaving you out here with him."

"Why?"

"'Cause I don't want to," Duke said, matter-of-factly.

Tristan stepped forward, nearly pushing me into Duke. "Man, why don't you go back in your room. I need to talk to Demi."

There was a time when I would've relished in being so

close to Tristan. Most women would be giddy with excitement to be in the middle of a Tristan and Duke sandwich. But it felt strange to be in this predicament, to be the catalyst of the beef between two brothers. I didn't want that.

"I'm not going anywhere," Duke said, his eyes locked on mine. "Never."

It was a callback to his promise earlier to never hurt me. My heart clenched in my chest, because… If I didn't know it before, I was pretty sure I was falling in love with Duke. I closed my eyes against the warmth that spread over my body. And when I opened them again, Duke was staring at me, a soft expression in his light eyes. No. He was staring *into* me. The emotion shining back at me stole my breath. "Duke," I whispered.

He swept his thumb over my jawline and down the column of my neck. "I meant what I said."

"I know." The urge to kiss him, to climb him like a tree and demand he take me back in his room was strong. But I needed to deal with Tristan. "Just a minute."

Tristan snickered. "You heard her."

Duke peered at Tristan over my shoulder. "Shut up, nigga. You had years to talk to Demi. And you fucked up every single time."

"You don't know anything about it," Tristan said. "You don't know anything about me and Demi. You just think you do."

Maybe it was the way Tristan had just basically intimated that there was something going on between us when we'd never even kissed. Or the sheer audacity he was displaying in this hallway. But Tristan pissed me the fuck off. The only thing that needed to be said today was *my* truth. And since Tristan wanted to play me for the fool, I would say what I needed to say to him in front of Duke. *I don't want him anymore.*

"Actually, he does," I scoffed.

Tristan blinked. "Demi."

"No." I placed both of my palms on Tristan's chest, shoving him. "Stop." Behind me, Duke brushed his hand over the small of my back, but he didn't speak. "I've had enough."

"I'm sorry," Tristan murmured.

"Keep your apology," I snapped. "You have some nerve, coming up here and inserting yourself like you have a claim to me. Duke is right. You have done nothing but lead me on since the beginning. That's on me, though, because I let you."

"I didn't lead you on," Tristan argued. "I do care for you."

"I care about you too," I admitted. "But I don't want you." I shrugged. "The best thing you could've ever done for me was not show up in Atlanta—or any of the other times you promised to be there, and you weren't." Tristan opened his mouth to speak, but I kept going. "You know who *was* there, though. Duke. He's never let me down—or let me sit in a damn hotel bar waiting for him."

Tristan narrowed his eyes on Duke. "That's what you think."

A remark like that about Dorian, or any of the other losers I'd dated would've given me pause. I wasn't fazed, though, because I was sure of Duke. He'd never lied to me. Did I think he'd told me everything? *No.* But he didn't lie. "I don't care. The fact is… he shows up. Even on his worst days. Even if he doesn't feel like it. That's all I need to know."

Tristan cocked a brow. "You sure about that?"

"Man, get the hell out of here," Duke roared. "I don't know what you think you know about me, but that shit doesn't matter. If Demi ever wants to know anything, she knows how to ask. I told you before… I'm not hiding. That's *your* M.O."

Raven bounded up the stairs. "Dad!" She paused when she spotted us.

Oh God. I should've just gone to my room and not hopped on Duke's dick again. "Hey, Raven," I chirped. "How are you?"

Raven frowned as she approached us. "What's going on?"

Asa chose that moment to open his door. He stepped out of the room eating a bowl of cereal. "Raven, you might want to go on downstairs," he said, chewing his Froot Loops. "This conversation isn't for you, niecy." He burped and patted his chest. "Damn, this shit is good. Mama knows she be making it happen in our snack cabinets."

Duke barked out a laugh. "You stupid for that, bruh."

"I'm serious." Asa hefted a spoonful of cereal to his mouth. "This is quite the show, though. I'm entertained."

Raven stopped. "Uncle Duke?"

"Hey, baby girl," Duke said. "You're here early."

"I came with Dad." Raven shifted her weight from one foot to the other. "Are y'all," she motioned between me and Duke, "getting it in?"

The vein in Tristan's neck bulged out and he balled his hands into fists. "Bubbles, why don't you go downstairs? I'll be down in a minute."

Raven crossed her arms over her chest. "Dad, I'm grown as hell. I don't need to stay in a kid's place. Clearly, Demi looks like she's been caught slippin'. I just asked a question."

Duke cleared his throat. "Do you really want to know the truth?"

"Obviously." Raven hunched a shoulder. "I asked."

"Duke," I warned.

"There is something going on here," Duke explained. "I know you think that Demi and your father are going to end up together. But, nah… That's not gonna happen."

I blinked, whirling around to face Duke. "What?"

Duke tipped his chin up. "Raven told us she hoped you and Tristan could be together."

Looking at Raven, I asked, "Really?"

Raven shot her father a sidelong glance. "Umm, yeah. Looks like Dad got beat to the punch, though. His loss. Uncle Duke, are you making breakfast?"

"What do you want?" Duke asked.

"Anything you make is good." Raven patted his shoulder. "Alright. I'm out." She walked away without another backward glance.

When she disappeared down around the corner, I muttered, "That was awkward."

"Hell yeah," Asa said, drinking the milk out of his bowl. "I'ma get dressed so I can eat breakfast. I think you should fix shrimp and grits, bruh."

"I got you," Duke said.

Asa closed his door, leaving the three of us in the hallway. We stood in silence for a moment, before Duke said, "I'll give you your minute."

I smiled up at him. "Thanks."

Finally, I was alone with Tristan. I swallowed. "I hate that this happened."

"Are you happy?" he asked.

His question caught me off guard. I half expected us to continue our heated conversation. "Yeah. I am."

"Duke, huh?"

"Yep," I confirmed. "I want to say I'm totally surprised, but I'm not."

"I'm not either," he confessed. "I do have eyes."

It was the same thing Ma had told me. And the sisters.

"I really do care for you. But you know that we would've never worked out. In hindsight, I knew it too." For so long, I'd had a singular goal. *Be with Tristan.* As I grew into a woman, I'd tried to hold on to that teenage fantasy. Maybe because it felt like a safe space, because I instinctively knew it would never happen. The reasons didn't matter now. My heart was clear, and it beat for only one brother. *Duke.*

"You're falling for him," Tristan said.

"Not *falling.*"

Tristan let out a slow breath. "I guess that's all that matters, then." He brushed his lips over my brow. "I never wanted to hurt you."

"Yeah, well… you did. But I'm not mad at you anymore. You did me a favor by stepping off that pedestal I put you on. Because now, I'm free."

"To be with him?"

I nodded. "Yeah."

"You should know that I've only ever wanted you to be happy, Demi. I just knew I wasn't the man to make you happy. I shouldn't have held on to you the way I did. I had my own selfish reasons, but none of that excuses my behavior. And I'm sorry."

"Thanks for that." I nibbled on my bottom lip, considering my next words carefully. "I hope that you and Duke can finally sit down and have a talk. You're brothers. You need each other."

Tristan flashed a sad smile. "Maybe one day. Not today."

I giggled. "Understood."

He squeezed my shoulder. "I'll see you at breakfast."

Tristan walked away. For the first time, I watched him go without sadness, hurt, or anger. I just felt happy. And free.

. . .

"There you are?" Dallas smirked when I joined the family at the kitchen table. "I thought you were going to miss brunch."

Duke was at the island cooking something that smelled divine. He met my gaze for a brief moment before he continued what he was doing. I sat next to Dallas. "I'm tired."

"I bet," Blake mused, biting a piece of pineapple.

Ignoring Blake, I scanned the room. "Where's Ma and Pop?"

"They left," Bliss said, feeding Naija. "Dad whisked her away late last night, for alone time."

That explained why they weren't around for the scene in the hallway upstairs. I also sent up a silent prayer that they weren't in the house while Duke was making me come.

I still can't believe I had sex with Duke. Good sex. I crossed my legs, shifting in my chair to ease the ache in my pussy. Apparently, I hadn't had enough. *Don't look at him.* Damnit, I looked. When I did, his eyes were on me, his intense stare providing the match to ignite my flame. The half-smile, half-smirk on his lips told me he knew it too. *Shit.*

"Hmm?" Dallas asked.

I hadn't realized I'd said that out loud. "Nothing," I mumbled.

Paityn waddled into the room, Bishop on her heels with their bags. "We made it!" She moaned. "Just in time for those grits. Did you put cheese in them?"

Duke grinned. "Gouda."

"Oh yes," Tyn groaned. "Is it almost ready?" Everyone greeted Paityn and Bishop with hugs and kisses. She finally plopped down in her chair, smoothing her hand over her growing belly. "I'm not gon' lie. Now, I know why Dallas and Bliss were trippin' when they were pregnant. This is ghetto. I have cankles."

Bishop massaged her shoulder. "Because you won't sit yo' ass down."

"And I can't back it up on my man without getting a crook in my leg," Tyn explained.

"Hey," Asa said. "Not at brunch, Big Sis."

"Baby brotha, you probably just snuck a woman out of your room." Tyn waved a dismissed hand at him. "You know what's up."

"I wasn't the one sneakin' out of rooms this morning. Right, Demi?"

I froze, leveling a glare on Asa. "Shut up."

Blake did a chair twerk. "Alright, nah, Demi."

"I told you," Dallas said, giving her a high-five.

"Traitor," I whispered.

Dallas patted my hand. "Sis, all I'ma say is… It's about damn time."

"Look at you." Bliss grinned. "Lookin' all flushed. Cheeks rosy."

I closed my eyes, taking a deep breath. "Fuck all y'all."

"Ah, shit." Blake cracked up. "You finally embraced your inner Young."

I laughed. "I hate you."

Dallas waggled her eyebrows. "I know *someone* you don't hate."

Tristan entered the room, taking a seat next to Asa. We hadn't all sat around the table in quite some time, and despite what had transpired earlier, it felt good.

"This is interesting," Blake mumbled.

Bliss cleared her throat. "Hi, brother. Long time…"

Tristan smiled. "Hey, baby sis."

My phone buzzed and I glanced at the screen just as Dex and Charlye walked into the kitchen.

Blake: *Don't let the fun killer ruin your fun, Sis.*

Dallas: *If you need to get your fuck on, I'll cover for you.*

I looked across the table, meeting their amused gazes. Rolling my eyes at them both, I typed: *Tristan is not killing my fun. I took care of that earlier.*

Bliss: *Damn. I missed it?*

Blake: *Mmm Hmm. Asa told me.*

Dallas: *Sissy, you were preoccupied with Naija. I'll tell you the story later.*

I poured a glass of water and responded: *Asa doesn't know shit.*

Dallas: *Asa heard shit. All night, Sis? Damn.*

I choked, spewing water on the table. I glared at Asa. "I'm gonna fuck you up."

"What?" Asa held his hands up. "What did I do?"

"You talk too much," I told him.

Blake sighed, a pleased smile on her face. "Yep. You might as well change your name now. Demi Young. Sounds good to me."

Dexter frowned. "What's going on?"

"Right?" Charlye said. "I feel like we missed something important."

Lennox cleared his throat. "You don't want to know."

"Seriously," Preston agreed.

"Nothing," I said, eyeing Duke. "They're just being silly."

Duke announced the food was ready. "I'm not serving y'all asses either."

Once everyone piled their plates high, we sat down and ate. Duke took the chair next to me and squeezed my knee. I bumped his shoulder. "Looks good."

He raised a questioning brow. "Good?"

"Girl," Dallas said around a spoonful of grits, "This shit slaps."

"Period," Blake added.

I tasted the grits and groaned. "Oh God, yes."

"That's what I like to hear," Duke murmured.

"You heard it all night too," Asa said, barking out a boisterous laugh.

I gripped the butter knife in my palm. Once again, Dallas slipped it from my hand. "He's annoying, no doubt. But I don't want you to butter him to death."

Raven hummed while she ate her shrimp. "Uncle Duke, I love you."

Duke held up a fist and she gave him a bump. "Love you too, baby girl."

"So…" Raven said. "…since the grandparents aren't here and we're all adults. Except Naija and Nique. Can we talk about the fact that Demi is getting dicked down by Uncle Duke?"

The room went silent as I scanned all their faces. Tristan set his fork down and dropped his napkin on the table. Paityn happily ate her food as if nothing was said, while Bishop avoided eye contact with me. Lennox dropped his head on Blake's shoulder, and she smirked at me. Bliss flashed a mischievous grin my way but played it off by nuzzling Naija's nose with hers. Dallas' eyes were wide, but her smile was genuine. Preston just gave me the you-know-how-they-are look. Charlye hid her smile behind her hand and Dex bumped his elbow with Duke's. And Raven… my sweet Raven. I remember when she was a baby. So cute, so innocent. Now, she was a woman, capable of putting me on blast just like everyone else in this family. *My* family.

Then, everyone laughed. Loud. Even Duke. And Tristan. *What the hell is happening here?* Mortified, I blinked a few times and sunk in my chair, covering my face.

Duke nudged me gently. "It's okay, Baby."

"It's really not," I said with a nervous giggle. "I'm so embarrassed."

"Don't be."

"He's right, Demi," Tyn said. "It's just your turn. We all have one."

Conversation shifted to other things, mainly the upcoming wedding, and we finished our meal without talking further about my sex life. The free feeling I'd had earlier exploded, filling every space in my heart. Because I was home. I was happy. And for the first time in a long time—*maybe forever*—I looked forward to life *and* love.

Chapter Fifteen

GET RIGHT BACK TO MY BABY

Duke

"It is my privilege as a minister and a friend, by the authority given to me by the State of Michigan, to pronounce you husband and wife."

Demi was so damn distracting, so tempting, so everything that I couldn't concentrate on anything the Pastor had said during the ceremony. I was focused on her, and only her. It had started that morning when her mouth around my dick served as the perfect alarm clock and finished with my face in her pussy as we showered together.

I'd spent the last two days familiarizing myself with her body in new ways. It had gotten so bad, so all-consuming that I hadn't been in a kitchen in twenty-four hours. My mind was on Channel Demi, all day, every day. And I wasn't sorry.

"Ladies and gentlemen," the pastor said, "it is my privilege to introduce to you for the first time, Mr. and Mrs. Young."

I met Demi's gaze from her seat on the front row. She was stunning in her rose gold sequin dress, matching the wedding colors. The dress was classy, elegant, but sexy, showing just the right amount of skin to make me want to hike her dress up and fuck her in the damn ceremony space. *Lord, forgive me.*

"You may now salute the bride," Pastor said.

Cheers erupted as Dex kissed Charlye. They jumped the broom to more roaring applause before Dex scooped her up in a fireman's carry and walked down the aisle and out of the room. I followed shortly after, linking arms with Charlye's sister, Elise. We paused at the front row to allow Charlye's parents and siblings to exit first, then my parents and siblings. Charlye and Dex wanted to honor the families in a different way.

When Demi brushed past me, I whispered, "I'll have you in five minutes."

Once the recessional was over, everyone gathered in a designated room for the family while we waited for the photographer. Charlye was glowing and Dex was the happiest I'd ever seen him. *I want that.*

When Paityn married Bishop, it wasn't a shock because she'd always wanted to be someone's wife. It was her second marriage, but Bishop was the right man for her. X fell in love with Zara when they were fighting over a promotion at Pure Talent. They'd been happily married for a while now, and parents to my sweet goddaughter. And Skye… she deserved happiness. Garrett had offered her that and more. Blake was the last person I expected to find someone she wanted to marry. Lennox was also the only man who could handle her. Dallas and Preston worked on paper and in real life. And

Dex had loved Charlye since we were kids. She was his heart.

Even as my closest friends and family linked up and moved into their new lives with their significant others, I'd never longed for the day I would be in the same position. In fact, I'd firmly avoided that shit at all costs. Until I realized I wanted Demi. Now, I was determined to spend the rest of my life making her feel as safe as she made me feel. My main mission in life had shifted from becoming a Top Chef to becoming *her* everything.

My father once told me that once he recognized how Ma made him want to be a better version of himself, he knew he had to lock that down. And he'd done just that. They'd recently celebrated forty years of marriage and still managed to make each other their top priority. As I watched Demi chatting with my sisters, smiling, laughing, I realized that she'd always been a priority for me. She'd been someone who'd offered understanding, unwavering support, and unconditional love. I loved her. *I'm in love with her.* The thought didn't make me cringe or want to fuck everything up. On the contrary, I felt stronger, solid in that knowledge. *I just have to tell her.*

"It's different, huh?" Dex handed me a glass of champagne. "Watching the woman you love from across the room, knowing that she wants you too."

I glanced at him. "Very different."

"Is this you admitting that you're in love with her?"

"You already know."

Dallas joined us, wrapping her arms around us both. "I'm super emotional today," she confessed. "But I'm so proud of you, Dex."

Dex kissed her cheek. "Thanks, sis."

Dallas looked at me out of the corner of her eye. "She's beautiful, huh?"

I raked my gaze over Demi. "Very."

"You better not hurt her," she warned.

"I couldn't," I said.

She grinned. "I know. Love you."

I kissed her other cheek. "Love you too."

The photographer snapped a pic of the moment. "Oh no." Dallas shook her head. "That's not my good side."

"Shut up, DD," Dex said, "and smile."

On cue, Dallas smiled as the photographer snapped a picture of the three of us. The Triples. Off to the side, my mother beamed. "My babies." She ran to us and posed. *Snap.* "Love you!" She blew kisses and zoomed off.

The rest of the pictures took forever because... Yeah, we were foolin' around. We were on time for the reception, though, which made the wedding planner, Taylar Cross, happy. After dinner, after the toasts, after the cake cutting, the party got started.

My sisters dragged Demi out to the floor to dance, and I smiled as Skye approached me at my table. "Finally." She sat in Demi's chair. "I've been waiting to talk to you."

"Why aren't you dancing?" I asked.

"I don't want to dance," she said with a shrug.

"What's up, Skye?" I draped an arm around her. "You've been watching me all night."

"Because I haven't seen you in so long."

"You just saw me a couple of weeks ago."

"Okay, I'm nosy."

"I'm just glad you're admitting it."

Skye bobbed her head to the music. "Demi, huh?"

"Yeah," I confirmed. "You have thoughts?"

"Some."

"Are you here to confess your undying love to me now that you know I'm with someone else that I actually care about?"

Skye cracked up, elbowing me softly. "I'm not Julia Roberts in this story," she said, referring to one of her favorite movies, *My Best Friend's Wedding*. "It's... You're different."

"In a good way?"

"The best way." She patted my knee. "I love her for you."

"Me too."

"I do have a question, though," she said. "I always assumed Demi was like me to you. Close, but not *that* close."

I barked out a laugh. "She is like you. In a way. Minus the sex part."

"That's what I'm saying. You never wanted to have sex with me."

Frowning, I asked, "Did you *want* me to have sex with you?"

"Hell, no," she scoffed. "I'm just curious. I think I'm pretty fine."

"You're beautiful."

"As long as you know that."

"Just not Demi."

Skye nodded. "I'll accept that."

I hugged her. "But you're still *my* Skye."

She leaned into me. "And you're still *my* Duke."

Demi walked over to us. "Hey."

"What's up, Demi?" Skye smirked. "Mmm Hmm."

"Oh no," Demi said. "What happened?"

Skye stood and gave her a hug. "Nothing. Sit there. He needs you." She pointed at me. "Don't fuck up."

I saluted Skye. "I won't."

"You can stay," Demi said, a confused look on her face.

"It's getting late." Skye yawned. "I'm old in spirit. I'm

usually in bed by nine. And I need Garrett to give me some, so there's that."

Demi laughed. "Okay." Skye walked away and Demi took her seat.

"More champagne?" I asked.

"Sure. I'll go with you." We walked over to the bar. "It was a beautiful wedding," she said, while we waited for her drink. "Charlye is stunning."

"She is."

The bartender set down a glass of champagne and a scotch on the rocks for me. "They're so happy." Demi sipped her champagne and set the glass down. Shifting toward me, she straightened my tie and smoothed her hands over my lapel. "There you go. Perfect."

I kissed her, chuckling at her wide-eyed look. "You look beautiful."

Demi scratched the back of her neck. "You just did that. I guess we're out there, huh?"

"I'm not hiding."

Wrapping her arms around my neck, she brushed her lips over mine. "Good. I don't want to hide."

"Dance with me." I led her out on the floor, stopping to drop our drinks off at the table. I pulled her close and rested my hands on her ass. "I have something to tell you."

Demi frowned. "Is it bad?"

"No."

"What is it?"

"I love you." Her eyes lit up for a second before she froze. "You have to keep dancing, baby," I whispered against her ear.

She blinked. "Oh."

We swayed to the music for a few seconds. I could see the wheels turning in her head, so I said, "Go ahead and ask me."

Demi blew out a breath. "Like… you love me with the love of the Lord? Or you love me because we grew up like siblings? Or you—"

I kissed her nose, cutting her off. "I'm in love with you. I love you, Demi."

"Already? It's kind of soon-ish."

"Not really. I told you… I know what I want. It's not a stretch."

"I guess not." The song changed, another slow jam. She pulled back again. "Why?"

"Why do I love you?"

"This is going to sound weird considering I'm now very acquainted with your dick. But… I…" She grumbled a curse. "You're the only man who's ever told me that."

Now it was my turn to be surprised. "What?"

"No one has ever said that to me. Not Dorian. Not anyone. Well, *our* family. No one I was sleeping with. Or even my parents."

I loved hearing her call *my* family *her* family. She'd once told me that she always felt like an outsider, even though we'd never done anything to make her feel that way. I pressed my mouth to hers. "I'll tell you every day." I kissed her again—once, twice, and a third time. A tear fell from her left eye, and I kissed her cheek there. "Every single day."

Demi hugged me, burying her head in my neck. Beyonce's "Dangerously in Love" played over the loud-speaker. As the song neared its conclusion, I heard Demi's voice against my ear. "I love you," she sang, repeating it over and over with Beyonce.

My heart pounded in my ears as she serenaded me. And when the song ended, I cupped her cheeks in my palms and kissed her. Hard. I didn't care who was watch-ing. I didn't give a damn who had an opinion. And I knew the entire moment was corny as fuck. It didn't matter, though. The only thing that mattered to me, the only *person* that mattered to me in that moment was her.

Finally, I broke the kiss and rested my forehead on hers. Vaguely, I could hear a whistle call and knew it was one of my siblings. Or my father.

"Damn," she whispered.

"We should probably get out of here," I suggested.

Demi looked at me then. Her eyes were glazed over, dark. "Good idea."

"We'll come back for the bouquet toss or whatever."

"We don't have to," she said. "I'm not into that. We should probably tell Dex and Charlye bye."

I scanned the room and found Dex and Charlye watching us. I threw up the deuces to my brother. He tipped his head to me. "He's good," I said. "Let's go."

D emi groaned. "Right there."

I massaged the small of her back, rubbing oil over her skin, taking my time with it. We'd already christened the hotel shower, which resulted in a little accident. Demi's legs had given out when I was eating her pussy, and she slid to the ground before I could catch her. She'd been walking gingerly ever since.

I trailed a line of kisses down her back, kneading her tender skin some more. "I'm sorry I didn't catch you. I couldn't concentrate on anything but how good you tasted on my tongue."

Demi trembled with laughter, then winced. "You're silly."

"I'm serious." I lifted myself up, allowing her to turn on her back. I kissed her stomach, then sucked a nipple into my mouth. "You should take that ibuprofen."

She wrinkled her nose. "I don't want to. It makes my stomach hurt."

"I'll run out and get something else."

"No." She tugged me forward and rolled into me. "This is perfect. Just being in your arms."

I wrapped my arm around her. "You know what else is perfect?"

"Hmm?"

"The phone hasn't buzzed."

Giggling, she said, "Right? I'm surprised."

"I'm not. Dex would cuss every one of them out for blowing up his phone on his wedding night."

"Dallas doesn't care."

"She does. Don't let her fool you."

Silence enveloped us, and my thoughts wandered back to the wedding. Pastor had recited the scripture I'd learned in Sunday School—First Corinthians. "...*love bears all things, believes all things, hopes all things, and endures all things, but above all, love never fails.*" I loved my family, my friends. No doubt. Yet, for the first time in my life, I had a different interpretation for that particular verse because I felt that type of love for Demi. My haunted memories, the crazy experiences, the bad decisions... none of that mattered. It almost felt like my life was starting fresh, starting new. The women in my life... Chastity, Carolyn, the random ladies in every city... none of them were her. It all came down to her. *Only her.*

"What are you thinking about?" she asked after a few minutes.

"You," I told her.

Demi perched herself up on her elbow, wincing a little. "Ouch. That hurt."

"Lay yo' ass back down then."

She searched my eyes. "Are you okay?"

I'd told myself time and again that I didn't need to tell anyone about my past because it was mine. I'd reasoned that I wasn't hiding, but I was. Because I could've shared it. I chose not to because I didn't want to taint my family's perception of me. But if I was going to be with Demi… *She should know everything.*

Letting out a slow breath, I said, "Remember when Tristan told you that I wasn't who you thought I was?" She nodded. "He was right."

Demi sat up, a confused frown on her face. "What are you talking about?"

"I've done things in my past that I'm not proud of."

"You've also worked hard to put those things behind you."

"How can I, though?" I challenged, shifting so that we were facing each other. "It's easy to hide pieces of myself when no one knows what I've done."

Demi didn't blink, she didn't even flinch. *I love her so much.* "You can tell me anything. I won't judge you."

"Even if you knew that I caused someone's death?"

Trinity. I wasn't driving the car that killed her, but I was the reason she was on the road that night. "Carolyn's daughter, Trinity. You remember her?"

"You dated her before you got with Carolyn."

I nodded. "She blew the whistle on us."

"I know all of this. And I know how she died. Her mother was driving the car."

"Trinity was driving the car. She was drunk." Carolyn had covered for her daughter that night with the hope that Trinity would be spared from prosecution. It didn't matter, though, because Trinity had died from her injuries.

"That's rough. I don't see how her death is your fault."

"Not directly. But my affair with her mother destroyed their family."

"Duke, I..." She sighed heavily. "You've carried this guilt with you for so long, but—"

"There's more."

"Okay?"

"The fallout from the affair could've been worse if everyone knew my role in Carolyn's company."

"You worked for Carolyn?"

"Yes."

"I assume you're not talking about the HR firm."

I nodded. "Correct."

"So you were an escort?"

"That, and other things," I admitted.

"Like...?"

"The business was solely under the table. Carolyn amassed a fortune without paying taxes, and laundered money through her HR firm. I helped her carry out the day-to-day tasks, including setting up the dates, collecting the money, and even resorting to violence if needed. Never toward a woman, though."

Demi nibbled on her thumb. "Why did you do it?"

"When I left medical school, it wasn't entirely because I wanted to pursue my dream of being a chef. Even if I wanted to go back, I couldn't because I flunked out. I barely even showed up my first year. Not only that, but I also gambled and lost the tuition money Ma and Pop sent me. I owed the school—and some very dangerous people—thousands of dollars."

Demi swallowed. "Oh."

"I was spiraling, drinking every day, getting into fights, fucking random women. Basically, trying to kill myself because I didn't see a way out. I just remember feeling so depressed. The shame..." I closed my eyes against the familiar feelings that swelled inside. Feelings that I'd fought hard to overcome. "Ma and Pop never knew about any of that. So when Carolyn approached me and asked me to work for her, I agreed."

"Were you having sex with these women?"

Hiring an escort wasn't illegal. What happened behind closed doors blurred the lines, though. While *I* didn't have sex with my clients, other employees did, with Carolyn's knowledge and encouragement. Which *was* illegal. "No. Just Carolyn. I didn't care either—about the fact that she was twenty-something years older than me, about her marriage, about her family. I just wanted what I wanted."

"In your defense, you didn't owe her family anything. *She* did."

"As you know, when Trinity found out, her father set about destroying Carolyn. Trinity was caught in the middle and started drinking to cope and—"

"Wait," Demi interrupted. "You were gone when Trinity died. How do you know all of this?"

"I checked on her. I know someone who's connected to them."

Demi seemed to understand that. "So whoever this person was, they told you what was going on? You weren't still seeing Carolyn?"

I shook my head. "Once I was done with the relationship, I didn't look back."

"But you went to see her on Thanksgiving."

"For closure. Like I told you before. She's sick," I explained. "Early-onset Alzheimer's, and a few other things. She thinks Trinity is still alive."

"That's sad."

"When Trinity died, I couldn't escape the reality that I had caused this. Carolyn had been in business for years before me. No one was the wiser until I entered the picture. The scandal of my affair with Carolyn set everything in motion. Now, Trinity is dead."

Demi's expression softened. "I understand why you feel the way you do, but it's still not your fault."

Hearing her say that, knowing she didn't look at me differently healed the part of me that had died with Trinity. All the guilt, whether misplaced or not, seemed to evaporate away.

"You were young and desperate to claw your way out of your predicament," she continued. "Carolyn took advantage of that. She knew better."

"I fucked up before I even met Carolyn."

"You did. She still sucks, though." She squeezed my hand, brushing her thumb over mine. "Duke, we all make mistakes. Then we try to fix them, and sometimes make it worse—when all we had to do was ask for help. But something good came out of it too. Medicine wasn't your calling. When you left, regardless of how it happened, you were able to pursue your passion. You can't regret that. If you'd stayed in medical school, you would've been unhappy, and I would've had to call you Dr. Duke."

I chuckled. "Don't do that."

"It's the truth. As far as the escort thing, it's not like you were innocent anyway."

Demi had said nothing but the truth. I wasn't a boy scout. I stayed in trouble for one reason or another. I definitely enjoyed women. And I'd had a lot of sex. I was never ashamed of it either. At least, not until today. "When you put it like that..." I said sarcastically.

She giggled. "Just being honest. I did live with you for years, and I know your old motto. What was it? 'Fuck them hoes and—'"

"Don't say it," I interrupted. "I was a cocky asshole back then."

"You were. You're better now, though. Which is exactly my point. Bottom line, we all have a past. Some of it is not pretty. What you've done doesn't define you or make you a bad person. It makes you human. I have no doubt that Ma and Pop would've told you the same thing if you'd shared this with them back then. They love you—and so do I. You're a big deal. Your face and body are fine as hell, but this," she pressed her hand over my pounding heart, "is what makes you beautiful. It's time to forgive yourself and move on."

I brushed my finger over her jawline before I tugged her to me, hugging her. "Thank you," I murmured, burying my face in her neck. For the first time in years, I felt peace about my past. "I've never talked about Carolyn like this to anyone." Xavier knew the story, but I'd hadn't given him this much detail.

Demi pulled back, searching my eyes. "I can see why. I'm glad you told me."

It felt good to get it out. "It was hard to see her like that," I confessed.

"You were in love with her."

Most of my family probably assumed I'd loved Carolyn back then. But I knew now that what I felt for her wasn't love. "I didn't love her," I admitted.

"Really?"

"The only woman I've ever been in love with is you."

Her eyes widened. "What?"

"You said that no man had ever told you they loved you. Well, I've never told another woman that I loved her."

She beamed at me. "I actually love that." She wrapped her arms around my waist, and we settled onto the mattress again, legs intertwined, bodies pressed together. She traced the faint scar on my side. "I'm your first."

A weight had been lifted with this conversation. As we fell asleep in each other's arms, I thought about her being my first. And my last. *My only.*

Chapter Sixteen

WHAT AM I GONNA DO?

Demi

I officially moved to Atlanta two weeks after the wedding. Between travel and work, Duke and I hadn't seen much of each other. But when we did, we'd made the most of our time together.

While neither of us were novices when it came to the opposite sex, it felt like we were discovering things as though we were. Not only was he the first man to tell me he loved me, but he was also the first man I felt comfortable sleeping with all night. He was the first man I could be quiet with, in peace without worrying about the things I didn't say. I wanted to be near him all the time, even on my bad days, even on the days I would've normally preferred silence. I woke up thinking about him and I went to bed with him on my mind. I even dreamed about him during the night.

Duke walked into my new condo, carrying a box. "Hey, baby."

I closed the dishwasher door. "Hey, love." I repurposed my own nickname for him. It was my way of telling him how much I loved him all the time—no matter what.

He kissed me once. Then again. And one more time. "You look like you're ready to sit on my dick."

I swatted him with my dish towel. "You're late."

"Not too late to fuck you on that countertop before I make dinner." He winked, then made his way to my bedroom. I followed him, shedding my clothes along the way as he talked about the traffic and the near accident he'd escaped. "I swear, Old Duke would've ripped that man's throat out of his neck." Finally, he turned around. He looked me up and down, his eyes blazing with desire. And it was all for me. "Take yo' ass over to the window. Slide them panties down and bend over."

Warmth bloomed over me, from the top of my head to my toes. I did as he said, sauntering to the window. Glancing back at him, I pushed my panties off and bent over. In the past, I liked to control the bedroom, but with him... I wanted him to take the reins.

I felt him behind me seconds later, the hard ridge of his erection pressing against my ass. I pushed back against him, enjoying his low groan. When I turned to look at him again, I immediately recognized the love in his eyes. But I also recognized the lust. It was hot, unrestrained. The world around me faded away. No cases, no tragedies. Only him. Only *us*.

He grabbed my hips, pulling me closer, brushing my clit with his finger. "Your choice. Nice and slow or hard and fast." His voice was a low rumble. The sound went straight to my core. "Scratch that. I'm going to take my time."

I let out a strangled cry as he slid his dick inside me. "Shit," I murmured. He filled me in a way that left no room for questions. He was perfect. We were perfect together. Two halves of a whole.

My body shuddered as he set a rhythm. The fire we made together was so hot, so intense, I felt like I was losing my mind. Our connection was deep. More than family, more than friends. As we made love, each thrust burning hotter and brighter, I knew I could never get enough of him, of this.

Soon, I was on the edge of a delicious orgasm, right on the brink of bliss. An ache only he could soothe intensified as he thrust in and out, over and again. My nerve endings fired off in anticipation of the main event because, at any moment, I was going to explode.

When Duke pressed his thumb into my ass, that was all it took. My orgasm hit me like a train, stealing my breath and snatching my soul. Seconds later, his dick shuddered in me as he growled my name.

Eventually, he picked me up and took me over to the bed, setting me down. "I'm not done with you yet."

"Oh," I gasped as he filled me again. "You're insatiable."

"Only for you," he told me.

The dance started all over again, and I gave up, handing control over to him as he brought me to another climax.

Duke kissed me awake and I jerked upright. "What time is it?"

He laughed. "Five o'clock."

I fell back on the mattress. "I thought it was tomorrow already."

"I'm good, but I've yet to make anyone feel like they lost twelve hours."

Cuddling into his side, I brushed my mouth over his jaw, then his lips. "I guess it's a good thing I made the bed first."

"You were thinking ahead."

"Always." I sighed. "How was today?"

Duke told me about his meeting with his agent. Recently, he'd created a line of seasonings that were selling well on his personal website. So well that he'd sold out on launch day. Now, a big corporation was looking to bring him in and distribute his products. "It's a catch-twenty-two. Take the deal and lose some control or nix the deal and burn out doing it myself."

"Maybe you can find a happy medium?"

"Bishop is looking into some things." Paityn's husband also worked for Pure Talent in Business Development, and he'd helped her launch her naughty toy business. "He wants to set up meetings with a few of his contacts."

"That's a start," I told him.

"It is, but…"

There was something about his voice, though. Lately, when he talked about his business, he didn't have the same light in his eyes. Almost like he was sad or conflicted. I perched myself up on an elbow to meet his gaze. "What's wrong?"

"The more time I spend on the business, the less time I spend in the kitchen." Over the past few weeks, he'd been complaining about not having the time to cook or even experiment with new flavors. "Don't get me wrong, I'm grateful. But I want to be able to work on my craft."

"What about your social media? It's full of videos of you making your favorite dishes. You still have the classes you teach too. And your personal clientele."

"Right. I've slowed down on that, though. This IG and YouTube shit takes a lot of time, and I don't necessarily want to be on camera every day."

"I get it. Have you thought anymore about restructuring your company so that you *can* spend more time doing what you love most. We've been telling you to expand your team."

"That's the next step." He shared the details about the meeting he'd had with Bishop that morning. After he'd voiced his concerns, they'd updated his business plan and started the process of *finally* hiring a business manager and a full-time assistant.

"Sounds like you're on the right track."

"I think so." He kissed me. "How about you? How'd that client meeting go?"

"It went." A former client of mine had recently contacted me about handling her third divorce. "The sad thing is she only wants the divorce so she can get back with her first husband. It's a mess."

"That's…crazy."

"I know, right?" Duke's phone buzzed, but he didn't answer it. "Are you going to get that?"

He shook his head. "Nah. It's not important."

"I'm so sleepy." I yawned.

"Get some rest. I'll make dinner."

Duke scooted off the bed. I raked my eyes over him, lingering on the tattoo on his back before letting my gaze wander down to his ass, then his strong legs. *So fine.* "I think you should stay in bed with me," I said.

He pulled on a pair of pants. Turning to face me, he winked. "If I get back in that bed, you won't get any sleep." He bent to place a kiss on my forehead, then my mouth. "I won't be long."

Once he disappeared around the corner, I picked up

my phone and checked my messages. I had fifty-plus text messages in the "Sisters" text thread. Against my will, they'd recently added me back into the group after an extended break. I hated being part of group threads, but Dallas had demanded that I stop acting like I'm not a Young sister. That meant I had to be subject to all the texts just like they did. They'd also added me back into the larger "Sibling" group.

I scrolled up to read from the beginning. Bliss had started the conversation with a pic of a man's dick. Well, it was more like a pencil. Apparently, she'd received it from a blind date that Ma had set her up with. The conversation segued into Blake's wedding. I was surprised when Blake finally announced her date. August 9. This year. After everyone chimed in about colors and programs and planning, Blake promptly told everyone to shut the fuck up.

Blake: *Just plan the damn wedding and I'll be there on time.*

Bliss: *Side-eye face emoji.*

Bliss: *Meaning the wedding will start at least thirty minutes late.*

Bliss: *I'll warn Taylar.*

Dallas: *'Bout damn time. #Siccadis.*

Blake: *That part.*

Blake: *Happy now, Sissy?*

Bliss: *Very.*

Me: *Finally*

Dallas: *She actually responded. Hey, sis!*

I sent a GIF of a woman saying, "Hey, girl, hey." Then I followed that up with another GIF of a woman waving goodbye.

After replying to a few emails, I turned my phone on FOCUS mode and burrowed into the mattress. To my right, Duke's phone buzzed again. Then, again.

I bit down on my bottom lip. I'd handled Duke's phone

before, but not as his girlfriend. *Did the rules change the minute we started having sex?*

The phone buzzed again, but this time someone was calling him. I let my curiosity get the best of me, so I peered at the screen. *Sasha Williams.*

I knew Sasha, but… *Why the hell is she calling Duke?*

A knot formed in the pit of my stomach as I considered the various reasons they could be talking, but the main one floating through my mind was… *Were they sleeping together?* That couldn't be it. I told myself that so many times, but the feeling wouldn't dissipate. *I should just ask him.* He'd tell me the truth. *He always told me the truth.*

I grabbed the phone right before another message popped up. The phone was locked so I couldn't see the message, but it was from her. I slid off the bed and walked into the kitchen, where Duke was seasoning two chicken breasts.

He eyed me. "Couldn't sleep?"

"Your phone keeps ringing." I handed it to him, but he didn't grab it.

"Sit it down. I'll get it later."

"It's Sasha," I told him, my eyes focused on him. He didn't seem fazed at the mention of her name. *Maybe I'm trippin'.* "She's texted several times and even called."

"You didn't answer?"

I planted a hand on my hip. "No."

"Hmm." He poured avocado oil into the skillet and washed his hands. After he dried off, he picked up his phone and looked at the screen. His face was unreadable, but I didn't miss the slight fall in his shoulders.

My chest tightened as I watched him process whatever she'd sent. "What happened?"

Duke let out a slow breath. "Carolyn died."

Duke

"Thanks for coming," Sasha said when I walked into her office.

The news that Carolyn had died hit me harder than I thought it would. I knew it was going to happen. After all, she'd been sick for a while. Even before her diagnosis, her mind had shattered into pieces the day Trinity died. What I didn't expect was her death to feel like a punch to the gut.

Sasha offered me something to drink, but I shook my head. "When did it happen?" I asked.

"Last night." She sat across from me and sipped her tea.

I leaned forward, resting my elbows on my knees. "Was it peaceful?"

"She died in her sleep," she explained. "Ola found her during one of her nightly checkups."

Carolyn Fuller had left an indelible imprint on every person that she interacted with. She was unforgettable, full of life, a shrewd businesswoman. The world might have turned its back on her, but she'd made her mark.

Sasha sniffed, dashing a tear from her cheek. "Hard to believe she's gone."

"I know."

"There was a time when I thought she was invincible."

Sasha and I had met Carolyn under similar circumstances. Both of us were young, both of us had found ourselves in precarious situations, and both of us wanted to keep our troubles from our families. Where we differed, though, were our motivations. Sasha was driven by her desire to rise out of poverty, and I was more concerned with getting out of trouble and being with Carolyn.

Sasha shook her head. "No one knows about that part of my life. But she helped me. I wouldn't be here if it wasn't for her."

Her words resonated with me in that they were similar to what Demi had told me after I'd spilled my guts to her. All in all, even through the scandal, the turmoil, my experience with Carolyn served as a catalyst for me to follow my dreams. *I'm Chef Duke Young, in part, because of her.* "Right," I agreed.

"Ola wanted me to give this to you upon Carolyn's death." She held out an envelope.

I opened it, peering at Sasha. "Do you know what this is?" She didn't respond, essentially giving me the answer with her silence. Pulling out the piece of paper, I scanned the document. My eyes flashed to hers. "What the fuck is this?"

"Duke, you have to understand the position she was in."

I read the document again. Then, again. Each time, I grew angrier. The sadness I'd felt only a minute earlier had been replaced with rage. "And you didn't think I deserved to know?"

"I absolutely thought you should know. But I just found out myself last year, right before Thanksgiving. I pressed her to tell you, but she'd completely blocked it out. She had no memory of it."

My stomach roiled as my mind raced with the possibilities. I thought back to the last conversation I'd had with her before I left for Paris and the way she'd talked to me during her lucid moments in November. Then, I thought of Trinity. *Is that why she was drinking?* "Did Trinity know?"

She shrugged. "I don't know. I don't think so, though. Carolyn knew that Trinity wouldn't be able to keep the secret."

Everything made sense now. "Where is he?"

Sasha handed me another envelope. "The address is in here. He's in Michigan. Ann Arbor, to be exact."

"You've got to be kidding me."

"I wouldn't joke about this."

What the hell was I supposed to do? How would I tell my parents? My siblings? *And Demi.* Something Tristan said came to mind, about people not knowing my shit, about Demi not knowing who I really was. "Does Tristan know?"

Sasha gaped at me. "You know I wouldn't say anything to him. He knows nothing about that part of my life."

"Are you sure about that? My brother is many things, but he's not stupid."

She let out a slow, measured breath. "No, he doesn't know."

"You wouldn't know if he did anyway," I muttered, standing. "I don't have to tell you how fucked up this is, but I'll handle it."

Sasha called my name, but I was already out the door, on my way to figure my shit out. Carolyn had died, but she'd left me a little surprise. A son. *I have a thirteen-year-old son.*

I drove around for an hour, torn between going to Demi's and telling her everything, and hopping on the first flight to Detroit. Instead of doing either of those things, I ended up in X's driveway. I'd been sitting out there for close to an hour before the front door opened and X jogged out to my truck.

He climbed into the passenger seat. "What's up?" He

gave me dap. "You've been sitting out here for too long. Zara told me to come and tell you to bring yo' ass inside and fry her some chicken."

I snickered. "Tell her I'm sorry. But I'm not in a cooking mood."

I stared at the garage. My bruh had moved from Midtown to the suburbs. He'd traded the luxury condo with stunning views for a mini-mansion with a three-car garage, a sunroom, and a deck for outside gatherings. And he was happy.

"Are you going to tell me what happened," X asked, "or just sit here and risk some nosy neighbor calling the police on your ass?"

"Carolyn died last night."

Groaning, X said, "Wow. That's… That's tough."

In the immediate aftermath of the affair, X had cleared his schedule, traveled with me to Paris, and stayed with me for a month. In that time, I'd shared mostly everything with him. From the beginning, he'd encouraged me to leave the past behind me and start fresh.

I rested my head on the armrest. "We went through a lot of shit together."

"Bruh, I understand that this might be a blow, but Carolyn wasn't a good part of your life. It's easy to romanticize the past when someone dies. But that relationship, and the subsequent fallout… It fucked you up. You weren't even the same person when you were with her. It definitely could've been worse had you not left when you did."

"I know. I told Demi about it," I admitted.

"Everything?"

"Yeah. She reacted how you would think she would."

"I hope she told you to let it go," he said. "I've been trying to tell you for years."

"She absolutely did."

"And you're listening, right?"

"I was, until…" I shook my head. "I have a son."

He frowned. "Wait… What? With Carolyn? Wasn't she like forty-something years old when you were messing with her?"

I glanced at him and nodded. "Which was why her getting pregnant at that age had never even crossed my mind."

"Apparently." X smacked his own forehead. "Bruh, that's fucked up. He's gotta be, what…thirteen or something?"

"That's right." The news I'd received today had rocked me. A few days ago, I'd contacted a jeweler. I had a singular focus—to make Demi my wife. Now, all I felt was uncertainty.

Clearing his throat, X said, "I hope you know that Demi loves you. If you're worried about how this will affect your relationship with her, don't. We all have a past. And sometimes that past comes back and slaps the shit out of us. Demi will understand."

X was intuitive like that. It didn't surprise me that he'd guessed my hesitation without me even saying anything. Since he'd gotten with Zara, he'd become some sort of relationship savant. Shit, he reminded me of me. And we were both just like our fathers.

"Will she really?" I challenged. "I have a son, bruh. That changes everything."

"It doesn't have to," he countered.

"I'm going to Michigan. I have to see him." I pounded the steering wheel with my fist. I could feel myself unraveling, losing control. And I hated it. "Fuck."

Eyeing me warily, X asked, "Is he in foster care?"

"A colleague of Carolyn's adopted him. I know her.

Donna Ware. She was a VP at The Fuller Group and a good friend of hers."

"Then she probably knows you're the father," he surmised.

Donna had been Carolyn's right-hand in business. There wasn't much that got past her. Carolyn had never confirmed it, but I had a strong feeling Donna even knew about Carolyn's side business. Donna had never had kids, so it didn't surprise me that she'd taken my son in and raised him as her own. "Definitely."

"What's your plan, bruh?"

I shrugged. "My plan is to show up. That's as far as I got with the planning."

"What did Demi say? She would know how to handle this type of situation."

Demi. I'd left her this morning to go see Sasha. She was probably waiting for me to call or come through. I couldn't go to Michigan without letting her know, but I was hesitant to tell her about this. Not until I'd seen for myself that this was real. "I didn't tell her."

"Why?" X asked incredulously.

"I feel like I need to take care of this first before I tell her."

"You're asking for trouble." X shook his head. "Listen, I almost lost Zara because I failed to communicate effectively. I got in my head and made a bad decision. You know this because *you* told *me* I fucked up. I thank God every day that she took me back, but it could've gone another way. Don't make the same mistake, bruh."

"I'll tell her."

"Tonight?"

"Eventually," I confirmed. "Right now, I just need to go home. I still have to figure out when I should tell my parents. And everybody else."

"Demi should be the first person you tell. Trust me."

As much as I wanted to argue with X, I knew he was right. I should've gone straight to Demi's after I left Sasha's office. But I didn't. And I wasn't going there tonight either. "I need to go."

X sighed. "You're going to leave without talking to Demi, aren't you?"

I nodded. "Headed for the airport."

"At least, call her."

"I will."

X reluctantly got out of the truck. "Get back at me when you get there."

I stopped by my house and packed a bag before I went to the airport. Once I purchased a ticket on an outbound flight and got past security, I called Demi.

"Hey, love," she said, her voice low.

"Hey, baby."

"Where are you?"

"At the airport."

Demi didn't speak for a moment. "What?"

"I have to go to Michigan."

"Tonight?"

"I have some business to handle."

I heard the rustling of fabric and imagined her sitting up in bed. "Are you okay?" she asked. "Do you need me to come with you?"

"No. I'm going to stay with Bliss." *Tell her tonight.* X's words replayed in my mind, but I blinked them away. "I'll call you when I get there."

"Okay. Love you."

"Love you too."

Chapter Seventeen

FOR THE LOVE OF YOU

Duke

I knocked on the red door in a quiet neighborhood, not far from my parents' place. A group of kids ran down the street, screaming with delight as they chased each other. It was March, but it felt like May, as was often the case in Michigan. Next month, it would probably be snowing on Easter Sunday.

Donna swung the door open, a smile on her face—until she recognized me. Her smile turned into a frown as tears filled her eyes. She hugged herself. "Duke. I should've been expecting you." She took a step back. "Come in."

I crossed the threshold into the house. The open floor plan gave me a view of the kitchen. It was always the first room I wanted to see in any house. The cherrywood cabinets and granite countertops were updated. There was a huge gas stove in the kitchen and stainless-steel appliances.

Donna motioned for me to follow her into the living room. "Have a seat."

I sat down on the sofa. "Thanks for not pretending you don't know why I'm here."

"Carolyn's death was bound to bring up some things."

"How are you?"

Brushing a tear from her cheek, Donna said, "I've been crying since I heard."

"When was the last time you saw her?"

Donna crossed her leg, rocking slightly. "It had to be last summer. I met her and Ola in the park. We had ice cream. It was hard to see her like that."

"Yeah."

"When I took Duke in—"

"Wait, his name is Duke?" The birth certificate Sasha had given me simply said Baby Boy Fuller. My heart swelled with a mixture of pride and despair. Because he had my name, but I wouldn't have known him if I'd seen him on the street.

"When Carolyn asked me to adopt him, she asked that we honor you by giving him your name. We decided on Nathaniel Duke Ware. Right around his tenth birthday, he demanded that we call him Duke because he said Nathaniel made him sound like an old man."

I chuckled. "I would've probably thought the same thing."

"He looks like you," she said. "Same skin tone, same light eyes."

"Does he know he's adopted?"

"Yes. We've always shared that with him."

"Did he know Carolyn was his mother?"

Donna sighed. "No. She never wanted to see him. I honored her wish and kept him away."

I swallowed. "Does he know about me?"

"No. He believes that his biological parents weren't able to take care of him, so they made the best choice and gave him to us so that he could have a better life."

I tried to control my temper because I wasn't that guy anymore. And I didn't want to chance my son hearing this conversation. "He could've had a good life with *me*—and my family."

"I know, Duke. I was haunted for so long about the decision to keep this from you."

"But you continued to do it."

"I love him," she cried. "He's my son. I've given him everything."

"Mom!" I turned toward the stairs as a tall boy bounded down the stairs, a basketball in hand. "Do you know where I put my kickz? I want to go to the park."

Donna's eyes widened in horror as she frantically darted her eyes from me to the boy, then back to me. "Um…" She cleared her throat. "I think they're in the mud room."

Young Duke frowned, concern in his eyes. "Are you okay, Mom?" He walked closer, his eyes finally landing on me. "Hi."

Words escaped me in that moment, and I blinked back my own tears as I took him in. She wasn't lying. He looked like me as a teenager. "What's up?" I managed to say.

"Are you a friend of my mom's?"

Donna's expression softened. "Yes, honey. He's a friend of mine."

"I'm Duke," he said, greeting me with a strong handshake.

"That's funny." I cleared my throat. "My name is Duke too."

He studied me for a moment. "You look familiar," he said. "Do you live in the neighborhood?"

I shook my head. "Nah. But my family lives close."

"Are you a coach?"

Confused, I asked, "A coach?"

"Did you come to one of my games?" he pressed.

My gaze dropped to the ball in his hands. "No. You play ball?"

"Yeah." He smacked the basketball in his palm. "Coach thinks I might be able to play varsity my freshman year."

I smiled. "That's good. I played varsity ball my freshman year too. Good way to get the girls."

He smirked. "I don't have a problem with that."

"Nathaniel Duke," Donna chided. "What did I tell you about treating women with respect?"

"I know, Mom." He glanced at me out of the corner of his eye. "Are you on IG?"

"I am," I replied. "I'm a chef."

He smacked a hand over his mouth. "Oh snap. You do videos. I watched you make some salmon bites. I've been trying to get Mom to try those joints."

"I'll have to give her the recipe."

"That's what's up? Well, I gotta go." He kissed Donna on her cheek. "I'll text on my way home, Mom."

Donna stood. "Okay. Be careful."

"I know, I know." He looked at me again. "Nice to meet you, Duke."

Desperate to hold on to the moment, to talk to him a little longer, I said, "Maybe I'll make it to one of your games."

"That's cool." He grinned. "I could show you some new tricks."

I smiled. Young Duke was definitely my son. He'd already mastered the art of talking shit. "You don't want to see me on the court," I told him.

"Maybe that was true back in the day," he teased. "Anyway, I'm out." He ran towards the back of the house.

Donna let out a sigh of relief. "Thank you for not telling him."

"I didn't do it for you."

"What are you going to do?" she asked.

I thought I'd made some hard decisions before, but this one... After meeting Young Duke and seeing for myself that he was healthy, happy, and loved, I knew I couldn't rip him away from his life. *I have to walk away from my son.* "My parents taught me a lot about nature versus nurture." Ma and Pop loved Tristan and Demi like their own, and I saw the value in being selfless when it came to a child's best interest. "I don't know my son, but I already love him. I can see that you love him, too, and he's well taken care of. I won't disrupt his life. But I need you to do something for me."

"What is it?" She was crying in earnest now. "Anything."

I fought back my own tears. "If he ever asks about me, please tell him that it was not my decision to give him up. If I had known that he was mine, I would've fought with everything I had to stay in his life." Swallowing past a hard lump in my throat, I continued, "Tell him that if he ever needs me, I will be there."

I walked to the door. I needed air. I needed to get out of that house.

"Duke, wait," she called. "Please."

I paused, my hand on the doorknob. But I didn't turn to face her. "Yes?"

"Thank you so much. I'll do my very best by him. And I promise to make sure he knows that his father loves him."

I didn't respond to that, I just left.

. . .

An hour later, I walked into my parents' house. I didn't even bother to check if Asa was home. Instead, I took the stairs, two steps at a time, and headed to my bedroom. I had planned to go to Bliss' house but decided against it. Ma and Pop were out of town, and I knew I'd have some privacy at their place.

I opened the door to my bedroom and froze. "Demi?"

Demi was seated on the bed, her glasses on and her laptop on her lap desk. She stopped typing. "You're back."

"You're here." I walked over to the bed and sat down next to her. "When did you get here?"

She glanced at her watch. "About two hours ago. I came straight here when Bliss told me you weren't there."

"You didn't have to come."

"Yes, I did." She set her computer down. "If anything, I came here to tell your ass off for leaving like that."

I chuckled. "I deserve that."

She smacked my shoulder. "What's going on with you, Duke?"

"Nothing," I lied. I immediately regretted that decision because she saw right through me.

"Wow," she said. "You just lied to me."

I dropped my head. "I'm sorry. I'm not used to sharing everything."

"Can I just tell you something?" she asked, scooting off the bed. She paced the floor. "We moved very fast with this. I mean, one day we were smoking an innocent joint together, and the next minute you had your mouth on mine and your hand in my pants."

"Demi, I—"

"No," she rushed on. "Let me finish. Maybe that was our mistake. Instead of taking it slow, taking the time to transition into this relationship, we forged ahead without a thought to how this change would affect us." Her shoulders fell. "Now, you're lying to me. And you never have before."

"It wasn't like that, Demi."

"It doesn't matter. I can't do this if you can't continue being the Duke that I've always known. If something is bothering you, either tell me or say you don't want to talk about it right now. Whatever you do, don't lie. And don't tell me it's nothing when I can clearly see that there is something wrong."

"Okay." I approached her. "I fucked up. X told me to tell you and I didn't."

"You told X before you told me?"

I blinked. "Demi."

"Wow. You're just fucking up all over the place."

Dropping my head, I murmured, "I'm sorry." I pulled her to me and tilted my head to meet her glare. "I was wrong."

"As hell."

"I didn't know how to tell you."

"Has that ever stopped you before?" she shot back.

I chuckled. "I guess not."

"Seriously, what the fuck happened that made you hop on a plane like a thief in the night?"

"It's big."

"Do you love me?" she asked.

Frowning, I said, "Of course, I do."

"Do you believe that I love you?"

I nodded.

"If I told you I had sex with my college English professor would you love me any less?"

"Did you?"

"No." She smacked me again. "You're missing the point. If it's something from your past, it doesn't matter to me. I still love you."

I led her to the bed, and sat down, pulling her on my lap because I needed her to be close to me. "When I found out Carolyn died, I went to meet Sasha."

"That part is the most confusing to me. I don't even want to know why Sasha knew that Carolyn died. But okay."

"She told me something that Carolyn had kept from me."

"What is it?"

"I have a son."

Demi's eyes widened slightly, and her mouth fell open. "As in Duke Jr.?"

"Kind of," I explained. "His name is Nathaniel Duke Ware."

"Oh, Duke. I know that had to tear you up inside." She hugged me then, offering me her strength and her comfort. "I'm so sorry."

I held on to her for dear life, as the first tear spilled from my eyes finally. "I met him today."

She pulled back, searching my eyes and brushing the tears from my face. "How was that?"

"Hard. He looks like me. Plays basketball, likes the girls. He's even seen my Reels."

Demi smiled. "He sounds like a wonderful boy."

I rested my head on her shoulder. "He's happy. His adopted parents take good care of him. I can't take him from them."

She trailed her fingers over my scalp and kissed my forehead. "I understand."

"I thought about you and how you had shitty parents, but they did one thing right."

Rolling her eyes, she said, "Just *one*."

"They didn't fight the guardianship."

"Not because they were altruistic," she muttered.

I drew back. "What?"

She pressed my head against her shoulder again. "That's a story for another day. Go ahead."

Sighing, I swept my hand over her thigh. "What would I look like if I came in there, guns blazing, demanding that he come live with me? I'd have to take them to court and put him through interviews, forcing him to choose between a virtual stranger versus the only parents he knows. I don't want to do that to him."

"I understand. What Carolyn did was fucked up, robbing you of the chance to be a father to your child."

"I did the math. She had him before Trinity died, during her divorce. She must've hidden the pregnancy to prevent her husband from having a claim to the baby."

"Still… she sucked. If she was alive and younger, I would beat her ass. Rest in peace."

Unable to help myself, I laughed. "You're silly. I wanted to tell you."

"You really should've." I squeezed her until she cracked up. "Okay, okay. You get one. And only because this was life-changing and traumatic." She jabbed her finger in my chest. "After this, you can't do that shit again. No lying. Not even by omission. Definitely no leaving without notice. I don't know what's wrong with y'all. Blake did the same thing to Lennox. That's bullshit and—"

I kissed her silent. "Got it."

"You hungry?"

I nodded. "I haven't eaten all day."

"Then you're in luck." She flashed a grin. "I feel like cooking."

Eyeing her skeptically, I asked, "What you gon' cook?"

"Stop acting like I don't know my way around a kitchen."

"You can't even peel an egg," I teased.

Frowning, she smacked my shoulder playfully. "Shut up. Those eggs were defective. I'll make a burger."

"And you won't burn it?"

"Medium well." She winked. "Mayo, mustard, ketchup, onion, tomato. No pickle. I'll even fry some potatoes and onions. I know what you like."

I wrapped my hand around her neck, tugged her to me, and kissed her. Once, then again. And another time. It was our thing. And I liked it. "I love you. I'm sorry."

"I love you too. And there's nothing you can do about it."

Demi

Summer, This Year

"We're going to be late for our flight." Duke jogged down the stairs, carry-on luggage in hand. "We'll make it."

Blake's wedding was next week. We'd decided to spend the next month in Michigan. The extended visit would serve two purposes—the wedding and the annual Young in Love Family Retreat. Duke also planned to tell the family about his son.

After months of avoiding the topic at family functions, I'd finally put my foot down and told him it was time to man up. He'd ultimately agreed, but wanted to do it when Ma was too busy to ask questions.

I could tell he was nervous, even though he'd tried to

play it off. So I decided to help him relieve some tension. Starting now.

Duke grumbled a string of curses as he looked for his wallet on the countertop. We basically lived together without really saying we lived together. He'd kept his place and I hadn't sold my condo, but we didn't spend nights apart unless we weren't in the same state. It was a foregone conclusion that we were going to be together. And I was here for it all.

"Baby, have you seen my wallet?"

"Nope," I chirped. "But I wanted you to see my new apron. I bought it so that I could be your sous chef."

"Pack it." He rummaged around in the junk drawer. "You can film with me when we get to the house."

We closed on Dex's house months ago and had recently completed a mini-reno of the space, with Preston's assistance. I couldn't wait to see it. "I think you'll want to see this right now."

"We don't have time," he murmured, his eyes still scanning the area. "I hope I didn't leave it at my place."

"I'm sure it's somewhere around here," I grumbled, frustrated that he'd yet to turn around. "Turn around, Duke."

Sighing, he whirled around, pausing when he finally noticed me. His eyes raked over me, from my bare feet to the apron that I wore. And nothing else. He smirked. "I thought you said we had a flight."

"We do. We got time."

He placed his arms on either side of me, caging me in. Leaning down, he sucked the base of my neck, running his thumbs over my nipples. He tugged at the string. "I like this. But you can't wear this to film."

I grinned. "I hadn't planned to wear it for the masses." The garment was a red, lacy apron *teddy*, complete with a matching thong. "But I'm willing to let you film me for your own personal collection."

Duke growled, sucking my nipple through the thin fabric. "Let me get my camera." He bolted up the stairs and returned a few minutes later with his setup. It didn't take him long to get everything ready and soon he pressed RECORD. He stepped in between my legs and ran his finger over my clit. I let my head fall back as he trailed wet kisses down my neck, over my breasts, and my stomach. I groaned when he buried his face in my pussy, licking me from front to back and dipping his tongue inside before he sucked my clit into his hungry mouth. I held his head there, riding his face until I climaxed against his tongue.

Duke stood, his thick erection evident from the tent in his jeans. I sat up, unbuckled his belt, and pushed his pants down. I hopped off the counter and dropped to my knees, taking him in my mouth. His low curse spurred me on as I took him deeper, my eyes locked on his. I loved it, watching him receive pleasure from me. I sucked him hard, alternating in suction strength as I cupped his balls in my palm.

"*Shit*," he groaned.

I hummed against him, reveling in the feel of him against my tongue, the taste of his skin. I wanted to draw it out, but I knew he would want to be inside me sooner than later. So I increased my pace, bringing him higher and higher, until he spilled his seed down my throat.

Standing, I wiped my mouth. "So good," I murmured.

Duke's gaze dropped to my lips a second before he kissed me, sucking on my tongue until my knees gave out. He lifted me in his arms, perching me on the edge of the countertop and sliding inside me. So slow, I could feel every inch of him. He thrust forward hard.

I gasped. "Duke," I breathed.

"I can't stop wanting you." He nipped my jaw. "I want

you like this every day." He accentuated each word with a thrust, and I fell back onto the countertop, giving him control once again. He fucked me hard, but slow. And I loved every minute of the magic we made together.

"Please," I begged as my orgasm built low in my belly.

"You're going to take it as long as I'm willing to give it. And I'm not done."

Duke dragged things out, slowing his movements to a snail's pace. I locked my legs around his waist and pleaded with him to let me come, to soothe the ache. Finally, he obliged, thrusting once, twice, and another time before I climaxed, coming long and hard. He followed me over soon after with his mouth on mine.

As our breaths evened out, Duke brushed wet kisses over my jawline, to my ear. "Love you," he murmured.

I wrapped my arms around him, holding him to me. "I love you too."

"I'll always want this," he told me. "There's nobody else for me. Only you."

I pulled back and smiled. "I feel the same way, love."

He brushed my nose with his. "We can always change our flight to tomorrow."

Laughing, I nodded. "Let's do it."

I hopped off the countertop, then took off up the stairs. Duke caught up with me easily, scooping me into his arms, and carrying me to the bedroom where he made me come again. Then, again. And another time. As we drifted off to sleep in each other's arms, I knew that it didn't matter where we were—California, Michigan, Georgia, or anywhere else—if I was with him, I was home.

Epilogue

ALL LOVE

Duke

Some Time Later

"Let's go!" I shouted as the team hustled down the court. The game had gone into overtime and the jam-packed arena was full to capacity with cheering fans on each side. The atmosphere was electric with so much on the line. A shot bounced off the net, with a rebound leading to a drive and score by the opposing team.

With forty seconds on the clock and their team down by two, all eyes were on the point guard as he scanned the court, trying to find an open player. Once he tossed the ball to the power forward, the hustle was on again. Soon, the point guard had the ball again and sent it soaring in the air. *Score.* Three-point shot, putting them ahead by one.

I leaned down, elbows on my knees as I waited while the coach used the last timeout to speak to his team. Next to me, Demi was transfixed on the action, bouncing our one-year-old baby boy in her arms. I couldn't help but smile at the sight they made, sitting by my side, supporting me, loving me.

Time had passed by quickly, but we moved through it slowly, savoring our time together. Once I decided Demi was the one for me, I never looked back. Neither did she. We'd settled into life together seamlessly, and I had no regrets. The icing on the cake was the birth of my son, Isaiah Jimyr Young. I smiled to myself as I remembered Pop's face when we revealed that we wanted to give our son his middle name, Isaiah. It had been a decision made in love and gratitude and honor to the man who Demi and I both called "father".

Demi elbowed me gently, pulling me out of my thoughts as the game resumed. I took a deep breath as I watched the point guard prepare to defend their one-point lead. When the other team sent the ball onto the court, the crowd erupted. I stood, pounding my fist into my hands. "Let's go, baby!"

"Come on, boys!" Demi shouted, standing.

Isaiah laughed. Initially, we had reservations about bringing him to the game, but he'd done a good job in the loud atmosphere. He would probably be asleep for the rest of the day, though.

Time was running out as the trailing team launched the ball down the court, just in time for their power forward to shoot the ball. It bounced off the rim. *Five-seconds.* The rebound went to their team, though. And right before the buzzer sounded, they shot a layup, winning the game by one point.

Demi let out a frustrated curse. "That's some bullshit," she muttered.

I shook my head as the fans around us roared their disappointment in the outcome. My eyes landed on the point guard, who was visibly distraught. Yet, even though he seemed devastated, he'd rallied his team as they congratulated the new state champions.

We waited several minutes before we made our way down from the bleachers to the floor. My stomach roiled as we waited. What happened next could be very good or very bad.

Demi tucked Isaiah into his stroller and turned to me. "Are you okay, love?"

I nodded. "I'm good."

She squeezed my hand. "Whatever happens, we'll handle it together."

As chattering people exited the arena, I noticed someone familiar on the other side of the court. I frowned as I zeroed in on the person. Correction. *Persons*. I nudged Demi. "Look at that."

Demi frowned, whirling around. On the other side of the court, my mother and father were seated on the bottom bench. Behind them were several of my siblings and their spouses. "Oh my goodness," she whispered.

I shook my head. Although, they made no move to approach us, my mother waved at me from her seat, then blew a kiss. "I did tell them to let me handle this, right?"

She shrugged. "Yes, love. But they have a vested interest in the outcome."

"Whatever you say."

Several minutes later, Young Duke emerged from the

locker room. He scanned the court and when he spotted me, he made his way over. "What's up?" he said.

I cleared my throat. "Nothing much. What's good with you? Good game."

I couldn't describe how it felt to watch my son command the court in the way he had. I wouldn't even try because my emotions were all over the place. After years of being on the periphery of his life, praying that he was happy and healthy, and keeping my promise to stay away, he'd reached out to me on my IG page. The message was short, to-the-point. An invitation to attend the Michigan State High School Championship game, where his team was favored to win.

Young Duke smiled slightly. "Well, we didn't win, but it was a good experience. I do have interest from a couple of colleges, some campus visits set up."

"That's good." An awkward silence settled between us for a moment. Demi cleared her throat. When I looked at her, she tipped her head, seemingly suggesting I needed to say more. So I did. "What schools are you looking at?"

My son smiled. "Actually, I'm interested in staying here, becoming a Wolverine. My mother told me that you attended University of Michigan too."

"I did," I admitted. "It's a family thing. Only a few of us decided to go elsewhere."

"A family thing, huh?" Young Duke said. "You have a big family."

It wasn't a question, so I figured he'd researched me. "Huge," I told him.

To my right, I noticed Donna standing there, watching. Young Duke glanced at her, then back at me. "My mom told me about you."

My heart swelled in my chest. The love I felt for him almost threatened to choke me with its intensity. When he'd asked me to come to his game, I had a feeling he'd somehow found out who I was to him. I didn't expect him to come right out with it, though. *Something I would've done.* "Did she?"

Young Duke nodded. "She told me you were my biological father." He looked at Isaiah in his stroller. "Is that your son?"

"Yes." I pulled Demi closer. "And this is my wife, Demi. Demi, this is Duke."

Demi grinned. "Hi, Duke." She gave him a hug. "It's good to meet you."

Young Duke bent down to Isaiah's level. He didn't say anything to him, just stared at him, before he stood to his full height. "Mom also told me you didn't know about me for a long time."

"That's true." I took a deep breath. "You should know that if I did, there is nothing and no one that would've been able to stop me from being in your life."

He stared at me, searching my eyes for the truth. It felt like I was looking in a mirror. His eyes, his face, his chin… that was all me. "I believe you," he said. "I was upset with Mom for not telling me."

"Don't be," I assured him. "She's your mother and she loves you."

"She told me that you agreed to step away so that my life wouldn't be turned upside down."

"I did," I confirmed. "Because it wasn't about me. It was only about you."

"Thank you." Young Duke sighed. "Since the truth is out, I want to know you."

I swallowed past a hard lump in my throat. "I'd love that," I croaked.

Demi leaned into me and gripped my hand, offering

me silent, strong support. Again. "We'd love to have you in our lives," she chimed in.

"I still have to learn to make those salmon bites," Young Duke said. "My girl watches your videos."

I barked out a laugh. "Oh yeah, I got you."

A young girl walked up on us and waved. "Are you coming?"

Young Duke told her he'd be right there. Turning back to me, he said, "I need to go take pictures with the team, but do you want to grab dinner or something?"

"Are you sure you don't want to hang out with them?" I asked.

He waved a dismissive hand. "Nah, I'm good. They're not talkin' 'bout nothing anyway. Besides, this feels more important."

We'd never spent more than a few minutes together, but I couldn't be more proud of him. *My son.* Confident. Intelligent. Intuitive. I found myself wanting to teach him everything I knew from recognizing bullshit to handling business to making a perfect pancake. So much to teach, so many years missed. I also realized that he would probably teach me a few things too. And I was ready to learn. "Sounds like a plan." When Young Duke ran off to take his pictures, I blew out a deep breath. "That was…"

Demi hugged me. "It was good." She pulled back, cupping my face in her palms. "It was great! Duke, this really happened. He wants to know you."

An answered prayer. "I can't believe it."

"I can." She wrapped her arms around me again and kissed me. "You're pretty amazing." Her eyes locked on something behind me. "Uh oh."

I turned around. No longer in their seats, my family had managed to make their way even closer in the short time I'd spent talking to Young Duke. My mother dabbed at her eyes with a tissue. Dallas held up her phone, presumably taking pics or FaceTiming someone.

"Gotta love 'em," Demi chirped.

"Yeah," I watched my father hand my mother more Kleenex, "I do." I glanced at Demi. "I love you too. *Only* you."

"I know," she muttered against my lips. We kissed once. Then, again. And one more time. "I love you."

Leaning in, I whispered, "I will have your pussy on my face and your mouth around my dick tonight."

Demi shoved me away playfully. "We have to wait until tonight?" She winked.

I cracked up, smacking her ass lightly. "You know I can go anywhere. Anytime."

She burst out into a fit of giggles. "You better." She lifted Isaiah out of the stroller. "He's getting a little antsy."

Running a finger over his cheek, I leaned down. "Since your Nana wants to be all in my business, you're going to spend the night with her tonight so I can have my time with your mama."

Isaiah flashed a toothy grin and clapped. "Da Da."

I took him from her arms and nuzzled his cheek with my nose. "I love you too, son."

Demi watched us, a soft smile on her lips, before she snapped a pic with her phone. "Sorry. I couldn't resist." My family inched closer to us. "So, I guess Young Duke is meeting the crew today, huh?"

"Guess so." I waved them over and my mother clapped with glee before rushing toward us. "Ma, y'all are not slick. How did you even know we'd be here?"

Ma shrugged, holding her arms out for Isaiah, who happily went to her. "I told you... I be knowin' shit."

Happiness. That's what I felt in that moment as my family gathered around us, offering us their support, their encouragement, and their love. It once felt out of reach to me. Marrying Demi, finding out she was pregnant with our son, and now getting to know Young Duke… Those moments had changed my life in ways I didn't expect.

A long time ago, my mission was clear—food, family, and freedom. I'd accomplished everything I wanted, except now my definition of freedom had changed. I was free from my past, free from my mistakes, free to enjoy life on my own terms, and free to love my wife and my kids with everything in me. And I wouldn't trade it for anything.

Be sure to keep reading for an excerpt from the next Young in Love Book, It's Not Forever, It's For Now (Tristan and Sasha's story).

Young in Love Series

Her Little Secret (Prelude)
It's Not Me, It's You
It's Not Love, It's Business
It's Not the Hookup, It's the Chase
It's Not Them, It's Only Her
It's Not Forever, It's For Now

Excerpt: It's Not Forever, It's For Now

*A*ll the warning signs were there. I knew the tools. Anger management had been ingrained in me from the time I could talk. Impulse control, coping skills, breathing exercises, calming activities, books. My father taught me that self-discipline would pay off in spades down the line. I never really believed him. Until now. *It might be too late*.

"What the hell did you do?"

My brother's voice filtered through the rage now simmering to a dull ache in my gut. I felt him move past me and finally my eyes were able to focus on the consequences of my actions. The man was sprawled out on the floor, his blood pooling in the ridges of the hard wood.

Glancing at me, my brother shook his head. I couldn't read his eyes, though. Most would react with horror at the sight. But not Duke ... He was a master at the poker face, which infuriated me because he'd learned it from me and somehow surpassed me in skill, even at fourteen years old. It wasn't horror. Not even disgust. Disappointment? Pity?

He ran a hand over his face. "I'm not going to ask what

you were thinking because I'm not even sure you know. But Demi can't see this."

Demi.

Tonight she'd come to us in need of help. She'd made a life decision, choosing freedom from her father in the middle of a torrential thunderstorm. A crack of thunder sounded in the distance, signaling the storm outside had passed. But a new one had started inside the moment my fist connected with Mr. Strong's jaw. I didn't *just* keep that muthafucka away from Demi. I'd essentially committed an act of assault on a grown-ass, family court lawyer with connections in high places. Demi's father knew people. He knew judges.

Closing my eyes, I tried to think of a solution. Unfortunately, I was out of good options. Or excuses. "Help me pick him up," I ordered Duke quietly, keeping my eyes glued to the man on the floor.

Duke stared at me incredulously. "Nah, man. That's not what we're going to do."

"Just do it!" I snapped.

Dropping his head, Duke rubbed the back of his neck. "The way I see it, Mom left you in charge. You handle that."

"Then get the fuck out of here!"

Duke didn't hesitate. He headed toward the staircase. Only he didn't go upstairs. Instead, he turned to face me. "Real talk ... You can't pretend you didn't almost kill him like you pretend you're not my brother."

The comment caught me off guard. I can't say I didn't deserve his ire. My behavior lately had put a strain on all my relationships. I'd always known I was different, but nights like this cemented the notion. Duke stayed in trouble, but he thought like *his* father. Because the man who taught me everything, the man who wouldn't hesitate to take a bullet for me, wasn't *my* real father. He was my uncle. And the woman who'd nursed me back to health when I was sick and put me to sleep every night with the sweetest rendition of "Baa Baa Black Sheep" I'd ever heard wasn't my mother. I wasn't even related to her at all. While they'd given me all the assurances that I was part of them, I didn't feel like it. Of their eight kids, I was the outlier. I wasn't destined for college. I hated school. I preferred solitude over crowds. Football was my sport, but I wasn't really a team player. Several of my siblings were probably going to follow the example set and become therapists. But they would make money helping people like me.

Sighing, Duke said, "Maybe you should just call Mom and Dad."

"If you're not going to help, leave," I whispered.

"If you won't do it for me, do it for Demi. She's already scared enough. Mom and Dad will know what to do."

Of course they would. Stewart and Victoria Young made a living knowing what the hell to do. They'd built an empire teaching others how to do the same. Growing up, I had never really appreciated their background in psychology. Mostly, I'd considered it my trap. Because I couldn't escape them. They seemed to know every tactic I used to get out of trouble or avoid communicating. All they'd ever done was given me a family, a place to call home. My imperfections, my mood swings, my expectations, my bullshit ... None of it ever mattered to them. And as crazy as it sounded, I'd resented it—resented *them*. Now I needed them.

Duke muttered a low curse. "At some point, you have to realize that you fucked up. You need help. In more ways than one. And this?" He gestured to the bloody man. "This shit isn't going away."

I stepped over to the man and bent low, once again

checking his pulse. "I need to get him out of here. Help me lock him in the guest room."

"What type of rock you been smokin', man? Accessory to kidnapping is not in my life plan. I'm not moving shit."

Mr. Strong groaned softly. "Demita," he mumbled, calling for his daughter. As if the sound of his own voice jarred him awake, the older man swung, throwing frantic air punches. He rolled around on the ground, trying to stand.

My brother glared at me. "This is some fucked up shit. Your ass is going to jail."

"You're done," Mr. Strong threatened, finally standing upright. "I'll ruin you."

As far as I was concerned, I was already ruined. But I wasn't going out like a punk. Before I could dig myself further into a shallow grave by kicking that asshole to the ground again, Duke's hand on my arm stopped me.

"Actually, *you* came to *our* house and tried to swing on him." He shrugged. "You were a physical threat— screaming like a crazed lunatic outside of our home in the middle of a thunderstorm, banging on the door, barging into the house uninvited as soon as he opened the door, and destroying my mother's antique vase in your haste to enter. I'm scared for my fourteen-year-old life," he dead-panned, indicating that he was the opposite of frightened but would make it work if the police asked about it. "My brother used reasonable force to protect himself, his minor brother, and *your* daughter who obviously was running for her life to get away from you. She's a bruised, bloody mess. You're an attorney. Sounds like self-defense to me."

I blinked, meeting my brother's unbothered gaze. The only thing I could do in that moment was nod in agreement. Duke always had the gift of gab. He could talk to anyone and remembered everything he read.

Mr. Strong's shoulders fell on a muttered curse. He looked at me. "You won't get away with this."

Duke pushed past him and opened the front door. "That's nice. Get the fuck out of here before I'm forced to defend *myself.*"

The long moment that passed as we all stood in the foyer seemed like an eternity, but Mr. Strong finally grabbed his shit and bounced.

Shaking his head, Duke said, "Do the right thing, Tristan?" Then he disappeared up the stairs.

Without a word, I walked over to the phone my parents kept in the hallway and dialed the number. When my father answered, I blew out a deep breath. "Dad, I messed up. When will you get here?"

An hour passed and I was seated on a bench in the foyer. I'd already checked on Demi, and she seemed fine with Duke. The smeared blood on the floor had darkened as it dried. My instinct to clean had been doused by my father's instructions to "not touch anything."

The sound of the back door opening drew my attention to the kitchen. Silence. Unlike every other time my family returned home. When the Young family entered a room, there were always loud voices, silly laughter, and annoying arguments. But there was nothing. No sound. My mother wasn't yelling for Asa to pick up his shit. Dallas wasn't telling everyone else what to do. Blake wasn't cussing anyone out. *Nothing.*

Seconds later, my "father" walked in the foyer. Assessing the damage, he picked up a shattered piece of Ma's vase and sighed.

I swallowed past a hard lump in my throat, fighting the

tears that threatened to fall. Despite everything, the truth was … I was relieved. Grateful. Seeing him walk into the door somehow made things better.

"Where is everybody?" I whispered.

He ignored me as he paced the area again, running his thumb over the thick glass in his palm. "In the car," he answered. "They'll be in when I give them the okay." Finally, he met my gaze. "Are you alright?"

"I blacked out," I explained. "He was shouting, threatening Demi. I couldn't stop …"

"I'm not going to beat you down tonight, but you've created a problem that needs to be handled."

"I defended myself," I argued lamely. It was the truth, but it wasn't the entire truth. The part of me that enjoyed the feel of my fist against that man's jaw, the part of me that loved seeing fear in that man's eyes … Although I liked to think I would've stopped myself, I wasn't so sure. Duke saved my life that night. And I hated him just as much as I was grateful for him.

Dad waved a dismissive hand my way. "I'm not worried about Alan Strong, son." He stood in front of me, prompting me to stand because I hated to not be on the same level as anybody. "Your anger has spiraled out of control. I've tried to allow you the space to find yourself, but I cannot allow you to disrupt this family anymore."

Over the years, I'd done plenty to destroy my relationship with my family. Fights at school, weeks-long suspensions, expulsion. I'd gone to three different high schools until I finally settled down enough to graduate. But …

Would he really make me leave?

"Are you kicking me out?" I asked incredulously. "For this?"

Squeezing my shoulder, Dad shook his head. "No. Never. And you know this, but—"

"Stew?" Ma called from the kitchen. "Baby, are you …" Her voice trailed off as she entered the foyer. "What the hell happened?" Gasping, she rushed over to me and touched my jaw with her soft palm. That small gesture was like a balm over rough, cracked skin. Over my heart. "Are you okay, babe?"

I stepped away from her, away from the contact. "I'm fine."

She wasn't deterred, though. Instead of taking the hint, she stepped closer, brushing her thumb against my chin the way she'd always done. "Did he hurt you?"

The realization that she wasn't mad at me, but concerned about me, was too much for me in that moment. I didn't deserve this. *I don't deserve her.* "Please stop," I mumbled. "I'm fine."

"Your father told me what happened," she continued. "I'm worried about you, son."

Her words seemed to ignite the fire of anger inside of me again. Because I wasn't *her* son. She knew it. I knew it. "Stop touching me!" I snapped, pushing her away.

Before I could say anything else, though, my father hemmed me up against the wall, feet off the ground. "We're not doing this, Tristan" he warned. "Not today. Not ever. I will put my foot up your ass if you disrespect my wife again."

"It's okay, Stew," Ma said, her voice soft, calm. "I'm fine."

Dad stared at Ma, but his thick hand remained around my neck. "Can you give us a minute?"

Ma glanced at Dad, then back at me. But she didn't argue. She tossed me one last backwards glance and left.

Once she disappeared into the kitchen, Dad's furious glare met my eyes. He squeezed my neck gently, but firmly.

"Don't try me, son. My fists still work, and you know I know how to use them."

I'd always heard stories about Dad as a young man. And I'd seen him in action myself a time or two. Despite the money and prestige he had now, life hadn't always been that way for him. He needed to fight his way through his childhood and had never forgotten where he came from. Everything he had today, he'd earned it with hard work and perseverance.

"I've had it with your bullshit." He squeezed my neck gently but firmly.

When he finally let go, I slumped to the floor. "I'm sorry," I grumbled.

Dad stretched his neck. "Last time we talked, you mentioned that you'd reached out to a recruiter."

I remembered the conversation we'd had right before they left town. The tense discussion had centered around my declaration that I had no intention of going to college and wanted to join the military. Dad and Ma had tried to convince me to take a different path, maybe pursue a trade or even join a police force. But I'd fought them because I felt that I needed to find my own way.

"Don't worry about cleaning up," Dad continued. "I'll take care of it. And I'll handle Demi and her father." He squeezed my shoulder. "The first step to healing is realizing you're sick. It's time for you to do the work. All that anger and resentment you carry will weigh you down until it takes you out."

The tears standing in Dad's eyes triggered my own. The first one streaked down my cheek, and I made no move to wipe it away. "I will do better," I promised.

He flashed a sad smile. "I don't want to see you destroy yourself or anyone else for that matter. I love you, but since you insist on 'finding your own way,' call the recruiter in the morning."

Dad pulled me in for a tight hug. Then, he left. And as I stared around the space, once again taking in the damage I'd caused, sadness threatened to choke me with its intensity. Glancing up, I noticed Duke standing on the landing in the hallway upstairs. The disappointment in his eyes was clear even from that distance, but he didn't speak. He simply walked away.

Now, it's time for me to do the same.

Recommended Reading

It's Not Them, It's Only Her is the fourth book in my Young in Love Series, but the Young family has been cutting up for a long time! If you'd like to get acquainted with this family before you read, I recommend starting with the following books:

Paityn Young found everlasting love in my novella, HER LITTLE SECRET. The twins, Blake and Bliss made their first appearance in her story.

IT'S NOT ME, IT'S YOU is book one in the Young In Love Series, followed by IT'S NOT LOVE, IT'S BUSINESS, then IT'S NOT THE HOOKUP, IT'S THE CHASE.

Want more of the Youngs?

Blake Young appeared as Ryleigh's friend in my Once Upon a Baby novella, BEYOND EVER AFTER.

Duke Young burst onto the scene in my Pure Talent novels, THE WAY YOU TEMPT ME and THE WAY YOU HOLD ME. And he stole the show.

Dallas Young made her presence known in my Once Upon a Funeral novella, FINDING COOPER.

Duke and Bliss also made an appearance in my novella, SOME KIND OF LOVE.

Meet their extended family in TEN CHRISTMAS SHOTS, which is a follow-up of my first historical romance set in the 1980s, MADE TO HOLD YOU.

Also, did you know that there was another set of Youngs? Yes, you heard that right. Aunt Vicki married someone with her same last name.

I introduced that side of the family in SMOKE IN LOVE, THE SECRETS WE HATE, and THE SECRETS WE CREATE - KNOX.

Please Note: Several of these stories take place around the same time. Some events may happen in multiple books from a different POV.

www.ellewright.com

Acknowledgments

I'm so grateful! God has been good to me!

To my hubby, Jason, you're my first love, my hero. Thanks for supporting me through everything.

To my lit sisters… Thank you for having my back!

A special shout-out to the awesome readers , bloggers, and writers that I've met on this journey. Thanks for your support. I appreciate you!

Connect with Elle!

Thank you for reading Duke and Demi's story! I love to hear from my readers. If you enjoyed *It's Not Them, It's Only You*, please consider posting a review or sending an email. They really do help. Don't forget to tell your friends!

Subscribe to my Newsletter
New Releases, Upcoming projects, and Freebies!

On Facebook,
Join my cocktail lounge for exclusive updates, drink recipes, and lots of fun!
bit.ly/EllesCocktailLounge

Visit my website: www.ellewright.com

Email me at info@ellewright.com

facebook.com/ellewrightauthor

instagram.com/lwrightauthor

amazon.com/Elle-Wright/e/B00VMEWB78

bookbub.com/profile/elle-wright

Also by Elle Wright

Contemporary Romance

Young In Love Series

(Very large family + Layered characters + Lots of heat + Laugh
out loud moments)

Her Little Secret (Prelude)

It's Not Me, It's You

It's Not Love, It's Business

It's Not the Hookup, It's the Chase

It's Not Them, It's Only Her

It's Not Forever, It's For Now

Smoke and Burn Series

(Smoking' Hot Heroes + steamy scenes + Lots of humor)

Some Kind of Love

Edge of Scandal Series

(Edgy contemporary romance + Heat + Humor + Scandal)

The Forbidden Man

His All Night

Her Kind of Man

All He Wants for Christmas

Wellspring Series

(Small Town Romance + Angst + Twists and Turns + Humor)

Touched By You

Enticed By You

Pleasured By You

Pure Talent Series

(Sexy + Steamy moments + High-powered executives + Drama)

The Way You Tempt Me

The Way You Hold Me

The Way You Love Me

Once Upon a Series

Beyond Forever (Once Upon a Bridesmaid)

Beyond Ever After (Once Upon a Baby)

Finding Cooper (Once Upon a Funeral)

The Secrets We Hate (Once Upon a Murder)

The Secrets We Create - Knox (Once Upon a Murder)

Standalones

The Closing Bid

Irresistible Temptation

The Baes

One More Drink

Ten Christmas Shots

Mr. Down for Whatever

Smoke in Love

Historical Romance

Made To Hold You (The 80s)

Suspense/Thriller

Basement Level 5: Never Scared

About the Author

There was never a time when Elle Wright wasn't about to start a book, wasn't already deep in a book—or had just finished one. She grew up believing in the importance of reading, and became a lover of all things romance when her mother gave her her first romance novel. She lives in Michigan.

Connect with Elle!
www.ellewright.com
info@ellewright.com